"Because I want you.

"I already admitted to that. Why do you think I'm so upset? All the time? About all the women that you bring into the winery, about the fact that my father gave the winery to you. About the fact that we're stuck together, but will never actually *be* together. That's why I had to leave. I'm not a fool, Jericho. I know you and I are never going to... We're not going to fall in love and get married. We can hardly stand to be in the same room as each other. But I have wanted you since I understood what that meant."

"Honey..."

"If you're going to reject me, just don't do it horribly."

And then suddenly she found herself being tugged into his arms, the heat from his body more intense than the heat from the sauna, the roughness of his clothes a shock against her skin. And then his mouth crashed down on hers.

* * *

***Rancher's Christmas Storm* by Maisey Yates is part of the Gold Valley Vineyards series.**

In Gold Valley, Oregon, lasting love is only a happily-ever-after away. Don't miss any of Maisey Yates's Gold Valley tales, available now!

From Harlequin Desire

Gold Valley Vineyards

Rancher's Wild Secret
Claiming the Rancher's Heir
The Rancher's Wager
Rancher's Christmas Storm

Copper Ridge

Take Me, Cowboy
Hold Me, Cowboy
Seduce Me, Cowboy
Claim Me, Cowboy
Want Me, Cowboy
Need Me, Cowboy

From HQN

Gold Valley

A Tall, Dark Cowboy Christmas
Unbroken Cowboy
Cowboy to the Core
Untamed Cowboy
Smooth-Talking Cowboy
Cowboy Christmas Redemption

For more books by Maisey Yates,
visit www.maiseyyates.com.

You can find Maisey Yates on Facebook,
along with other Harlequin Desire authors,
at www.Facebook.com/harlequindesireauthors!

New York Times Bestselling Author

MAISEY YATES

Rancher's Christmas Storm
&
Seduce Me, Cowboy

HARLEQUIN
DESIRE

HARLEQUIN®
DESIRE™

Recycling programs for this product may not exist in your area.

ISBN-13: 978-1-335-45521-5

Rancher's Christmas Storm & Seduce Me, Cowboy

Copyright © 2021 by Harlequin Books S.A.

Rancher's Christmas Storm
Copyright © 2021 by Maisey Yates

Seduce Me, Cowboy
First published in 2017. This edition published in 2021.
Copyright © 2017 by Maisey Yates

This edition published by arrangement with Harlequin Books S.A.

For questions and comments about the quality of this book, please contact us at CustomerService@Harlequin.com.

Harlequin Enterprises ULC
22 Adelaide St. West, 40th Floor
Toronto, Ontario M5H 4E3, Canada
www.Harlequin.com

Printed in U.S.A.

CONTENTS

RANCHER'S
CHRISTMAS STORM

Chapter 1

As Honey Cooper looked around the beautiful tasting room that—other than the vineyards themselves—was the crown jewel of Cowboy Wines—she thought to herself that if she had a book of matches and just a tiny bit more moxie, she might've burned the entire place to the ground.

Not that it could ever be said that she was lacking in moxie—maybe it was just the desire to avoid prison. Perhaps not the best reason to avoid engaging in the torching of her family winery. Scratch that, her family's *former* winery.

Until it had been sold to Jericho Smith. Jericho Smith, who was the most infuriating, obnoxious, sexy man she had ever known.

He made her itch. Down beneath her skin where she couldn't scratch it. It drove her crazy. And now he had

her legacy. Just because her brothers were no longer interested in the day-to-day running of Cowboy Wines
and her father wanted to retire, Jericho had offered to
buy and her father had sold. Sure, she had a tidy sum
of money sitting in her bank account that her father
had felt was her due post sale, but that didn't matter. It
wasn't the point.

Maybe she should go find a matchbook.

Instead, she looked down at her phone—she had
bought herself a smartphone with her ill-gotten rage
money—and saw that it had lit up again. She had a
message.

It was from Donovan. Which thrilled her a little bit.

Donovan ran an equine facility up north, on the outskirts of Portland. She had met him on a dating app.
A dating app. Yes, Honey Cooper had signed up for a
dating app.

But the thing was, she was really sick of the pickings
down in Gold Valley. She was sick of cowboys. She was
sick of everybody knowing her brothers. Her father.

Jericho.

She was untouchable here. They might as well up
and put her in a glass case. Everybody acted like they
were afraid of getting punched in the face if they came
within thirty yards of her. In fairness, they probably
were in danger of getting punched in the face. Jackson
and Creed weren't exactly known for their measured
temperaments, and when it came to Jericho… Well, he
was the older brother that she absolutely didn't need.

He twisted her up in ways she hated, and had for as
long as she'd noticed that boys were different from girls.
Of course, the problem with knowing a man that long

was that he could only see you as the pigtail-wearing brat you'd once been and would never really see you as a woman.

There was also the fact she knew all too well that Jericho's personal policy when it came to relationships was that they were best as a good time, not a long time.

But he was just so hot.

So was Donavan though. You know, if the pictures that she had gotten from him weren't a lie. No, they weren't those kind of pictures. He had not sent her his nudes. She wasn't sure if she was offended by that or not, as she had it on very good authority—TV—that men often sent women their anatomy when they wanted to hook up.

Not that they physically sent their anatomy, but pictures of them.

Still, she was on the road to getting out of Gold Valley, to getting away from the winery—without setting it on fire—and getting away from Jericho once and for all.

That was part of the problem. The proximity was killing her. She still lived at Cowboy Wines. And she felt surrounded—absolutely surrounded—by her father's perfidy.

So she was going to run away to Portland. Take a job at a different ranch. Maybe lose her virginity to Donovan.

No, she was *definitely* going to lose her virginity to Donovan.

For Christmas.

And she would forget all about Jericho and the fact that she thought he was hot. And the fact that he had devastated her by buying the winery. The winery that had been her only dream, her only goal for as long as she could remember. She'd knuckled down and worked the land, worked it till her knuckles bled, the same as the rest of them, for years. And now it was gone.

To add insult to injury, she still thought he was hot. Even while furious with him. Even while he took a new woman into his bed practically every night. Which didn't matter.

She didn't care about that. She didn't care. Because she didn't actually want to date him. She just wanted to climb him like a tree.

And who didn't? Honestly. He was incredibly beautiful. Tall, broad and well muscled. Sin in cowboy boots. And in a cowboy hat. And a tight T-shirt. And as much as she would like to actually be sick of cowboys, it was kind of her aesthetic.

She'd lost her mother when she was only thirteen, and it had stuck with her. There was something about the loss that was a lot like the bottom of the world had fallen out, and she'd done her best to cling to what she could.

She had her dad, she had her brothers and the most important thing to her had been to fit in with them.

She knew that dealing with her in her grief had been hard for her dad so she'd done her best to be more stoic. She'd pushed off her desire to experiment with makeup or clothes or anything like that.

She'd become the cowgirl she needed to be.

But it hadn't gotten her anywhere. Now she was ready for something else.

To see what else she could do and be.

Donovan was different. He was sophisticated. The

place he ran was an *equine facility*. It wasn't a *ranch*. She wouldn't be a ranch hand. She would be a horse trainer. She would be fancy. She would be free.

She would not be a virgin.

If her father didn't think that she needed a winery, then she didn't need to be around them.

That made her heart clench tight. She wasn't… She wasn't going to fall out with her family. Not entirely. Her mother had died when she was so young, and her father had taken good care of her. But he just didn't understand having a daughter. He loved her. She knew that—no matter how difficult things had been around the time of her mother's death, she did know that. But it didn't occur to him that she might want a piece of this place. Even though she had worked it most of her life.

And her brothers… They were pains in the butt. They really were. But they loved her. She needed distance though.

She so badly needed distance.

And she had a plan to get it.

She picked up her phone and looked at the message.

What's your estimated date of arrival?

I was thinking the week of Christmas.

She was actually thinking she'd leave tomorrow. That was what she was thinking. Leaving tomorrow. Getting out. Getting gone. Pulling off the Band-Aid.

She had never missed Christmas with her family before. But this was part of her defiance. She wasn't going to consult them on her leaving. She was going to just… She was going to go. She was going to do whatever she wanted.

She didn't need to ask their permission, and she hadn't. She hadn't told them any of what she was thinking, or let them know how furious she was, because why would she?

Her dad didn't want to deal with her emotions anyway.

Plus he was rarely around anymore. She had no idea what was going on with him, but he was never home. Her brothers were married now—and to the Maxfields at that. Which meant they would be off doing things at their fancy winery. Or worse. Expecting her to join them.

It wasn't that she didn't like her sisters-in-law. They were just…a lot. A whole lot. Cricket was her age—she supposed they ought to be friends. It was just… She had a difficult time thinking about how she was going to cozy up to a girl who was sleeping with her brother. *Ew.*

That would work just fine. I'll have a room ready for you.

She hoped that it would be a room *with* him.

She had to do something. To erase this place, her pain, her stupid, pointless attraction to Jericho, the man who had stolen her whole future from her. The man who owned way too much space in her head.

Her stomach twisted in defiance of that thought.

She did hope there was a room ready for the two of them to share. She *did*. She was ready. She was ready for this. For a change. For something new. For a chance to be different.

She was going to make her way in the world. And she did not need Cowboy Wines to do it.

Jericho was tired. Down to his bones. And he only had a day or so before he had to leave for the Dalton family Christmas.

He would love to resist it. Hell, he would love to be an asshole and just stay away entirely no matter how many times the Daltons reached out. But two months ago, he was contacted by West Caldwell, who was apparently his half brother, telling him about his connection to the Dalton family.

Apparently Hank had expected Jericho would be too mad to speak to him, considering it had come out that his various half children were under the impression he'd known about them and denied them, even though that wasn't true.

West had been the voluntary envoy, meeting him down at the Gold Valley Saloon, explaining the situation and how he himself had come to be in Gold Valley and come to be part of the Dalton clan.

The thing was, Jericho had already known about his connection to the Daltons. He'd known about it from the time he was old enough to understand that everyone had a father—it was just that his own didn't give a fuck.

But it turned out he'd gotten that wrong.

Hank Dalton hadn't known. The infamous retired rodeo cowboy was apparently the father to a whole passel of kids he didn't know he had. Owing to his wild years, when he had been philandering and cheating on his wife—and apparently not understanding condom usage—he had a spread of kids in their thirties. Some of whom were with his wife, Tammy, others of whom were not.

Apparently, he was the last one who hadn't been tracked down, owed to the fact that Hank hadn't known his first name, and his last name was so common.

Hank was infamous in Gold Valley, and his mother had made no secret of the fact that he was his father.

But then, his mother had died when Jericho was only sixteen, and it had been the Cooper family that had taken him in. Finished raising him. Made sure that he never wanted for much of anything.

Cancer was a bitch and it had taken his strong, caring mother from him far too soon. A pain he had in common with the Coopers. They didn't talk about it—feelings weren't high on their list of things to deal with—but they all just…knew. That was enough.

They'd been enough.

And he had just never… Hank had rejected her as far as she was concerned, and Jericho had never wanted to take a damn thing from Hank.

But the story was more complicated than that. It turned out it was Hank's wife, Tammy, who had dealt with the former mistresses who'd all had his children. Hank himself had never really known.

And so he was… He was doing this. He was heading up to this family Christmas thing. And he didn't know what the hell was in store for him. But he'd spent his life without any real family. He was curious, frankly. To see this whole big family that was his.

Thankfully, Honey would be around to see to the

running of the winery. Plus, Jackson and Creed could get their asses in gear to give them some help. They were like brothers to him.

And Honey was...

Under his skin in ways he didn't like to acknowledge. He'd known her since she was a scrappy, spiky kid, and now she was a scrappy, spiky woman who ignited his blood and made him question if hell was really all that hot, or if it was something he should risk.

Lord knew, if he ever touched her, Jackson and Creed would have his head on a pike. And if he were the kind of man who could offer something extra, it might be different.

But in his mind, love was a sacrifice. And he'd bled out all that he could on that score.

So he kept his fly up and his hands to himself. Around her anyway.

Unwanted attraction aside, she was a good worker, and she would be more than up to the task of seeing to the place around the holidays. In fact, since he'd bought the place, he swore she'd been working two times as hard.

Being here without him wouldn't be that difficult either, especially because it wasn't exactly prime wine tasting time. They had a couple of private parties, but otherwise, people were getting together and sitting outdoors and watching music every week during this time of the year. Maybe his success in life was part of the reason he'd agreed to meet with the Daltons.

Because hell, he'd gotten pretty far in life without Hank.

He pulled himself up from nothing with bloody

knuckles. Bought his first ranch after years of working it. Bought another one. Expanded. Made profits.
Got to the point where he could buy the winery. And
now he had several different business ventures relating
to ranching and agriculture.

And he was successful. No matter how you looked
at it.

He didn't need the Daltons' pity or their money.
There had been a time when his mother really could've
used it. They had gotten a single settlement from Hank,
but her cancer had bankrupted them.

He'd been a kid left with nothing in the end. And
yeah, he'd spent some time being bitter about it. Until
he'd decided the best revenge could only ever be living well, and he'd done whatever the hell he could to
make sure he was living as well as any man could be.

He worked hard, he played harder. Family, marriage… That shit wasn't in the cards for him.

He walked into the winery tasting room, to see
Honey leaning over the table on her phone. She was
wearing a pair of blue jeans that seemed on a mission
to hug her ass as tightly as possible.

No. Honey was not his sister. She was also barely
over the age of twenty-two, too damned young, too
damned earnest and more likely to bite him on the wrist
than kiss him. She was like a wild mink.

And damn if it didn't appeal.

He knew exactly when the switch had flipped, and
he did his best to never think about it. It had been back
last November when Creed had announced he was marrying his rival—because she was pregnant.

Honey had been incensed, a furious little ball of rage.

"You don't marry somebody just because you lust after them. That's silly."

"Fine. The pregnancy."

"I still don't understand how you could be so stupid. You're not a kid."

"Honey, I pray that you always keep your head when it comes to situations of physical desire."

"I would never get that stupid over a man."

She'd said that with total and certain confidence and something had broken inside him. Shattered. She was a woman.

And he wondered what sort of man could make her that stupid.

His immediate, gut response had been…

Him.

He'd wanted to run out of there like his pants were on fire and his ass was catching. Instead he'd stayed—like it was nothing—and tamped it all down to a manageable burn.

It was what he'd been doing ever since.

"Afternoon."

She lifted her head slowly, then turned to look at him, her expression cool. "Jericho."

"Did you practice that face in the mirror?"

"What face?" she said, the coolness evaporating immediately, her eyebrows locking together.

"There you go. Now you look like you. I'm going to need you to oversee things while I'm gone over Christmas."

"Excuse me?"

"You heard me."

She blinked wide, whiskey eyes. "Do you think that you're my... Do you think you're my boss, Jericho?"

"Honey," he said, realizing that he was tempting fate. And her temper. "I own the winery now. You do work for me." He was the one that would be signing the checks once that first pay cycle ended. So maybe she hadn't realized it. But it was true.

"I... I quit," she said.

"Excuse me?"

"I quit. I'm leaving, actually. I'm leaving."

"You're leaving?"

"Jericho, do you always just repeat what women say? Because if so, I find it hard to believe that you have such good luck with them."

"Women don't gravitate to me for my conversational skills," he said.

A streak of color flooded her cheeks. And he would be a fool to read anything into that.

"I don't really care why women seek out your...company. I'm not seeking your company out. I'm leaving. I got a job."

"You..." He realized he was about to say *you got a job*. "Where?"

"Up near Portland."

"What are you going to do? Work at one of those assy coffee shops that only serves drinks in one size? And sells more macho than coffee?"

"It's not in the city. It's a ranch on the outskirts. An equine facility. I got a job there as a trainer."

"Sight unseen?"

"Yes."

"What the hell is this place called?"

"None of your business."

"Does your father know?"

"My father is too busy with… Well, he seems to have taken to my brothers marrying into the Maxfield family with a lot of enthusiasm."

"What's that supposed to mean?"

He knew what it was supposed to mean. Cash Cooper had carried on a youthful affair with Lucinda Maxfield years ago. Time and misunderstandings had separated them. But since her marriage to James had fallen apart, and Cash's wife had passed, he suspected the two of them had rekindled things.

And it seemed Honey suspected it too.

"Apparently the Maxfield women are universally irresistible to the men in my family." She shook her head. "But I don't want to spend my Christmas at Maxfield Vineyards. I don't want to be part of their fancy ass… whatever. I don't want you to own Cowboy Wines. I want everything to go back to the way it was. But it isn't going to. Which means I'm going to take myself off. I got a place. And I really like… I really like Donovan."

"Who's Donovan?" he asked, eyes narrowing. Jackson and Creed weren't currently in residence, which meant that it was up to him to make sure she wasn't doing anything dumbass.

Honey was open; she was honest to a near fault. If the thought was in her head, it was out of her mouth just as quick.

The fact that she'd been keeping secrets set off big loud alarm bells.

"He owns the equine facility that I'm going to," she

said, sniffing loudly. "And I've been talking with him on an app."

His stomach went tight. "Explain."

"Well, if you must know, I met him on a dating app."

"You met a guy that you're going to go work for *on a dating app*?"

"Yes."

"This is an HR violation waiting to happen."

"I think he might be HR."

"All the more reason for you to turn tail and run. This doesn't sound like a safe situation at all."

"I'm not a *child*, Jericho. And anyway, I'm going up there with the express intention of violating HR mandates."

"Hell no." Anger burned in his gut. Honey might not be for him. He knew she wasn't. But even so, he was not going to let Honey Cooper run off up north to shack up with some guy who owned an equine facility—that was the most pretentious little bullshit he'd ever heard—and…start sleeping with him immediately. The very idea made him see red.

"No," he said. "You are not doing that. You are staying here."

"It may shock you to learn, Jericho, that you don't get to control my life. You don't get to tell me what to do. You don't even get the tiniest say in what I do with my time. Because it isn't your business."

"You are my business, Honey Cooper, whether you like it or not."

She rounded on him, her expression a fury. "You're not my brother, asshole. You're not my boss, and it isn't your decision. I'm leaving. I'm leaving tomorrow. I've got everything packed up."

"That's a problem, because I'm also leaving tomorrow."

"Sounds like a you problem."

"Honey…"

"No," she said. "I'm out. I should've been the first in line to buy the winery. My father never consulted me. You never considered it. You never considered my feelings at all. Acting concerned for me now, when you bought out my family's winery without thinking that I might want to…"

"I didn't realize Cash didn't consult you." He felt slightly guilty about saying that, because Jackson had basically told him that Honey wouldn't be happy about the decision. And he'd chosen to ignore that. He'd chosen to go ahead with it, because it was what he wanted. There wasn't a whole lot in this world that he could claim as a legacy. His mother was dead; his father had never wanted much of anything to do with him—so he'd thought. Cowboy Wines was the closest thing he had to a family anything. The Coopers were the closest thing he had to a family.

Which meant that getting a piece of it had mattered to him. And when Cash had wanted out…

He never mentioned the possibility of selling it to Honey. It wasn't like he had taken it out from under her deliberately. And she hadn't said anything, not a damn thing, in the time since.

But Honey's happiness meant something to him. The Coopers meant something to him. Which was why, no matter how nice Honey's ass looked in a pair of jeans, he'd never do anything about it. There were plenty of women out there. More than willing to warm his bed for a few hours. He wasn't going to mess with his friends' sister. He also wasn't going to let her go off half-cocked to warm some other dude's bed just because she was mad.

Not that he didn't figure she'd be warming beds, or that she hadn't. It was just that this was a bad idea. Clearly, up front from the start. And there was no point doing something that was so clearly this dumbass right from step one.

"It doesn't matter whether you knew or not. You should talk to me. You all should talk to me."

"The thing is, I wanted it." He figured honesty was the best policy here. "Whatever was going to get it. Whether you're happy about it or not."

"Well, I'm not happy. But it doesn't matter, because I won't be around to be unhappy anymore. Fuck you."

She turned around and stalked out of the room, and he resisted the urge to go after her. Honey and her tantrums weren't his problem. He had bigger issues. Like making sure everything was covered before he went up to deal with the Daltons. Of course, if he called Creed and Jackson about it, he would blow Honey's operation. Which was probably for the best.

He took his phone out of his pocket and dialed Jackson. "Hey. I'm going to need your help with the winery for the next week."

"All right."

"I'm going to meet my family."

"Your family?"

"Yeah. My father. Hank Dalton."

"Well, hell."

"Don't say it like that. It's not that big of a deal."

"It *is* a big deal," Jackson insisted. "He finally acknowledged your existence?"

He didn't particularly want to talk about this. But it was reality right now, so he supposed there was no avoiding it. "He didn't know about my existence. Apparently."

"Hell."

"I don't see it as that big of a deal. So I don't see why you should."

"Because it's a big fucking deal."

"Only if you think I'm going to make a big, happy family out of it. I'm going up for some big Christmas thing. That's it."

"Well, I don't mind helping out." And he thought about selling Honey out just then. But he didn't.

"Thanks."

He might pay for that later. But he would deal with her. No point sending Jackson off after her.

She was already angry enough. He wouldn't make it worse. And hell, she would see reason. He couldn't actually imagine Honey taking off and moving up north. She wouldn't do it.

No. She would come to her senses and see reason.

She had to. He didn't want to think too deep about the alternative.

Chapter 2

Honey flung a suitcase into the bed of her truck and slapped her hands together. She had every box in her bedroom all packed up. And she was ready to go. She had left a note for her dad.

The boxes would be picked up by a moving company—she was really enjoying the fact that she'd gotten a bit of money from the sale of the winery—and driven up separately.

She would be taking her truck and an overnight bag. Traveling light. And she was ready. Especially after that discussion with Jericho yesterday. Which couldn't even be called a discussion. He was such a high-handed dick. And she was over it. Honestly, completely and utterly over men acting like they thought they knew what was best for her life. *If it was only acting like they knew what was best for my life, it wouldn't be that bad.* But they actually made decisions that impacted her life and didn't seem to get it when it infuriated her. More than infuriated. She was so… She was just so hurt by the whole thing with the vineyard.

She didn't know that she would ever really get over it.

Getting ready to leave this place now… She wished that it felt more triumphant. Instead, it felt sad. This place housed the few memories that she had of her mother. And so many happy ones with her father and her brothers. And yes, even Jericho.

They were a close family, and they always had been. But this move by her dad had driven such a wedge between them.

A wedge she hadn't told anyone about. But she didn't know how. Didn't know how to do it without flying off the handle, and after a decade of keeping it all to herself, the idea of letting it all out terrified her.

And her brothers had gone off and got married… It was just that everything was different. She didn't think it could ever go back to the way it was. No, she knew it couldn't. So she might as well start over. She might as well.

She put her hands on her hips and looked back at the room that was neatly stacked with boxes and then looked at her truck. There was no point delaying it now. She was on her way.

She walked around to the other side of her truck and started when she saw Jericho standing back next to a tree, his arms crossed over his broad chest.

His black hat was pulled low over his face, his dark eyes glittering. "And where exactly do you think you're going?"

"Lake Oswego," she said.

"Oh please," he said. "You're going to last about five minutes there. You're going to die of hipster."

"I don't think Lake Oswego is renowned for its hipsterdom."

He arched a dark brow and it made her stomach feel funny. "You're really leaving?"

She frowned deeply. "My shit is packed. What do you think?"

"Stay," he said, the word low and rumbling, and it tugged at her and she hated it. She had to get away from here. From him. She'd wanted a whole bunch of things for years. To be an equal to her brothers, to work this winery as they'd done and be able to have a piece of it someday. For Jericho to look at her with heat in his eyes. She wasn't going to be able to find new patterns if she didn't change things. Everything. "Don't be rash about it."

She really wanted to punch him for that. He had no idea. This wasn't rash. It was the culmination of so much stuff. Of realizing that she was going to be treading water in Gold Valley for the rest of her life.

She had no career here. Not like she'd believed.

Her crush—toxic attraction sprinkled with a dash of irritation… Whatever you wanted to call it, it was on him.

"I'm going to go."

"Look. I asked your brother to come here and handle things while I was away, and I did not blow your cover. So now I want you to be reasonable."

"*Reasonable* meaning do exactly what you want me to do?"

He lifted a brow, which she had privately deemed his most arrogant eyebrow some years ago. "Hell yeah."

She huffed. "Jericho, I don't owe you the reality that you want. You sure as hell didn't care about what I wanted when you bought the winery."

"It wasn't that I didn't care."

"It was. You didn't talk to me about it. Nothing. My entire world felt like it had been pulled out from under my feet."

"How is it different? You didn't own the place when your dad ran it. Why is it so different working for me?"

"Because I…" It hurt, this admission. But she was going to have to practice it because she was going to have to tell her dad eventually. Tell him without dissolving. She might as well practice on Jericho. "Because I expected someday that maybe my father would leave this to me. To us. I don't have any problem with you having a piece of it. You've been part of us from… For a long time. But me being cut out of it…that's what I can't understand."

"You got some money."

"I did. But it's not the same as getting this land. I can go earn money anywhere. Which is what I'm going to do."

"And you're going to sleep with this guy?"

That spiked a wave of fury in her blood. He had her vineyard. He had her desire. He didn't deserve to be spared her honesty. "Yep. Lots of times."

"Honey…"

Her eyes collided with his, and there was something about the look on his face that made a reckless heat careen through her blood. Because while she was talking about sleeping with Donovan, she couldn't actively picture it. Yes, she'd seen photographs of him, but they couldn't compare to Jericho standing in front of her in the angry, hard, hot flesh.

His mouth firmed into a grim line.

"What?"

"It's a bad idea," he said, his voice hard.

"So what?" she asked. "Has every one of your ideas been good?"

He cleared his throat. "Well, no."

"Why do I have to make good decisions all the time? I want to make a bad decision. I want to try something. I don't think it's up to you to decide whether or not I get to do something crazy. So, I'm off."

"Dammit, Honey."

"Damn *you*, Jericho." She walked past him, and then he grabbed her by the arm, whirling her to face him. She felt like all the breath had been sucked out of her body as she stared into his thunderous face.

She took stock of him. Of his beautiful features. His dark brown eyes and skin, the black stubble that covered his square jaw. And she felt like he was taking up all the space. In addition to having taken this winery from her, he had stolen her ability to breathe. Her ability to think. And right now it just enraged her.

"Let go of me."

She wouldn't allow him to steal this from her too. He had been her most secret, most shameful fantasy for far too long, and she was on her way to make something new, to get something new. She was going to have what she wanted. And she did want Donovan. Or at least, she really wanted to want Donovan. And that was going to have to be enough, because she couldn't have Jericho.

Ever.

He was now the emblem of everything ruinous.

And she had called her brothers out for being dumbasses more than once, too many times to ever let herself be a dumbass over a man.

You don't think that you're being dumb about Donovan?

No. She wasn't. Because the simple truth was… He was handsome, and maybe having a fling with him would be fun. But it wouldn't devastate her. There was no way that it could. Because the ranch wasn't the family winery.

And he wasn't a man that was so close to her brothers he was practically family.

And he didn't… He didn't make her itch under her skin.

He didn't get to places that she couldn't reach.

So there was no risk involved. Jericho represented too much risk. Every risk. Every risk she couldn't take.

So yes, she could run away to Lake Oswego. She could hook up with a guy who may or may not be permanent. But she could never… She could never.

She jerked away from him and climbed up into the cab of her truck, defiant. Then she slammed the heavy door and unrolled her window. "I'm leaving."

"Yeah, you're doing a real convincing job of it too."

"I'll run your ass over if you get in my way."

"Honey…"

"Look, Merry Christmas and whatever. And good

luck with your family. I don't hate you." Her throat suddenly got tight. "I just can't be here."

She started the engine, and before she could think better of it, she put the truck in Drive and punched the gas. And then she was leaving. Driving away from the little house she had called her own for years. From the winery that had always been her home. From the man who had given her butterflies in her stomach since before she knew what it meant.

This was better. Because she couldn't stay here. Held back, held in place, not anymore. Everyone else had moved on. And she would have to watch Jericho bring an endless succession of women to the winery for sex for the rest of her life. And never resolve the feelings that she had... Never move on. She hated how much this was about that. How much it was about him.

So she drove away, and she challenged herself not to look back. She was not going to look back.

And pretty soon the road became less familiar, winding and lined with trees. And as she went up in elevation, what had started as a light dusting of the snow turned into big banks of it piled up on the sides of the road.

Luckily, it wasn't cold enough right now to turn anything to ice.

She was on her way. She was on her way. She had quite a few miles of the middle of nowhere before she hit the interstate, and so she plugged her new phone in and cranked some country music, singing along with Luke Bryan, but pretty soon the lyrics of the song made her too sad. And she couldn't even say why, because it was a party tune about someone being excited to hear her song playing on the radio. Maybe it was because it reminded her of warm nights at the winery and sitting around with her family. Sitting with Jericho. Making s'mores and dancing up on the tailgate.

But the problem was, somewhere deep in her soul, that it always felt a little bit electric because he was there. And she just couldn't…

Why are you really mad?

She didn't want to think about that. She did not want to think about why she was really upset. Why she really needed to leave. Because him buying the vineyard had shown her something. That he really didn't think about her. And that she thought about him far too much. Way more than a woman should think about a man who had never showed any interest in her at all.

The road wound along the river, and she took in the beautiful scene. The rapids rolling over big smooth rocks, pine trees lining the banks and even a bald eagle giving her a patriotic show as he went fishing in the water.

And you're moving to the city.

It was not the city. It was the outskirts of the city, and she would be at an equine facility. Really, it was completely up her alley. It was great. It was going to be fine.

Better than fine. Better than fine.

She was really full of affirmations today.

Sadly, she did not feel all that affirmed.

Suddenly, her truck sputtered slightly and gave a jolt. She startled, looking around as if there would be answers for what the hell was going on out there in nature.

It sputtered again, and she pulled over to the side of the road, letting it idle as she started breathing hard.

It would be fine. It was fine.

She put it in Drive and started to maneuver back out onto the road, and it made a horrible grinding sound and then stopped.

Well. Shit.

She grabbed her phone to call her brothers and saw that she didn't have any bars.

What the hell? Had she driven back into 1996?

She got out of the truck and looked around. It was freezing. The wind whipped up, the sky going gray.

It felt ominous.

She couldn't walk back to Gold Valley. She had driven more than an hour, and it would take her all day. On the route that she had driven, there was no town back or forward for at least fifteen miles.

This was...terrible.

Horrible.

No one knew where she'd gone, that she'd left, that she was coming...

Only Jericho knew and he wasn't expecting her to get in touch anytime soon. Donavan didn't even know to be expecting her.

Someone would happen down the road, she was certain of that.

She was not going to panic. There was no point panicking. She just had to deal. She had protein bars in the glove box. She reached over and opened it, grabbed one and opened it immediately, suddenly feeling ravenous. Because, of course, the prospect of being stuck here did not agree with her at all.

Someone would come by. It wasn't like she was in the middle of nowhere.

She tore open the bar and shoved the food into her mouth.

She was fine. It was fine. Forty-five minutes into sitting there, she felt much less fine. Especially when the first light snowflake tumbled from the sky.

Great. She was going to freeze to death on the side of the road. A frozen pathetic virgin, whose last thought wouldn't be the man she was going to have sex with, but her older brothers' best friend, whom she had left behind.

She laid her head back against the seat and groaned.

And instantly, her mind conjured up summer. Summer, and Jericho half naked at the ocean. Wearing nothing but a pair of swim shorts, low on his hips. She could still remember the way that line cut right there, lowering her IQ by several points. His washboard abs, his chest, with just the right amount of dark hair.

And his skin… She wanted to lick it. And she had never licked another person in her life, but she was absolutely confident she wanted to lick him.

And punch him. In fairly equal measure most of the time. And what the hell was that?

She pounded her head against the back of the seat now.

"And here you are, just beginning to be responsible and take control of yourself. Here is your reward."

Freezing in her truck.

She heard a truck engine before she saw one. She turned sharply, opening the driver's-side door and stumbling out of the cab of the truck quickly. She didn't even bother to put her coat and mittens on.

She just started to wave.

She was a motorist, and she was in distress. And she was going to make sure this person knew that she was distressed.

She hopped up and down, feeling ridiculous, but her desperation outweighed the ridiculousness by a fair amount.

It was a red truck, sort of a rusty red. And it did not take her long to realize…

No.

Of course.

The bane of her existence. The object of her desire. That damn pain in the ass.

He turned his blinker on, and she took a step back, and then he pulled right into the outcropping where she had parked her truck.

"What the hell?"

She looked into Jericho's stormy face.

"Well," she said. "I am having some car trouble. And I have no cell service."

"Shit," he said.

"What are you doing?"

"I told you that I was leaving. I'm heading up north to go to this… Big Dalton family shindig. They rented some complex up in the mountains."

"Oh really?"

"In Washington."

"In Washington?"

"Yeah."

"Can you drop me off?"

"Drop you off?"

"We're repeating again. And yes," she said. "In Lake Oswego. That would be perfect. I could have a tow truck bring my truck up there. But then I don't have to delay anything."

She really badly needed to get there. She needed to see Donovan in person. She needed to get this all taken care of. She just really needed it.

"You want me to drive you up to your fancy equine facility booty call?"

"How many times have I watched you pick up squealing, giggling bridesmaids at bachelorette parties?"

It was a fair question. Because she had watched him. A lot. In fact, she had something of a running tally in her head. And she didn't like it. It made her want to vomit her guts out every time.

She hated the idea of a woman touching him. She hated it.

Some woman running her hands over those abs. The ones that she wanted to lick.

The ones that she hated herself for wanting to lick.

Because there was just no point to it. He was Creed and Jackson's best friend. He was basically a surrogate son to her father, and try as she might, she genuinely could not see Jericho as a brother. She just couldn't.

And he wasn't… He was never going to marry her.

She didn't want to marry him anyway. She wasn't even sure she wanted to get married. She didn't know what she wanted. She had been certain that it was the winery, but now that wasn't going to happen and she had to reevaluate things. Wanting to lick somebody's abs did not equate to wanting to marry them.

But they couldn't just… They couldn't do anything. Not given the proximity of their lives. Not given just how enmeshed they were.

But that did not mean that she liked knowing that he was off fucking some other girl.

"It will be a few," he said.

"How many times have you watched me pick up a guy?"

She could practically hear him grinding his teeth together. "I haven't."

Her cheeks were hot, but she was determined to be bold in this. Her brothers had never been discreet about their sex lives, and Jericho certainly hadn't been. Why should she? "Drive me to my booty call," she said.

It was poetic in a way.

She would use Jericho as a vehicle to get rid of her virginity. Not… Just in the way that he was going to actually drive the vehicle that would lead her up to the guy that was going to take her virginity. And that would be perfect.

"Your brothers…"

"Can hardly expect that I don't have a sex life," she said, lying, since she clearly did not have a sex life, but she hoped that Jericho didn't know that.

"They probably aren't going to want to know about you having a sex life with some guy who's going to be signing your paychecks."

"Right. Like you've never had an ill-advised love affair."

He huffed a laugh. "I wouldn't call anything that I've ever had 'a love affair.'"

"We can stand around debating the semantics of where you had your dick, Jericho, or we can get out of the cold. I would like to get out of the cold. Can you give me a damned ride or not?"

She was incredibly proud of herself for not falling apart completely for saying the word *dick* in his presence, especially not when she meant his actual dick, which made her feel sweaty and hot and more than a little bit excited. She wasn't going to think about his dick. No. She was not.

She really needed to take care of her virginity.

Not in the way she had been taking care of it, which had been like a preservation project. This was eradication.

"Yeah, I'll give you a ride."

"Brilliant," she said. She took a photo of exactly where the truck was and the mile marker it was by, grabbed her suitcase and hefted it out of the bed, slinging it over into Jericho's.

Then she climbed up into the passenger side.

Thankfully, the truck was warm. And she buckled up, snuggling into the much more comfortable seats.

"Your truck's fancy ass," she said.

"I'm rich as fuck," he said.

She raised her brows. "Must be nice."

"Didn't you get a bit of money from the sale?"

"Yeah," she said, idly adjusting the heater knob on the truck.

"So, why don't you buy yourself a new truck?"

"Well, I don't really want a new truck. I mean I don't really need one. I mean, I don't really know what I want. It'll take some trying to figure it out."

"Right. Hence the taking the new job with the guy that you're…"

"I like him," she said.

"Great," he said. "Happy for you."

"You don't seem happy for me."

"Did you want me to throw you a party? A 'Honey is going to get laid' party?"

"That's all you're thinking in terms of. Maybe I really like him."

"Sorry. But you don't seem like you do."

"You don't…" She sputtered. "You don't get to decide what I sound like."

They drove down the road, fat flakes building as they hit the windshield.

"Is this four-wheel drive?" she asked.

He shot her a sideways look. It clearly said: *What do you think?*

She continued, "I do like him."

"You have shown a lot more emotion over generally being pissed off with me than you have over being with him. Being horny for somebody is not the same as being into them. Like into them completely."

"Excuse me," she said. "I'm not horny for him. I am not a fourteen-year-old boy."

"If you're not horny, what's the point?"

"I oppose the terminology," she said.

"Oh, I'm sorry. Did you want to split hairs about your sex language?"

"I would rather not get into sex language with you. How about that?"

"Suit yourself."

She cleared her throat. "It doesn't bother you to use it with me?"

"Hell no. I say it to anybody. I'd say it to your brothers."

"So I am…the same as my brothers to you."

"Yeah," he said.

"Bullshit," she practically screamed, but she was losing her mind here. He was not one of her brothers. He was being a possessive, demanding jerk, and he wasn't even one of her brothers. But worse, he was a man she wanted to be possessive of for all the wrong reasons. Still wrong. Still not what she wanted. Never what she wanted.

"You would not want Jackson or Creed to go sleep with somebody that they were working with. Hell, Jackson was working with Cricket when he started to have sex with her. She's my age. Also, Creed was working in opposition to Wren when he had unprotected sex with her in a wine cellar. He got her pregnant. They're ridiculous. They are so irresponsible with sex that even I know all about their sex lives, and I really shouldn't. I am their sister, and I oppose that I know so much about it. But because they've been such idiots, the entire town is aware of it. So the fact that you're trying to warn me off sleeping with somebody just because I'm going to work at his ranch proves definitively that you don't actually think of me the way that you do Jackson and Creed."

He looked at her for a moment, lifting a brow. "Who said I didn't tell them they were being dumbasses?"

"Did you?" she pressed.

"Not in so many words, no, but I didn't really want to get punched in the face."

She turned, balled her hand into a fist and slugged his shoulder. He was so muscular his flesh didn't even budge. It was like punching a granite wall.

"You tool," she said, shaking her hand.

"Honestly, language. And you were upset about *horny*."

"And fuck you," she said.

"All right, I don't think of you as your brothers," he said. The windshield wipers on his truck were moving faster now. Working overtime. Trying to keep up with the snowfall.

"You wouldn't want me to anyway."

"You don't get to say what I want," she said.

"You're awfully spiky," he said.

"I have a right to be spiky," she returned. "You're being patronizing."

"I'm not intending to be patronizing. But the fact of the matter is, you are younger than us. And I worry a little bit about you."

That last comment made her feel like she was on uneven ground. But her fury still lingered, even while his concern wound its way around her heart. "You worry about me so much that you took my livelihood out from under me without a second thought."

"I didn't the hell know you wanted the winery, Honey, and I'm not invested in you not having it. We should've talked about this before you went off half-cocked."

"I'm about to go get a whole cock, thank you very much."

"I'm sorry, but *horny* was offensive?"

She chewed the inside of her cheek, feeling red and embarrassed and mad. She was just so… It wasn't fair. None of it was fair.

"This weather is getting intense," she said.

"Yeah," he said.

But something about the way he said that made her think that he wasn't really thinking of the weather.

They ended up not talking for a while, and she fiddled with the radio until she eventually gave up and just plugged her phone into his cable, firing up her country playlist. But he didn't complain.

It transitioned from Luke Bryan to Mickey Guyton, and she tried to focus on the song lyrics and not on the fact that the cab of the truck suddenly felt too small.

But about fifteen minutes into their determined silence, making commentary on the weather wasn't just to deal with awkwardness. It actually really merited a comment.

"This is crazy," she said.

The snow was beginning to truly pile up on the side of the road and starting to actually cover the road in earnest.

"It's fine," he said.

"I'm glad that you have so much confidence in your truck. That seems just like a man."

"No, it's spoken like a woman whose truck gave out a few miles back in good weather. I have a decent vehicle. It's going to be fine."

But the snow escalated until they couldn't see in front of them. Jericho slowed his truck to a crawl, maneuvering over the road as best he could.

"Shit," he said. "I might have to pull off. I can't see a damn thing." Just then, a big truck hauling logs came by in the oncoming lane. They didn't see it until it was right on top of them. It breezed by them so close, hugging the yellow line and making Honey jump.

She put her hand on his forearm, breathing hard.

"Good Lord," she said.

"Yeah," he said. "I'm going to have to pull off till it eases up. Assuming I can find a spot. See a spot."

"Where the hell are we?"

"Somewhere between Gold Valley and Lake Oswego," he said.

She thought she should probably laugh at that comment, because obviously… But her heart was still beating too quickly.

He took his phone out, and she could see that he didn't have any bars. She didn't hold out any hope that it meant she would either. He pulled off slowly, and she could feel the truck slide, then sink.

"Oh…" she said. "We're not going to be able to get back out."

"We'll be able to get back out."

Not today.

Not soon.

He didn't say that but she knew it. So did he.

The snow didn't ease.

They sat there, the engine idling, the heater doing its best to keep them from freezing.

"I thought I was going to die in my truck all alone. But it turns out I'm going to die in your truck sitting next to you. I have to tell you, it is not an infinitely more cheering prospect."

"We're not going to die," he said.

"You don't know that."

"No," he said. "I don't know that on any given day. But I don't figure as a matter of course that I'm going to die, and I don't really figure it now."

"But again," she said. "You don't know."

"For the love of God, Honey."

He didn't say anything after that. He was just breathing in irritation.

Hard and heavy, and she became very aware of her own breathing. Of her heart beating. She turned to look at him, suddenly afraid.

"What are we going to do?"

"Not panic," he said.

"This is how people die," she said.

"Yeah," he said. "It is. But I'm not going to let anything happen to you. You understand?"

His brown eyes were sincere, and that was so unusual that it twisted up her insides. Plus she was afraid.

And for some reason, it was stirring deep truths and longings inside her. Making her feel shaken.

She suddenly felt very aware of how close they were. Of the heat coming off his body. Especially as things outside began to cool.

"I'm not going to let anything happen to you," he said. He moved his hand across the empty space on the truck seat and placed it over hers. "I swear."

She shivered, looking away. "Okay."

"It's going to be all right."

"I believe you," she said.

She jerked her hand away, feeling suddenly beset by his touch.

It didn't mean anything to him. He was comforting her like he would a child. But it made her too hot. Even in all this cold. They both knew that no one was going to happen by. Because everybody was getting off the road. There was not going to be any help coming for them unless it was somebody specifically looking for people who were stuck.

And neither of them were relishing the prospect of sleeping outside, she was sure.

"I'm going to get out and take a look around."

"No," she said, leaping forward, grabbing onto his hand. "People do that and they don't come back."

"I'm going to come back."

"They always think they will."

"I will not get away from the view of the truck. I promise you."

"Promise," she said. "You know… You know that happened to that man… The family got stuck and he walked away and…"

"I know," he said. "But I'm not going to lose sight of the truck. I just need to see if there's anyone else around here. Or if there's a house even."

"This is the middle of nowhere."

"It's the middle of we don't know where. That's a fact. So I'm just going to see."

And then Jericho opened up his truck door and stepped out into the snow.

Chapter 3

The weather outside made a witch's tit look like Hawaii. It was cold. And he was not prepared for a blizzard. But then, he didn't figure there was going to be a blizzard. Sure, there had been a forecast for snow, but it was Oregon. The much talked about snow apocalypse was always only ever a few flakes. If anything, you might get a foot, but nothing like this. Nothing like this. This was unprecedented. And crazy.

He kept his word to Honey, keeping one eye on the truck as he walked up and down the side of the road, then took a step into the woods to see if he could see houses.

Under the cover of the trees there was less snowfall, and there was better visibility. That was good.

His hand burned. From where he had covered hers with his. Ill-advised. But she had been afraid. And he'd have been a bigger jerk if he hadn't tried to comfort her.

There was something about the fact she was telling him all this when she'd told no one else that made it feel different.

There was also something about being away from the vineyard, sitting with her in his truck, that made her feel different. It made things between them feel different, and he couldn't say that he liked it overly much.

It was just... Not what it was supposed to be.

Right, and you need to be thinking about this while you're in a survival situation?

He kept thinking of the way she'd said *dick*. *His* dick, in fact.

Honey used vulgar language all the time. It was kind of her thing. She was surrounded by men, and he kind of assumed that she tended to overdo it a little bit to prove that she was one of them.

But that was different. It felt different.

He felt it right on the aforementioned body part.

Just find some shelter, asshole.

All right, so he'd lied to Honey a little bit. He took hold of his scarf, unwrapped it from his neck and set it right next to a tree that was parallel to the car. As long as he kept a visual on that, he would be fine. The visibility was just so much better in the woods.

He pushed forward, always keeping the scarlet red of that scarf in his view.

He was looking for a house. Someplace that would have a phone so that they could call.

Anybody out here would have a landline. Or a phone that managed to get service somehow.

And then he saw it, just barely visible under the cover

of the trees. A cabin. It was huge, but there were no lights on. It didn't look like anyone was there.

Well. He was not sitting on the side of the road with Honey. And... Hell. If he had to break into the place to use a landline, he would.

He crossed the expansive trees and went up through the back of the house. He knocked just in case. But there was nothing. No one.

There was a lockbox on the door, like it was something that was for sale. He checked every window and found one in the back ajar. He pushed it up, popped the screen out and climbed in.

And he really the hell hoped that he didn't trip a burglar alarm, or anything of the kind, because he didn't especially want to get shot, either by a homeowner or a cop, in the pursuit of shelter. But this was an emergency. He laughed, because no cop was going to come out here even if a burglar alarm was tripped.

So there was that. The weather had caused the problem, but at least it was helping with this part.

He walked through toward the front door and saw a big basket sitting there. There were bottles of wine in it, and there was a piece of paper sitting in a plastic sleeve.

He looked down at it. Welcome to Pineview. There were instructions for everything in the house, plus a list of amenities.

A vacation rental. He'd stumbled on a vacation rental. Hell.

He went to flip on some lights, and realized there weren't any. Then he looked down at the paper again.

In this off-grid retreat...

Well. Shit. However, he could see from the amenities

paper that there should be a way to start a fire. A way to get lights going. And there were generators. For the hot water and for the toilets. All in all, it could be worse.

The paper also had a code to access the lockbox, and he did so, taking the keys out with him, before going back and replacing the screen on the window and closing it.

Wine in hand, he walked out the front door and back toward where he left the scarf.

From there, he made his way to the truck.

The visibility was so poor. He could hardly see.

He jerked the door open on the passenger side of the truck, and Honey jumped. "Oh," she said. "I did not see you."

"This is ridiculous," he said, pulling the door open with great effort. The snow was up to the bottom of it, piling higher and higher.

"Come on out," he said.

She did, as best she could. But there was a fair amount of wrestling with the snow in trying to get the door to open.

"Crazy," she said.

"I know it."

They both had suitcases in the back that were now covered with snow.

"What exactly are we doing?"

"I found a house."

"And they're letting us come inside?"

"Kind of."

He hefted her suitcase out of the back of the truck and handed it to her. Then he took her free hand with his and led her into the woods. She was wearing gloves, which offered a barrier to their touch. But he still felt the fact that he was holding Honey Cooper's hand.

She dropped hold of it when they were beneath the trees. He stopped and gathered his scarf.

"What was that?"

"A marker. I didn't keep the truck in sight. But I kept that in sight, and I knew that the truck was just parallel to it."

"Of course you couldn't just be safe," she said.

"Hey, I found a house," he said. "You should just be thankful."

"That's a very male thing to say," she said.

"I'm a man," he responded.

"Sure," she said.

He gestured in front of them. "It's just through here." They went through the trees, and the house was still there, standing dark.

"I thought you said…"

"I didn't say anything. It's a vacation rental."

"A vacation rental."

"Handily, with a list of amenities right inside."

He pushed open the door, and she followed behind him.

"Damn," she said. "It's as cold in here as it is out there."

"But dry," he said. "It's off-grid."

"Off-grid," she squeaked.

She looked so distressed it might have been funny if there was anything funny about it. "Yeah," he said. "But there's fire starter. And it's designed to be this way. So, if the power goes out in the broader world everywhere, we'll be just fine here."

"Because the power's already out," she said.

"But again," he said. "Set up for it." He gestured around. "Lanterns."

"Seems a fire hazard," she said.

"Are you going to get overly excited and knock any of the lanterns down?"

"No," she sniffed.

"Well then, I expect it's fine."

He watched as Honey wandered around the room, setting her suitcase down and ferreting about.

He looked down at the paper. "So if we get the generators to fire up, you can use the bathrooms."

"Well, thank God for that. I wouldn't have relished going outside to take care of things."

"No," he said.

"What else have we got?"

"There's a store of food. A root cellar and some evaporative cooling. Apparently. The off-grid experience is enhanced by the foods that they stock and provide. There is salted meat."

She looked around as if everything in the room might be a potential threat. And damned if he didn't find it... cute.

What the hell. He didn't do cute.

"Well," she said. "I feel like a pioneer."

"You don't sound thrilled about it."

"In fourth grade we had to spend an entire year playing *Oregon Trail*. I had enough party members die of dysentery to be cured of this fantasy."

"I always liked *Oregon Trail*."

"Sure. As a game. Less so as something I actually

have to experience. I do not have an endless supply of bullets with which to go hunt buffalo."

He leaned into the humor of the moment because it was that or lean into the tension, and he didn't want to do that. "You wouldn't be able to find any buffalo in this weather anyway."

"Maybe they have some of the salted meat," she said.

"I guess we'll have to find out."

"Right now I'm more cold than I am hungry. I stuffed a protein bar in my face before you came to pick me up."

"Why?"

"I felt imperiled. Which made me feel hungry."

"Right. Well. Fair enough."

She scampered into the living room and he followed behind her. And saw that she was already taking out the fire starting gear from the basket near the hearth.

"Looks pretty good."

In this room there was a large fireplace. And he had noticed that there was a den off to the side where there was a woodstove.

That would actually likely produce more effective heat.

He assumed that whatever they cooked on in the kitchen also ran on wood heat. And it might benefit them to fire everything up.

"You got this?"

"Of course I've got this," she said. "I'm a country girl."

He chuckled. It was getting dark outside, and he took one of the lighters and a little lantern and decided to carry it with him.

The cabin was cavernous, massive, but it was also

solid and sturdy and fairly well insulated from the cold outside. Rustic, but comfortable.

The furniture was expensive, very nice. There was a big bedroom with a large king-size bed. And furs covering what looked like a pretty plush mattress.

And instantly, he pictured laying Honey down on those furs.

The image was so stark, so clear, that it made him jerk back. Shit. He could not be having thoughts like that. That just wasn't going to fly.

There was a big fireplace in there, which was good.

The other two bedrooms did not have a heat source.

He assumed that this place was mostly for rent during the summer. He couldn't imagine people going to the trouble of trying to rent it this time of year. And with weather like this it was basically a liability. He went back down the stairs, and there was a raging fire going in the living room.

"Well done," he said.

"I'm not entirely useless," she said.

"You're not even a little bit useless. I'm pretty damn sure you know that." Their eyes met and held for a long moment.

And it made him conscious of how alone they were.

And how beautiful she was.

He looked away.

"I don't know. Sometimes I feel a little bit like I might be useless."

"Is this about the winery again?"

"It's hard for things not to be about the winery right now."

"I get that. I really do. I get it. But I don't think it

was actually a commentary on you. Your dad wanted out from under it. He told me…he hasn't really been happy there for a long time. You may not believe this, but he approached me about it. I'm not sure that he's thinking any deeper than that. He's not capable of seeing the winery as a dream right now."

"Well, but…"

"He cautioned me plenty, even as he offered it. But the thing is, it's in a much different state now than it was all those years ago when he first started. It's profitable, it's got a full staff. Asking Jackson to look after things is kind of a formality. I think your dad sees a younger person wanting to take over the winery and remembers himself at my age…"

Honey snickered.

"What's so funny?" he asked.

"A younger person."

"I'm young," he said.

This was just insulting. He was in his midthirties, for heaven's sake, and this child, who was not a child at all, but a woman he found incredibly attractive, was laughing at him.

"Not really."

"Wow."

"Well. I'm just saying. You're not as young as I am."

Damned if he didn't know that.

"No," he said. "I'm not."

"Just making sure you remember."

Suddenly, that statement took on an edge, and it sliced through his gut like a knife.

"All right," he said. "Quit mouthing off and let's figure out something to eat."

"I hope that nobody's going to show up," she said.

"I don't think anyone's showing up. Even if they had a reservation... If we can't get out, people sure can't get in."

"Fair. This is so wild."

She stood and looked out the window, and he gazed at her, silhouetted by the waning light. The snow was beginning to pile up in earnest, even with the cover of the trees.

"There's no internet. Obviously. And there's no service. So until we are able to get out of here... We're not going to be able to get in touch with anyone."

"Great. So my truck is just going to be sitting up where we left it. Good thing I brought my stuff."

"Good thing."

"What are the Daltons going to think when you don't show up?"

He laughed. Hard and without humor. "Probably that I had second thoughts. About joining that circus."

"Well, I guess that would be fair."

"Yeah. Definitely."

"You never seem to be really affected by anything, and I guess I didn't really appreciate how weird it must be to find out you have this whole big family."

"I've known," he said.

"Oh," she said. "Well, I guess it must be weird to get an invitation to join it then."

"It's all weird. But... On the scale of things I've been through in my life, it doesn't really register. I felt like why not go." But even to his own ears that sounded hollow. If he didn't care, he wouldn't be going. But the truth of the matter was, he wasn't entirely certain why he was going. He just didn't have a good answer. Not for himself. Not at all. He didn't know what he wanted to prove, though he would like to think that he wanted to prove nothing. That he literally didn't care at all about Hank Dalton or what he thought. That he didn't have any desire to get to know his half siblings.

But there were a lot of them. And nieces and nephews too. And... Yeah, all right. Once you had an invitation to join in with the big family, it just seemed... He just wanted to see. He wanted to see what they were like. He wanted to see if he was like them.

Hardheaded and stubborn and determined.

He knew that Hank and Tammy Dalton were white trash from way back, and then Hank had done good in the rodeo and gotten a lot of money. That the money had managed to buy them class.

He knew they were hardscrabble and determined people, whose fights had always been legendary in town.

Jericho himself had a hot temper, he was more determined than most and he had been certain that he was meant for better things than what he was born to. And he had done all that he could to make that possible. He'd worked with his hands and used his brain to figure out the best usage of his work ethic. Basically, he had to wonder if he got some of that from Hank.

Granted, he knew he got plenty of spirit from his mom, who had been a beautiful woman, and a fighter. All the way to the end.

"Sorry," she said.

"No need to apologize. It's a weird situation. But it is what it is."

"You know," Honey said, wrinkling her nose. "For a while there, Cricket thought that she might be our half sister."

Jericho sputtered. "Really?"

"Yeah. She's not."

"Yeah, judging by the fact that she is now engaged to your brother, and they're having a baby, I figured."

Honey shrugged. "Well. It's just… Families are complicated. Is my point."

"Yeah. I know. Though I've always been kind of short on family."

She looked away. "You've always been like family to us."

He arched a brow. "Right. You just love me."

"Well, when you're not being annoying."

"Why don't you make yourself useful and start a fire in the woodstove. I'll go dig around for food?"

And then Honey left him sitting there, pondering the moment. And pondering the strange interruption to his life that this was. He been on his way to deal with this family stuff, and now he was here.

With her.

Far too much temptation for him to consider.

He didn't know what the hell any of it meant. And he had to wonder if by the end of it he would have a better idea, or if it would just be one of those things.

Not everything in life means something. Sometimes it's just a shitty detour.

Yeah. Well. He just hoped the shitty detour had decent food.

Chapter 4

Honey managed to find the root cellar, and in it the evaporative coolers. There were vegetables in there, remarkably well-preserved. Which only reinforced her theory that the house had been intended to receive visitors.

She hummed as she dug around for food, trying not to overthink the moment that had happened in the living room.

She really hadn't given a lot of thought to this whole situation with Jericho and the Daltons.

But then, she didn't know what to make of it. And they didn't exactly confide in each other. Mostly they just…bickered.

Because he made her feel strange, and if she wasn't saying something, they were sitting in silence, and she didn't like sitting in silence with him.

She found bacon and eggs, and some potatoes, and decided to go with breakfast for dinner. Unfortunately there was no pop can of biscuits, which would've made everything complete, and she wasn't about to go scrounging around for baking supplies.

There was a basket sitting by the door of the root cellar, and she grabbed hold of it, put her spoils inside and walked back up the stairs to the main level of the house.

The whole place was beautiful. High-gloss logs that built a sturdy, impressive-looking house. She just couldn't understand why anybody would choose to put a house this beautiful right out in the middle of nowhere with no amenities. Though, she supposed these were amenities. They were just a lot more work than the amenities she was used to.

She walked into the kitchen, and he was standing there, stripped down to a T-shirt, stoking the fire underneath the woodstove. His brown skin gleamed in the light, his muscles shifting with each movement.

He took her breath away.

And that was silly. She really needed to get a hold of herself.

"Breakfast for dinner," she said, lifting the basket.

"Perfect," he said.

"I did find ketchup."

"Well, that is the important thing."

"Absolutely. You can't have eggs or hash browns without a whole bunch of ketchup."

"On that we agree."

"Well, glad to know there's something. Maybe the secret to world peace is ketchup."

"Somehow I doubt it."

"What would it be then?"

He frowned. "Ranch dressing?"

"They don't have ranch dressing everywhere."

"All the more reason to use it as an agent of world change. People just need to know about ranch dressing," he said.

"Also true."

His dark brows shot up. "Two agreements in under a minute. We may survive this."

"Yeah, and I have bacon in this basket. So…" He chuckled. He straightened and crossed his forearms over his broad chest.

Her heart thundered.

"I turned on the generator. For the bathroom. So, all that's functional. And if you want to shower…"

"Oh," she said, suddenly feeling a little bit fluttery. "Thank you. That's great."

"As far as I can tell, it's got enough gasoline to run for a bit. But we probably don't want to run it constantly."

"The appeal of off-grid living escapes me," she said.

"I have to say, I like a modern amenity."

"Careful, I'm going to start thinking we're friends."

"Oh, God forbid."

She forced a smile, then started to root around through the cabinets, producing a frying pan, some cooking oil and the cheese grater. She found a potato peeler and stuck it in Jericho's hand. "Care to make yourself useful?"

"Amend that," he said. "I have been very useful this entire time."

She rolled her eyes. "Oh certainly," she said.

He moved alongside of her, grabbing the potatoes and starting to peel them into the trash. His muscular forearms flexed and shifted, and she did her best not to be distracted by it. And she did her best to ignore it while she sliced the bacon off the slab—which she had never done before—and cracked the eggs into a bowl, whisking them around.

It was a little bit of a learning curve, figuring out how to get everything onto the stove without burning it or causing huge drama, but owing to the basic nature of the meal, she managed to put together something nice. The dishes were camp plates. Blue tin with white speckles, and she found herself overwhelmed by nostalgia holding on to them. She couldn't even quite say why.

Until an image came into her head of her mother sitting at the table in the kitchen, holding a mug made of the same material. She smiled. "My mom used to like this kind of thing."

"Living off-grid?"

"No, these camp dishes." Her heart squeezed, and the image in her head got fuzzy around the edges. "My memories of her are so thin. I wish there were more. I wish I'd understood I was losing her so I would have held on to every memory more than I did."

"I'm sorry. From what I remember of her, she was great," he said. "I... I was glad I got to know her even if it was for a short amount of time."

She cleared her throat. "Yeah. I'm glad too. She really loved you, you know."

"That's how I met your brothers, you know."

"How?"

"Because both of our moms were sick. That sucked.

And of course at school… That was something people talked about. Then I lost my mom. I related to what they were going through with your mom's illness… It's not a great thing to be bonded over, that's for sure. Because it just kind of sucks."

"Yeah," she said. "It does."

"But your dad… He found out about my living situation, and he took me in. I don't know if you realize just how much I depended on your family."

She frowned. "No. I didn't. I didn't think about it. It was just that one day you didn't really leave."

"Well, if not for your dad, I was either going to have to figure out becoming an emancipated minor or possibly going into the system. And I didn't really relish that. He became my legal guardian… He made sure that I had everything I wanted. He did what Hank Dalton never did. He was like a father to me."

"Jericho…" Guilt twisted her. Because she hadn't realized all this. She'd been a kid, and she'd been consumed with the changes in her own family, and of course consumed with the fact that she thought he was handsome. And the associated torture therein.

She had never really thought about his losses. About the strangeness of his relationship to Hank Dalton. About…

You've never thought about him as a person. He's been an object. There to be good-looking to you, irritating to you…

Yeah. Well, turns out he wasn't exactly the crappiest person in their relationship. It was her. It left her feeling rocked. Because she had spent so much time absolutely certain no one understood her. But how much of an effort had she ever made to really understand the people around her?

She was sure she was stoic because they all simply were.

Were they also trying to protect her? Protect themselves?

"I'm sorry that I never thought about that," she whispered, the words coming out raspy. "It's pretty much inexcusable."

"It's fine, Honey."

Her chest felt sore, and her heart was beating hard. She didn't like it. "No. I've been a brat to you. Always."

He stared at her, long and hard. "You know I never forgot. That you are just a little girl who lost her mom the way that I did. I didn't forget. Because I'm older than you. Because I got to have some perspective along with my grief. You were a kid. And…"

"I'm not a kid now. And it seems that I haven't done a very good job of recognizing…the full picture of things."

"I think that's pretty normal."

"Stop absolving me for being a jerk. I don't deserve it."

"Since when is any of this about what we deserve."

"I don't know. I just know that… I should've been a better friend."

"You're a pretty good friend. You made some bacon."

"Yeah, well you saved my life. What if you hadn't of happened by? I would be completely stuck in my truck in this blizzard. Nowhere to go. No cell service, no hope of rescue. Because at a certain point people that were smarter than us got off the road."

"Well, I did happen by. And here we are."

She looked around. "Yeah. Here we are."

"I guess there's not really much to do up here."

"There's some bookshelves."

"Yeah, I noticed that. Maybe I'll finally get around to reading *Lord of the Rings*."

She wrinkled her nose. "I think I'll stick with the field guide of birds that I saw earlier."

"Birds, huh?"

Why couldn't he just let her find a thing to do to distract herself so they didn't have to talk?

She sniffed. "I like birds, Jericho."

"Like *particularly*, or in comparison to how much you like hobbits?"

She huffed a laugh. "No. *I like birds.*"

"What's to like about birds?"

"They're…cute. Or majestic. Or *menacing*. Birds can be all three. I admire it." Then she added, "I aspire to it."

"They're also good fried," he said.

She scowled. "Yes. But that isn't… I'm not reading a recipe book. I am reading a *field guide*."

"Well, enjoy your field guide."

"Perhaps I will."

They finished eating, and she gave thanks for the running water, rinsing off all the plates while Jericho dried and put them away. Then they retreated to the living room, where they had built a big fire, and she pretended to peruse the illustrated guide to birds while he did a good impression of somebody reading a thick fantasy novel.

And really, she was just suddenly overwhelmed. By the isolation. By his proximity.

By the fact that she had intended to be with another man tonight. Losing her virginity.

And suddenly the idea made her feel strung out. On edge.

Suddenly it made her feel… Way too much of everything. She also thought of her suitcase, which was currently full of lingerie.

And she swallowed hard.

She turned her focus to the Mott Mott. Which was an interesting enough bird. But not half as interesting as the intrusive thoughts swirling around in her head. Which should not be interesting, but problematic. Very, very problematic.

"Well," she said. "I'm sleepy."

"It's probably about that time," he said.

"We'll let the fire die out."

"Oh."

"I started one upstairs a bit ago."

"Oh good."

Except her throat was dry, and it didn't particularly feel good. It felt…like something, and it shouldn't feel like something. They were just out here surviving together. There was nothing happening. No undertone to the offer of preparing beds and fireplaces.

She followed him upstairs, and it took a moment for things to begin to dawn on her fully.

"Wait… You started one?"

"The other bedrooms don't have fireplaces," he said. "If you want to stay warm… This is the room."

He pushed the door open and revealed a master bedroom, with a roaring fire and a massive bed covered in blankets and furs.

"Oh but…"

"It's not a big deal," he said. "It's a huge bed."

"But…"

"Is it a problem?"

A thousand thoughts cascaded through her head. Yes, it was a problem. She had never shared a bed with a man in her life, and now she was supposed to sleep next to the most beautiful man she'd ever known. Now she was supposed to… What the hell? How was she going to survive this? How was she going to survive this?

"You seem bothered," he said.

She did her best not to sputter outrageously. "I am *unbothered.*"

"I brought your suitcase up too. If you want to get in some pajamas."

She thought about the pajamas she had brought. All of a rather lacy nature. Because she had been planning on…

She swallowed hard.

"You know. I think I'm just going to sleep in this. For warmth."

"Suit yourself."

"Do you need to… You need to change into…pajamas?"

He fixed her with a hard stare, his dark eyebrows lifted. "No. I think I'll stick with this."

"It's okay…"

"I don't wear pajamas, Honey."

"You don't…"

He slept naked.

The truth slammed into her hard. And she felt it between her legs. Oh gosh. She was failing at not making this sexual. This thing that would never be sexual to him because of course he didn't feel that way about her at all.

"Well, then." She coughed. "Stay in your jeans."

"Somehow I thought that might be your stance."

She decided she just better rip the Band-Aid off. She got into the bed quickly, lifting at the edge of one of the furs and sliding beneath it, huddling on one edge of the bed.

It was so warm. It was luxurious. There had been a slight chill to everything, and the quilt, combined with the furs, took the edge off.

She was far enough on one side of the king-size bed that she didn't even feel it when Jericho got in.

She gave thanks for that. If she stayed on her edge, she should be all right.

She closed her eyes and tried to make her breathing sound normal. Tried not to sound like somebody who was faking being asleep.

"I'll tend the fire."

She opened one eye. "You don't have to do that by yourself."

"It's no big deal."

"But it's not… I mean…"

"Honey, don't worry about it. Get some sleep. If this turns into a multiday thing, then we may have to have conversations about who's manning the fire and who's not. But right now… We don't need to make a big deal out of it."

"Oh. Okay."

"Get some sleep. Because tomorrow is going to be a full-time job to keep ourselves warm. And fed."

"Hopefully the snow will have stopped by then." How long could it possibly do this? It had to stop. Tomorrow it would warm up and things would melt.

It had to.

"Hopefully. But I don't have any way to check the forecast. So I've a feeling we'll be walking down to check the road intermittently."

"Yeah." She sighed. "You know, nobody's even going to realize that we are missing except for the Daltons. And since they're just going to think that you blew them off..."

"I know. Thankfully your truck is sitting there closer to town than mine. So, it's possible that somebody will realize."

She blinked. "Right."

But neither of them said what they were both thinking, which was that they might be stuck here for a pretty long time. And that if they were, there wasn't going to be a whole hell of a lot that they could do about it.

They were just going to have to be very comfortable with each other.

And on that note, she curled up as close to the edge of the mattress as she possibly could. And closed her eyes tight.

Chapter 5

Jericho woke up and realized that the room was cold. And that he was *very* warm.

She wasn't touching him, but there was only a scant foot between the two of them, and he could feel the heat radiating off her body. He had tried initially to get under only one layer of the blankets, but it had just gotten so damned cold, that he had ended up surrendering to the need to get beneath them. And that put them far too close for his comfort.

And he needed to get that fire going again.

He stood up and looked out the window, pulling the curtains back. It was gray, early. The sun would probably be up in another half hour or so. But he wasn't quite ready to face the day. Not considering what they had ahead of them.

Because the snow had piled up impossibly high underneath the trees, and one thing was certain, even if the snowplow had been out this far, his truck was stuck on the side of the road. And he was going to have to get to a space where he could get a tow truck.

And right now, none of that was looking likely.

So he got the fire going again, and eyed the bed. And the space Honey had crowded into.

He lay back down, one layer beneath the blankets, and stared directly up at the ceiling, trying to ignore the way her breath fanned over his neck.

She was Jackson and Creed's little sister. She was practically a sister to him. And what he'd said to her last night had been true. He had always known that she was just a kid grieving her mom.

And it had never really bothered him that she didn't treat him like there was something grieving and broken in him. It was funny to see her distress over it. Like she thought she should've been sweeter and kinder for some damned reason.

As if he was suddenly breakable, because she realized they shared a common grief.

He'd always known that.

The fact that she was such a determined person. The kind of person who did just sort of get along with things… That was one reason he… Well, he recognized it. Because life was hard, and somehow you had to keep going. She was good at that. And he admired it.

Gradually, he realized that he wasn't going to be getting back to sleep. And he decided the better part of virtue would be getting the downstairs warmed up and figuring out some breakfast. And most especially coffee. He figured round two of bacon and eggs wasn't the worst thing in the world, and did that up quickly, and then gave up a prayer of thanks when he found a percolator and some coffee.

He set that on to steep and then decided to go back to the bedroom.

He didn't grab a lantern because the light was gray, and he could see more or less, and he'd taken decent note of the layout of the place the night before.

He pushed the bedroom door open and saw Honey, now curled up firmly in the middle of the bed.

He started to cross the space, but bumped against the dresser and knocked her suitcase down. It popped open, landing on its end, the contents spilling out.

"Shit," he muttered, bending down to pick it up. He reached down to begin to shove the items back inside and recognized the texture of the handful of things that he grabbed.

Lace.

He had an entire handful of lingerie. Because the suitcase was… Well, hell, it appeared to be 90 percent see-through underwear.

He was frozen. Completely and totally frozen, and grateful for the fact that he couldn't see all that well, because if he had too much of a sense of the kind of panties Honey was into, he might just die of a heart attack. And he didn't need that kind of drama, not on everything else.

He didn't have that kind of restraint; he damn well did not.

But it was too late. Because he was already figuring out exactly what these panties consisted of from just a casual touch, and his mind was constructing highly visual fantasies.

He heard a squeaking sound, and then she sat up, just in time to see him crouched there, holding on to her clothes.

"What the hell are you doing?"

"I knocked your shit over," he said. And he shoved it back into the suitcase as quickly as possible and turned the thing flat.

"Don't go through my things," she said, climbing out of the bed and scrambling over to the suitcase, viciously pushing the clips back down.

"Sorry," he said. "I didn't mean to. I just came to tell you that I made coffee. And bacon and eggs."

"Well, fine," she said.

"I'd suggest you get changed, but I don't think you have a change of clothes in there."

"Oh, you had to say something."

"Yeah. Apparently I did." He had meant to say something, because at the end of the day, it was his bad that he knocked the suitcase over and it wasn't really his business what was in it. But he had seen it. He couldn't unsee it. Not even a little bit.

"A gentleman wouldn't comment."

"I never said that I was a gentleman."

"Well, that is… That is very clear and obviously true."

"Settle down, Honey."

"Do not tell me to settle down. Do not tell me to settle down when you're the person who…who has been manhandling my things."

"Were you planning on actually working up there?"

"I was going to have the rest of my things sent. But in point of fact, I was intent on launching a seduction."

"Hell. I need coffee."

He turned and stomped out of the room, went down the stairs.

And he heard her furious footsteps behind him.

"Not that it's any of your business," she said. "I was on a mission to lose my virginity."

Everything in him went quiet. Still.

He turned, and he couldn't really make out her face in the dim light. Couldn't tell if she was angry or horrified that she let that slip. Couldn't tell what she'd been thinking by doing it.

Virginity.

She had been going up there to lose her virginity to…

To some random dude.

And he would never, ever, be able to get that image out of his head. That Honey Cooper was a virgin.

That she was ready to lose it. That she had a whole bunch of lingerie designed for that very thing in that suitcase up there.

He was only a man. And what really worried him was that he might have more in common with Hank Dalton than he had previously realized. Because he was a little bit of a womanizer and always had been, but this was something else. This felt like a compulsion. A tug.

And he didn't want to think about it. But it was there. And it was driving him.

And he felt…

It was deeper than the attraction he'd felt before.

Something in him felt like he would never really be

satisfied if he didn't strip her naked right then and there, kiss her lips and…

Coffee.

"I am getting coffee," he said.

"Does that bother you? Does it bother you to know that I was taking control of my life and my sexuality?"

"I was happy to previously have never thought about your sexuality," he said through gritted teeth.

Such a damned lie.

But a virgin? A virgin. He had not considered that. Not ever.

"Well. How nice for me. That's the problem, Jericho. I could stay in Gold Valley and remain a sexless, boring object that just sits around the winery, not seen as somebody who could take over, not seen as somebody capable of being the boss, not seen as an actual woman, or I could go off and make a life for myself.

"So maybe you don't understand why I might want to get a new job, or sleep with the man who gave me that job. Honestly, those things are accidentally linked. I met him on a dating site. I wasn't going to take work from him, but the offer came up. And it…it seemed infinitely better to what I had. Seemed infinitely better than dying on the vine out in Gold Valley."

"Let me tell you something," he said, breaking his own rule and mandate about going to get the coffee. "There's a whole lot out there in this world, good sex and bad sex, and none of it makes you who you are. You make you who you are, and there should be no reason to go out and fling your virginity at the nearest person you can find just because you're unsatisfied with the state of things."

"It doesn't matter, and yet you are lecturing me on the fact that I shouldn't throw my virginity away? Can you see how those two things conflict with each other?"

"Dammit," he said. "That's not the point of anything. Just sit… You don't need to find the first guy you're remotely interested in and…"

He didn't like any scenario, but for some reason he extra hated Donavan.

"You don't know who I'm interested in. You don't know who I have been interested in. And who I haven't been. You don't know as much about me as you think. Look, I admitted that I don't know as much about you as I should. That I kind of just saw you as… It doesn't matter. But the fact that you knew that I was a grieving little girl doesn't mean that you know me now."

"No. It doesn't. And if I'm honest… I figured that you… I mean… You're twenty-two."

"I know how old I am," she said.

"I figured you had." He gritted his teeth. "You know. If pressed to think about it."

"Well, I know you have, because you flaunted all over the place. And that's what I don't understand. How is it okay for you to do that, but you're all up in arms about me."

"I don't want you to get hurt," he said.

"Why do you think I would get hurt?"

"Because women *do*," he said. "They end up making rash choices about sex and they get hurt."

"Wow. That is the most… You are infuriating. And you have no right to comment on anything. None at all. I didn't want you to see that suitcase, I didn't want you to know about any of this."

"Why did you tell me?"

She sputtered. "I need coffee."

She brushed past him and went into the kitchen, grabbing hold of the percolator and the camp mug—that was identical to the plate she'd used last night—and pouring an amount in. "I guess it would be too much to hope that they had half-and-half."

"Sorry. Nothing quite so civilized."

"Well, that's just terrible."

She just served herself up a heaping portion of eggs and bacon, then retreated into the living room, where there was a fire going. He stayed in the kitchen, stood while he ate.

This was fine. It was early, and the situation they were in was weird. They didn't need to carry on talking about her hymen, or whatever. He didn't care about things like that. He never had.

So why his brain should be stuck on Honey and her sexual status, he didn't know.

Maybe because he'd been too damned fascinated by her to begin with, and now that he knew for a fact no man had ever touched her…

The idea of being the first one to do it…

Hell.

And no.

As if she hadn't been off-limits to begin with.

After he got the coffee into him, he felt a little more balanced. And he took himself into the living room, where Honey was sitting, her giant bird book on her lap, her empty plate beside her. She was studying the birds.

"How are the birds?"

"Much the same as I left them," she said, sniffing.

"Good. Good." He looked at her. "You know speaking of birds. And bees…"

"No," she said, holding up her hand. "I could happily never have this discussion with you, Jericho."

"Why not?"

"Because it's awkward. Because I'm going to die of being awkward."

"It's just…" He didn't know why he couldn't leave this alone.

He had to…deal with it. Talk about it until he wasn't so preoccupied with it. Make it feel like something normal and not taboo and definitely not the source of a host of new fantasies surrounding a woman he never should have had any fantasies about in the first place.

Let alone fantasies about being her first.

"Look," he said. "It's just that… Women get a lot of feelings around sex."

"Oh," she said. "*Women.* Women get a lot of feelings around sex. Which is why you are prowling around like an angry cat unable to drop the subject."

"I'm not prowling. Most especially not like a cat."

"Panther."

"Not less offensive."

"Why?"

He knew why. Because he felt like a predator all of a sudden. Stuck in the house with her. Like a fox in the henhouse, if he had to choose. No. He had control over himself. He was not Hank Dalton.

He looked at Honey, who was staring yet more resolutely at the birds.

"Are there new birds?"

She didn't look up. "I can report that there are no new birds since yesterday."

"But you seem very committed to the book."

"Just let me deal with the awkward situation by pretending to be engrossed. I think we both know that's what I'm doing. Why can't you do the same?"

He didn't know.

"Because. Ignoring stuff doesn't make it go away."

And that was the biggest load of bullshit he ever spewed in his life, because if he was good at one thing, it was ignoring feelings until they went away. Because he had been a lonely, sad kid who had just pushed those feelings aside and made himself tough. Because he had been forced to be grown before he ever should've been, taking care of his mother and missing so very much being the one that was taken care of. Because he had developed resentment heaped upon resentment at the father who wasn't there.

Who hadn't given them enough money to survive the medical bills that were piling up. Because his mother—because of her pride—refused to accept any money from Hank, or to allow Jericho to ask for any. Yeah. He was a champion at ignoring emotions. A damned *king*.

And he flashed back to the moment in the winery before he found out that Honey was leaving. Before she yelled at him. And he suddenly had an inkling as to what was going on here. It was an excuse. An excuse that his body was latching onto like a champion. She had introduced something interesting, and he had taken that as an opportunity to swing wide the door on the attraction that had been building there for longer than he cared to admit.

It was harder right now to deny how attracted to her he was than it ever had been. His blood felt hot with it.

It had become harder and harder to think of her as the little girl she'd once been.

The image of her now had fully replaced the one of the past, and it was even hard for him to think of her solely as Jackson and Creed's little sister. They worked together. They spent a lot of time at the winery together. And he saw her, her moods, her work ethic. Her strength. She was snappy and feisty and every inch the kind of woman he'd love to tangle with if she weren't…

No. That was a lie. She was not the kind of woman he'd want to tangle with if she weren't Honey Cooper. Because she was too… She was too earnest. Everything that she felt and did came from a very real place. Including all the anger she'd spewed at him back at Cowboy Wines, and…even her running up north to go sleep with some guy. Because she was put out about the situation at the winery.

Like she was trying to shed her skin, shed her expectations. And he didn't do earnest. He didn't, because there was nothing he could do in the face of it. Because he had spent so many years deadening his own feelings. And he didn't know what to do with the person who simply…hadn't.

"Isn't there something to do? Like some manly homesteading thing? That will get you out of my grill."

"I made you breakfast," he pointed out.

"And it was appreciated. The coffee was good. But… Isn't it a full-time job survivaling?"

"*Survivaling* isn't a word."

"It is. It's what we're doing. We are survivaling."

"We're *surviving*."

"No. Because it's like—" she waved a hand "—survivalist stuff. It's not just like surviving."

He huffed out a laugh. "Has anyone ever told you that you're ridiculous?"

But the ridiculousness didn't ease the tension. She was too cute, sitting there on the overstuffed couch by the fire, woolly socks on her feet, her brown hair in a loose knot on her head. As she held a giant book that opened across her whole lap and pretended to read it.

She looked up at him. "Oh. All the time."

"So, you want me to go survivaling. And what are you going to do? Sit here reading about birds? How is that useful?"

"A solid database of avian knowledge can always be useful, Jericho."

He stared at her for a long moment. At the way the sun glowed on her skin. The curve of her cheekbones, her round, pink mouth. Her whiskey-colored eyes.

She was a pretty creature. No doubt about that.

The kind of pretty, delicate thing his hands could easily spoil. And he would do well to remember that.

"For what?"

"For example, I will know which birds we can cook and eat if it comes down to it."

"You know, I think I'm going to go ahead and hope we skip that part. There's no way the weather's going to keep up like this."

"I wouldn't have thought it would have kept up overnight," she said, putting the book down and scrambling to the window, looking outside. "I've never seen anything like this."

He didn't want to say that he hadn't either. Didn't want to acknowledge that this was outside of his scope of experience. "It'll be fine. We are really very okay with our setup."

"Yeah. Except for the whole being out of touch with civilization."

"We don't need civilization. We have each other." He paused for a moment. "And bacon."

"The bacon won't last forever." Her voice sounded thin and it made his gut tighten.

They were talking about bacon.

"No." And he was a little afraid of what might happen if the two of them kept on in close quarters. But no, there was no reason to be afraid. He was in control of himself. In control of his body. Brief flashes of attraction, and a newfound fascination with her sexual status did not get to dictate what he did next.

And what he would do, was go chop wood.

Because that was useful. And it was not sitting here ruminating on things that he shouldn't.

"I'm going to go chop some wood. Best make me some bread."

"Bread?"

"Yeah, that's your women's work. For the survivaling."

That earned him her anger and damned it if didn't ignite a fire in his blood. He needed to go jump in a snowbank.

Good thing there were so many handy.

"*Really*," she said.

"Well, once I'm done chopping wood I'm going to have expended a lot of calories."

"All right," she said. "I'll make you something. I can't promise it'll be bread. I don't have… Anything. And I'm not good at that stuff anyway. I know just enough to keep myself fed."

"Well, maybe it's your chance to expand your skills."

That hit. And it hit hard. And in spite of himself, he caught himself holding her gaze. Lingering.

It hit him deeper than it should.

Made him think of all kinds of skills he could help her expand.

His hands on her skin. Her body against his. He'd denied it for so long now it was second nature. Wanting what he couldn't have was his natural state.

As a boy he'd wanted a father. He hadn't had one.

He'd wanted his mother to be well. He'd wanted to not be a caregiver, and he hadn't gotten that either.

Wanting Honey was just a piece of all that same longing he'd lived with his whole life.

No.

"Wood," he bit out.

And then he strode out, like the fire had leaped out of the fireplace and was chasing at his heels.

Chapter 6

Honey felt prickly and perturbed. As she had, ever since this morning's explosion with Jericho. She had not meant to tell him about her virginity. But then, he shouldn't have looked at all of her lingerie.

Still, the lingerie had not necessitated her confession. She didn't really know why she'd done it.

Maybe wanted to see what he'd do…

That made her breath quicken.

It was a strange thing, being trapped here with him. It was a lot like being in the den with a lion. And the problem with that was, she kept getting tempted to… feed herself to him.

The problem was, in close proximity like this it was difficult for her to forget that she was attracted to him. Wildly. But what had started as a fluttery sort of teenage feeling had lately become extremely adult and quite *imagination after dark.*

But she…

The fact was, she wanted him, and Donovan had only ever been a surrogate for that. Because she felt like her attraction to Jericho was emblematic of the fact that she had held on to her virginity for too long. But she had convinced herself that she could rid herself of her issues by just losing it to anybody. And now she was beginning to wonder.

It was a really distressing thing to have to admit to herself. Especially while she was trapped here with him.

Especially while it felt a lot like the universe was giving her an opportunity to exorcise the actual demon that was hounding her.

The problem was that she had a job lined up with a man who certainly thought that she was coming to also have a physical relationship with him. And that, she supposed, was where Jericho's concern for her well-being in that regard had come from. She could suddenly see how very sticky it all was. Because if she slept with Jericho now…

Well, she wouldn't expect them to have a relationship. No. Far from that.

They could barely be in the same room without bickering. They were a very bad match, actually. It was just that she happened to be very particularly attracted to him. It was just that she couldn't imagine touching him and then… And then touching someone else.

Well, he has given no real indication that he wants to touch you, barring his strange and deep fascination with your virginal status.

It was true. He had not given a real indication that he wanted to touch her. Everything that she was thinking was based firmly in the realm of fantasy. Firmly in her head.

She started to open up the pantry doors and search around for dry ingredients. She found a cookbook and was successful at finding the ingredients necessary for a quick bread. There was no yeast. And she supposed that was a gift. The Irish soda bread would be quick. And the odds of her screwing it up, even with the wood-stove were low.

She was thankful now that her father had made her learn basic survival skills. And that he had made sure she knew how to keep a fire going.

And she just had to wonder…if what Jericho said was true. If what was happening with the winery didn't have anything to do with the fact that she was a girl, or the fact that her father doubted her competence. But everything to do with the fact that he was simply done. That it had become an albatross to him, and he had nothing left to prove.

She knew that the reason that he'd started the winery in the first place had been to get at James Maxfield, her sister-in-law's father, who had stolen the love of her father's life away from him many years ago.

Her father's obsession with proving that he was good enough had driven a wedge between her parents; at least, that was something that her father had been talking about lately. His own shortcomings. The ways that he hadn't managed to be the husband that he wanted to be because he was so lost in what could've been. The way that he had never really appreciated what he'd had.

He had the woman he'd always loved now, but she knew that getting there hadn't been the easiest of journeys.

So maybe that was it. Maybe he just couldn't separate his own feelings from the equation.

She mixed together all the dough, which in her opinion formed kind of an unattractive lump, and put it in a cast-iron skillet, which she then slipped into the oven.

She had no idea how to gauge the heat or the doneness in a wood fire oven, so she kept a continual eye on it. But much to her gratification, the smell that filled the kitchen was lovely.

By the time lunch rolled around she had a beautiful-looking round of bread that she was ready to slather in butter.

But Jericho hadn't returned.

She felt the prickle of worry.

The snow was still coming down pretty hard outside, and while she didn't think he could've gotten lost, she didn't really know.

Neither of them knew this area, and the visibility was poor. She had no idea where the wood was that he was supposed to go chop. And he might've injured himself. It was icy outside. Him walking in the ice with an ax was a whole different thing to concern herself with.

And it just didn't matter how fine everything seemed. She knew that better than most.

Good people were taken away for no reason. All the time.

No one was safe. Nothing was truly protected from harm.

With a bit of panic building in her breast, she grabbed her coat and slipped out the front door.

The silence was eerie. All noise insulated by the dense cover of snow all around. It was still falling, and every so often she would hear a tree groan beneath the weight of it.

That was another thing to worry about. Falling trees and limbs. The snow here was so wet that it fell heavy and thick on the branches. And could easily create a disaster. Downed power lines and trees, mudslides...

She sucked in a sharp breath and regretted it, when the cold touched the back of her throat and made her cough.

It was so cold.

Snow like this was such a rarity that she really wasn't used to it. They got a light dusting now and again down in Gold Valley, but anything thicker and heavier typically fell up in the mountains, where she did not live. So it was just all very unusual.

She would like to enjoy the novelty a little bit, but it was essentially impossible, given that the novelty was pretty well stripped away by the reality of the situation.

She paused for a moment and heard a loud crack. One that she hoped was the sound of Jericho chopping wood, and not the sound of a tree limb giving way.

She scrambled that direction, slipping and sliding in the slushy snow that went past her knees.

Her boots were insufficient, and snow went over the edges, down into her feet.

She shivered. But she kept on going.

She heard the crack again and was reasonably certain that it had to be Jericho. But she pressed on anyway.

She came up over a snowy ridge and saw him, swinging the ax and bringing it down unerringly on the log piece, splitting it in two.

Then he dropped the ax, and picked up the stack of

wood that he had produced, lifting it easily and beginning to walk up the hill. He stopped when he saw her.

"What the hell are you doing?"

"I came looking for you."

"It's freezing," he said.

"Yes, I know. It's why I was worried about you. I'm fine." Except for the snow in her boots.

"You don't look fine."

"I am." But her teeth began to chatter.

"March yourself back to the house."

"I was worried about you," she said. He walked up the hill, and she waited for him to reach her. He was laden with wood.

"I can take some of that."

"No, you can't. Go on."

"I could," she insisted.

"Your feet are about to fall off. Don't tell me those boots are waterproof."

"Fine. They're not. But my feet are not going to fall off."

"Go."

"There are fires and everything back at the house," she protested. "I'll be fine."

"This isn't a joke," he said. "I understand that we landed ourselves in a really cushy situation, but this is the kind of weather that kills people, Honey, and you were worried about that when we were stuck by the side of the road, but I feel like you're not as worried about as you should be now."

"Oh no, that's not fair. Because I went out looking for you because I was afraid that something happened to you. Because I know that this is the kind of weather that kills people."

"And if you found me, what were you going to do? Were you going to carry me back to the cabin?"

She looked up, all the way up, so she could meet his gaze. "Yeah. I think I could have."

"You think that you could've carried me back. Through the snow."

"Women lift cars and stuff when their children are in trouble. I'm pretty sure that I could drag you if I had the kind of adrenaline that… Well, I'm sure it's less adrenaline than a woman needing to lift the car off her child. But I bet it's an appropriate amount to move you."

"You're infuriating."

"How am I infuriating?"

"Because you keep overestimating yourself. You keep acting like you know the way of the world when you damn well don't. You don't know the state of anything, Honey. You just don't. You don't know as much as you think you do, you don't…"

"I'm fine. I made bread."

"No. You're acting like a child. Because why? Because you're mad that I have the winery?"

"Because I am furious," she said. "Because I'm furious that you have the winery, and that I had been fixated on your ass for at least ten years. It is ridiculous, and I'm over it. How can I… How can I want you when you are such a jerk, and I don't even like you."

He looked like she had picked up a ball of that wet snow and hit him in the face with it.

And she realized that she'd said it. She had actually

said it. And it was more awful and horrible than the revelation of her virginity ever could have been.

"Oh…"

"What do you mean you want me?"

"It's just that…" She stopped.

"Don't stop," he said. "Your feet are wet. Explain yourself."

She felt she was being frog-marched through the snow, and she had gone and embarrassed herself so deeply that she was sweaty along with freezing. Which was just a terrible combination. And it couldn't get any worse.

So some small part of her felt compelled to try to *make it worse*.

"I'll explain myself… It's just… I wanted to sleep with somebody else to get away from you. And to get away from the way that you make me feel. And to get away from…everything."

They arrived back at the house and he opened the door, propelling her inside. "Go take your clothes off."

"What?" It came out as a squeak.

"You heard me."

"I… I said that I… I didn't say that I wanted to…"

"We'll deal with that later. Right now you need to get warm. There's a sauna outside. Get those boots off, strip yourself down and put on the robe in the bathroom. I'll start the sauna."

"Oh… But don't you want to…"

"What I want is for your feet to not fall off," he said. "That's what I want. The rest of all this running off at the mouth you're doing we'll deal with later. But right now, you keeping your feet is the important thing."

Shivering, she shut herself in the bathroom and looked at the shower. She knew that it theoretically had hot water. She could just refuse to do what he said and get in the shower. But instead, she found herself stripping down and putting on the thick robe that was hung there. There were a pair of boots that looked soft and fuzzy, and the label over the top said sauna slippers.

She slipped her feet into them. They were lined with wool, and appeared to have a treated, waterproof exterior.

When she exited the bathroom, Jericho was nowhere to be seen, and it was probably all for the best, because she was naked beneath the robe and it made her feel uncomfortable, even though she was naked beneath all of her clothes, if she thought too deeply about it.

She picked up the paper that had all the directions for the house and saw that it stated there was a map on the back. She flipped it over and saw a hand-drawn guide to how to get to the sauna.

She shuffled out into the snow, thankfully not into any parts that were as deep as where she'd been a little earlier. So her feet stayed dry.

She saw smoke coming out of the top and was curious. She did not know how an off-grid sauna worked.

She opened up the door and Jericho was inside, his jacket cast to the side, his shirtsleeves rolled up as he fed wood chips into the fire. Then he took a ladle and poured water over the hot rocks at the top of the stove, steam coming off them in waves.

"This is how you do it," he said, pouring more water over it.

It was already toasty inside.

"And you need it."

"Thanks," she said.

She had closed the door behind her, because leaving it open seemed… Well, it seemed counter to the point of getting the sauna warm. But now she realized that she had gone and enclosed herself in a very tight space with the very man she was feeling completely self-conscious about.

And also that she was wearing only a robe.

"If you're in here for longer than twenty minutes, I'm going to come looking for you."

"Right."

Wherein she would be naked.

She shifted uncomfortably, heat building between her legs. Why was it like this? Why was it so…

It wasn't inevitable. She wanted it to be. And that was the problem. She was so hung up on him that she was pushing in a direction that she probably shouldn't go.

But all this… All this blurting she was doing, she didn't actually think that it was organic. She was obviously pushing the conversation. Holding herself back from saying the thing that she actually wanted, but saying everything but.

The fact of the matter was, what she really wanted was for him to be her first. What she really wanted was for him to be the one to introduce her to…to sex.

Because for all that he infuriated her, he was the only man that she had practically ever really wanted. He was the only man that she could really imagine herself being with. And imagine it she had. Repeatedly. In vivid detail.

Her chest felt tight, and her whole body flushed.

And then suddenly, she realized. She was going to do it. She was going to do it, become it, because she had already embarrassed herself. She had already told him that she was a virgin. She had already told him that she wanted him. She was just going to do this.

So she reached down to the belt of the robe and undid it. Then she let it drop to the floor. And she was standing before him, wearing nothing other than ridiculous shearling boots and a smile.

"Maybe you could stay." Her voice felt scratchy; she felt scratchy. Her heart was pounding so hard she could barely hear, and the steam filling up the room seemed to swallow her voice.

But she could see his face. She could see the tightness there. The intensity.

"Honey…"

"No. I just… Maybe this is the time to have a conversation, actually. The one that we decided to have later. Because I'm getting warm. I'm very warm."

"Put your robe back on."

"What if I don't want to?"

"Why not?"

"Because I want you. I already admitted to that. Why do you think I'm so upset? All the time? About all the women that you bring into the winery, about the fact that my father gave it to you. About the fact that we're stuck together, but will never actually be together. And that's why I had to leave. I'm not an idiot, Jericho, I know that you and I are never going to… We're not going to fall in love and get married. We can hardly stand to be in the same room as each other. But I have wanted you since I understood what that meant. And I don't know what to do about it. Short of running away and having sex with someone else. That was my game plan. My game plan was to go off and have sex with another man. And that got thwarted. You were the one that picked me up. You're the one that I'm stuck here with in the snow. And I'm not going to claim that it's fate. Because I can feel myself twisting every single element of this except for the weather. The blizzard isn't my fault. But I'm making the choice to go ahead and offer… Me."

"I…"

"If you're going to reject me, just don't do it horribly."

And then suddenly, she found herself being tugged into his arms, the heat from his body more intense than the heat from the sauna, the roughness of his clothes a shock against her skin. And then his mouth crashed down on hers.

Chapter 7

He was being an idiot. He was being a damned idiot. There were so many women out there in the world that he could sleep with and suffer no consequences for doing so. She was not one of them. She was in fact one of the few women who wasn't in that number. The only others were his friends' wives. And then there was Honey. And she was clinging to him like she wanted him. Like she wanted him and needed him. Like he was air.

He'd tried to resist. He'd told himself to.

But she wanted him.

That changed everything.

And she was so damn soft. And he was powerless not to rub his hands up and down her curves. From her rib cage just beneath her breasts, down her slender waist, to cup her ass, which was the most delightful handful he could've imagined.

And back up again. She was divine. And sweet. Just like her name suggested.

She might be vinegar when she talked, but when she kissed…

She shivered in his hold, her response to his kisses so intense it floored him. She was trembling with need. And it was… It was intoxicating. And maybe because she was a woman that he shouldn't want, he wanted her all the more. Maybe that's what made her skin so soft. Maybe that's what made her cries of pleasure so sweet. Maybe that was what made her so damned irresistible.

He moved both hands down to her ass and squeezed her tight, pulling her up against him so that she could feel how hard he was. And he knew it was too late. Knew that it was too late for better judgment and smarter decisions. There was no decision to be made. She was naked, she was in his arms and he wanted her.

He lifted her up off the ground, sat down on the wooden bench there in the sauna with her legs parted wide, her thighs on either side of his. He tilted his head back and looked at her, as best he could in the steamy room. Her breasts were small and round, beautiful, her nipples the same color as her name.

Tight and begging for his attention. Her stomach was flat, muscled from all the hard labor that she did, her thighs just the same. And that thatch of curls between her legs… It was all he could have ever asked for.

He gripped her hips, stared at the way his hands looked against her skin, moved them up beneath her breasts and slid his thumb across her nipples. She was beautiful. Delicious. He leaned forward and kissed her, right between her breasts, and she arched.

"Tell me if you want me to stop," he said, his voice rough.

"Don't stop," she whispered. "Please don't stop."

He lowered his head and sucked one bud into his mouth, flooded with relief. Because all this tension that had existed inside of him had suddenly unwound, tension he had known was there.

The denial that he wanted this. The denial that he wanted her. He did. And there was no denying it or hiding it. He had tried. He had put it down to a few errant moments of looking at her ass, but it was a hell of a lot more than that.

It had been building. And he knew it. It was why he'd been so furious when she said she was going to sleep with someone. It was why he'd been so obsessed when he'd found out that she hadn't.

Because he was full of this. This deep, dark, forbidden desire for a woman that he knew he wasn't supposed to touch.

But he was touching her now. Tasting her.

And it was a hell of a thing.

He moved his head from her first breast and then paid equal attention to the other, where she was just as sweet, just as filled with desire for him. She let her head fall back, and a cry of need escaped her mouth.

He didn't have a condom in here, so it wasn't going to go all the way. But he could take her there.

He curved his forearms up beneath her knees, pressed his hands to her lower back and lifted her from his lap as he slowly laid her down across the bench, parting her thighs and gazing at all of her feminine beauty.

"Jericho," she whispered.

She said his name. She said that she wanted him.

This seemed to prove it. Beautifully.

This was insanity. But he was neck-deep in it and feeling fine. Feeling ready to be submersed. He kissed her inner thigh, and she shuddered. Then he lowered his head, flicking his tongue over the source of her pleasure.

She gasped, arching against his mouth.

And she tasted sweet, and he knew that he had overdone it on the references to Honey, but it kept being true.

And he didn't know how he had ever thought of her as simply Creed and Jackson's younger sister. She was Honey and herself. And right now, she felt a whole lot like his. Right now, he didn't want to think of what moment followed this one, where she was so perfectly sweet and aroused for him. Only for him. All for him.

So he kissed her there, and teased her, until she was writhing against him, until she was begging.

Until she was crying out her pleasure, and he could feel it. Deep down inside. He could feel it.

"Jericho," she gasped.

The scene was all around them, between them. And she sat up. She looked dazed, filled with wonder. Her skin was dewy from the heat and the steam, and he wanted to lick every inch of her. And he had never seen a more beautiful sight.

Forbidden fruit. Pleasure deferred. Whatever you wanted to call it. It was damn sweet.

"Jericho…" And then suddenly she basically flung herself at him, kissing him, touching his chest, and he was so hard it hurt. She settled herself on his lap, the slick, wet heat of her hot against his denim-covered arousal.

He moved his hands over her curves, over her softness. And he knew that he would never get enough. Not of her. Not of this. Ever.

It was a scary thought, considering he shouldn't even have another bite, let alone gorge himself on the feast like he wanted to.

"I don't have a condom," he said.

"I have tons of condoms," she said.

"I meant I don't have a condom in here."

"Right," she said. "Oh… Oh. But we should get one."

"We should go back to the house."

"To get a condom."

"Maybe to take a breath," he said. But he would rather have a condom.

"I don't want to take a breath."

And she was looking at him expectantly, and he realized if he stopped now it would be… Well, it would be because of something other than her.

Sure, some of it was because of him. Some of it was because he was the last man who should be taking someone's virginity. He didn't have the sensitivity for that. He didn't have the sensitivity or the emotional… Anything. To be the person who should be handling something like this. But a lot of it was about Creed and Jackson, and at the end of the day, that wasn't fair. Because Honey was her own person, and the fact that her family seemed dedicated to not treating her like her own person, capable of making her own decisions, not even bothering to check with her before her dad sold the winery… All of that… That was… Well, it wasn't fair. She deserved to be treated like she knew her own mind.

Right. And that's the thing that will get you laid.

He wasn't going to claim he was being altruistic about it. But he was looking at it from a different angle. That was all.

The angle that let him have an orgasm.

But no. It would never just be that. She would never just be that. She was Honey Cooper, and he wasn't going to pretend otherwise. If he wanted to get laid, he could get laid. But she said she'd always wanted him. She'd said…

Well. You're a little bit sad.

Because the fact that she'd always wanted him, that meant something to *him*. This girl, this beautiful woman, who was part of the best family he'd ever known, wanted him. He couldn't deny that did something to him. Made something inside of him that had previously felt shattered feel fixed. And the fact that he wanted to chase some feeling of redemption in her arms was messed up as hell. The fact that he seemed to believe on some level that the gift of her body was going to wash away a world of hurt… Yeah, well, he had never claimed to be the most emotionally well-balanced person. Quite the opposite. He knew that he was a mess. He'd always known.

The kid who'd never really been a kid. The kid who'd been rejected by his father. Who'd lost his mother. Yeah, he never claimed to be real balanced. So he might as well just embrace it. Because hell, they were snowed in. What else could they do? And he could turn away from it now, but the odds of them resisting were low. Unless they were going to be rescued in the next ten minutes, and the way the snow continued to come down didn't make it seem likely—well, he might as well just go with it.

So he wrapped her in the robe, scooped her up in his arms, realized that she had never taken those boots off and pushed open the door to the sauna. It was still freezing cold outside. The snow was continuing to dump down in buckets, and he didn't know how long they would be stuck here.

"This is an extraordinary circumstance," he said, carrying them both through the snow. "And when we get rescued..."

"Right," she said. "I get it. Only during the snowstorm."

"Only during the snowstorm."

"What if we end up here for Christmas?"

"I don't know. I guess we'll cross that bridge when we come to it."

"I would like to cross this other bridge first."

"Seems like a good idea to me."

He kicked open the door to the cabin, then closed it behind him with his heel. They would need to get a fire going again in the bedroom.

He carried her up the stairs, and she clung to him, her arms around his neck, and her eyes took on a strange, soft look.

"What?"

"Well," she said. "No one has ever... I mean... No one has ever treated me like this. I had to be tough pretty much this whole time."

She had been. Tough, mouthy Honey, and everybody did treat her that way. He knew that was so. Even he was guilty of it. But did nobody really treat her with any softness? That was all he wanted to do. Wrap her in furs and make sure she was warm. Well, that was not all he wanted to do, but it was definitely the more gentlemanly thing he wanted to do.

He hadn't felt compelled to care for anyone in years. He'd been burned out on it. But Honey always seemed so invulnerable. And he knew she wasn't. That much had become clear on this little trip together.

It brought out tenderness in him he'd thought long gone.

He didn't say anything. Instead, he just kissed her. He kissed her because she was beautiful. He kissed her because he wanted her to feel that.

He kissed her because there weren't words to say that he was sorry for all the softness she'd missed out on because her mother had died. Because she had then been surrounded by people who were as wounded and hard and hurt as she was.

That was the truth of it. They had taken him in, but they were all in the same boat. Grieving and wretched and in general some of the least emotionally conversant people around.

And they'd all been there for each other, but clearly something was missing. For her.

Something no one had realized.

He would make it his mission for her to feel it here. For her to feel it this week. *Week. You don't know how long it's going to be.*

No. He didn't.

Someone could come knocking on the door right now—which he found he really didn't want—someone could find them in a week. Two weeks. They might be able to get the car out in the next couple of days. They didn't know.

But right now, it didn't matter. Right now, he was determined to dedicate everything in his power to making Honey feel all the things that she hadn't before.

That's a power trip.

Maybe. Maybe it was a power trip. Because he was a kid who—at the end of the day—felt like he had never really been able to offer much to anyone. He had tried, but his mother had still died. His father hadn't been there. The Coopers had given to him. And in the end, he felt like, to an extent, he had given back by buying the winery. Except he had still hurt Honey. And that did matter.

Sure, his own success was important. But so was her happiness.

And for the first time, he felt like he might be giving more than he was taking, and that was a pretty good feeling. Even if it was trumped up, all things considered. Since he was also getting sex and it wasn't like this was a mission of charity.

He was hardly the Mother Teresa of orgasms.

The bedroom was cold, and he laid her out gingerly on the bed and wrapped her up in the furs there.

She burrowed beneath them happily and kept her eyes on him as he began to build the fire.

The urge that he had to suddenly just…give her everything that he could think of… It was almost overpowering. He wanted her to have…every good thing. Every good thing. He got the fire going, nice and big, and when it was done, he straightened. "Okay. So tell me where the condoms are."

Chapter 8

Honey fought the urge to burrow deeper beneath the covers. She was… She was so desperately aroused, so desperately excited that she could barely breathe. Jericho had kissed her. Well, she had kissed him. After stripping naked. And then he had… Hell. He had kissed her. And places that she hadn't even got around to fantasizing he might kiss her.

It had been transformative. And now this. This realization of her deepest fantasy. She wanted this man. She wanted this man in ways that defied her experience. That far outstripped anything she'd ever done, anything she'd ever fantasized about in a concrete fashion.

It was real. But it was ephemeral and unformed. A mass of feelings that made her breath quicken and made her heart beat faster.

He was beautiful. She had always thought so. But it

was the way he looked at her. That was what truly left her in awe. That was what made it so she couldn't think.

Because he wasn't looking at her like she was just Honey, the same woman that he'd seen every day for the past who knew how many years. He was looking at her like he'd never really seen her before. And that made her feel new. The kind of new that she had wanted. The kind of new that she had believed might be out there for her, but it was better than finding it with a man she had never met before. She had found it with him.

She had found it with him, and she hadn't been expecting that.

Oh, how she wanted this man, this man who looked at her as if he had never seen her before, all the while he was a man who saw her all the time.

It was the fulfillment of her deepest need. Her deepest fantasy.

He was everything.

But she was nervous. And she found herself shrinking into those furs and that soft mattress.

They had shared this bed last night, but they had kept a healthy amount of space between them. Just a few moments ago in the sauna there had been nothing between them at all. And now...

"Are you okay?"

"Yes," she said, doing her best to sound emphatic.

It came out with just a little more tremble than she would've liked.

"Are you sure?"

"I am absolutely sure. I did say."

"You can always change your mind."

In those words, coming from the strongest, hottest

man she had ever known, who was essentially sex and cowboy boots, did something to fire up her arousal even more.

He was strong enough to take what he wanted, to do whatever he wanted. He was strong enough to break her if he wanted to, but he didn't want that. He wanted to use his hands to give her pleasure, and only the pleasure that she wanted.

He was more than any fantasy she'd ever had. And she was so unbearably aware, not of his strength then, but of the way that he kept it leashed.

That was power. And the intensity of it was enough to make her combust.

"I am 100 percent sure that I want to have sex with you, Jericho. I have been 100 percent sure of that for a very long time."

"And yet you're so mean to me."

"It didn't stop you from wanting to have sex with me," she pointed out. And then she suddenly became very afraid that he didn't actually want to have sex with her. What if she was just a charity case? What if this was just pity? Or worse, some misguided overprotective instinct because he didn't want her to have sex with a man she didn't know, a man that she was going to go work for. What if this was…him using his penis as a protective shield. Like parents who wanted their kids to drink at home if they were going to drink. Maybe he wanted her to have sex with him if she was going to have sex with anyone.

That would just be a whole lot of a hot mess. And she did not want that.

Except she didn't really want to question him either.

Because she wanted him. But of course, him not really wanting her would be unbearable…

"Is this about me? I mean, at all? Do you… Are you attracted to me?"

He huffed a laugh. "I have spent the last little bit trying not to notice just how beautiful you were. Because the fact of the matter is, there's a lot of women that I could be with who don't present as much of a complication as you do."

"That is not very flattering," she said, wrinkling her nose.

"I'm not trying to flatter you. I'm trying to be honest with you. And honestly? This is a terrible idea. If your brothers find out, they're going to kick my ass. Your dad's gonna kick my ass. Hell, maybe when I come to my senses, I'm going to want to kick my own ass. But I want you more than I care about that."

He hesitated for a second. As if there was something else he wanted to say, but then he didn't.

"All this is insulting, and deeply flattering at the same time. I'll take it." Because her chest burned. With satisfaction. With triumph. With the knowledge and desire that whether or not she was a terrible idea, Jericho Smith wanted her. He could have any woman. Fundamentally, he often did.

But right now he wanted her. Right now, she was the thing that he craved. Right now, she wanted to luxuriate in that more than just about anything. "The condoms are in my suitcase."

"The lingerie suitcase."

"Yes. I have several boxes, and I bought different kinds. Because I didn't know… You know, they say ribbed on some of them. And I didn't really know what that meant, so I got that. But I got regular kinds too." She felt silly all of a sudden.

"As long as they're not hot pink, I'm fine."

"What if they are? Would that be a deal breaker?"

He shifted. "At this point, nothing is a deal breaker. I'm too far gone."

The fact that he couldn't reject her over a hot pink condom was another spurious compliment, but another one that she would gladly take.

He got up close to the suitcase and bent down in front of it, taking out a couple of boxes. "Did you choose the ribbed?"

"No."

"Why not?"

"Because I think I can manage your pleasure just fine without them." His lips hitched upward into a grin that made her stomach flip. "In fact. I know I can."

"You are very confident. Has anyone ever told you that before?"

"Yeah. Though, usually the word is *arrogant*."

"You don't sound bothered by it."

"The question I always have about arrogance is why is it a problem if you can back all your claims up?" He grinned. "Am I arrogant? Or am I just telling the truth."

"I feel that I will not be able to comment upon that until after… After."

"If you're still able to comment after, I'll consider it a personal failure."

He took a whole strip of the condoms from the box, dropped it back into the suitcase, then deposited the protection on the end of the bed. Then he stood there, pitched his cowboy hat up off his head and pulled his shirt up directly after.

Her mouth went dry. She knew that he was beautiful. She had known. But the last time she had seen him shirtless, it had been all fruitless longing and furtive, embarrassed attempts to keep herself from staring too intently. And now she just looked her fill. Because why not? Why not just look? His dark brown skin, with hard ridged muscles and just the right amount of dark hair was the perfect representation of all things masculine. And it called to everything feminine in her. To her softness. A softness that she'd had to deny more than indulge, because she had been dropped into a world that was hard. A world she knew was hard.

And all of her soft feelings had always felt twisted around that reality. Around the truth that there was no reward for being sad or grieving, and there was no special prize for having lost much in life. She'd made the mistake of getting lost in all that once, and she'd only caused other people grief.

So she had just done her best to cover it up, to get along.

And it had all come to a head in an explosion of anger when her father had sold him the winery, but there was just so much more to her than that. So much more to her than anger. And she didn't often let herself explore that or feel that. And maybe that was partly why her attraction to him had often come out as an expression of anger or aggression. Because it was easier. Because if it wasn't that, it was softness. And it was the softness she had always feared. But there was something about him, and all that masculine hardness that made her want to luxuriate in everything about herself that was different.

And she found herself slipping out from under the covers. Not quite so embarrassed now to show herself. She kicked the boots off beneath the blankets and shoved them down off the edge of the mattress, then slipped out from beneath the furs, parting her robe as she did. Exposing her breasts on a rush of air. She had done the same thing in the sauna, but she had felt insulated by the steam then. But there was nothing concealing her now. The firelight glowed over his skin and hers. And it added to the intimacy of it. To the mood. To the magic of the moment.

She climbed out from beneath the covers completely, slipping the robe away, showing him her.

He sucked in a harsh breath through his teeth. "You are so damn sexy."

He saw *her.*

Not what she had been able to show the world up until this point. Not the things her brothers wanted other people to see, or that her father thought. He saw her. A piece of herself that she wasn't even fully comfortable with. Because even when she had made the decision to go up north and sleep with Donovan, she hadn't been driven by an overwhelming surge of attraction. Or by being in touch with her sexuality. Rather it had been anger. Just more anger, fueling her and firing her on. And right now she wasn't angry. Right now, she was soft and she was vulnerable, and if he said something pointed, she had a feeling that he could rent her in two.

But he wasn't. Instead, he had said just the right

thing. Just the perfect thing. Instead, he had made her feel like more, not less.

She was very unbearably conscious just then of all the things that she had missed in her life because she hadn't had a mother.

The conversations, the shopping trips. She wondered if her mother would've shifted her focus just enough so that this feminine piece of herself didn't feel quite so foreign.

So that her focus hadn't been so squarely on simply fitting in with her family. Because there would've been someone else like her. Someone else who was different. And maybe she would've still been the same her, but maybe the feminine mystique wouldn't have been quite so...mystical.

It didn't feel mystical now. It felt simple.

But she was safe with him. The stranger who was also familiar.

He put his hands on his belt, while he kicked his boots off and shrugged off his jeans and underwear in one fluid motion. Her mouth went dry.

Because in his entirety, he was the most gorgeous thing she had ever seen.

A friend of hers in high school—just a casual friend—had once said that she had seen a penis in person and was not going to rush to buy artistic renderings of it for her room.

She really thought that she might buy some art if it was fashioned to look like him.

He was art all on his own. Thick and strong and large.

His thighs were muscular, his waist lean, every ounce of hard work that man did etched deep into his muscles.

He was a sculpture come to life, every loving detail on his body seemingly handcrafted into an ideal human form.

She had done a bit of time on the internet, trying to prepare herself for what was going to happen. Not with porn, obviously—she knew better than to try to consult male fantasies for what she should expect out of sex. But she had done a bit of reading on how sometimes the first time hurt—but probably not if the woman was a little older and had ridden a lot of horses—she qualified as an older virgin, and she had certainly done her fair share of horse riding.

She also knew—because she wasn't a child—that a man would fit.

But right now, inexplicably, she felt a bit nervous about that. Just a bit skeptical. But then he came down on the bed beside her, and he was kissing her, the length of his naked body pressed against hers, and she forgot to be nervous. She forgot everything but the way that it felt to be touched by him. Kissed by him.

And suddenly, ridiculously, her eyes filled with tears. Because this was… It was different than she had imagined it would be. He was different. There was no fighting, no banter, no ridiculousness. None of the things that they threw out between each other to keep the other distant. That was what she did. All the time. Throwing down gauntlets and throwing out outrageous statements to keep him standing back. So that she wasn't challenged. So that he didn't see.

But he could see now. And he knew. He knew that she wanted him. And the world hadn't collapsed in on itself. Rather, a whole new world had opened up to her.

Rather, everything had become brighter and brilliant and more beautiful.

And, oh, how she wanted him.

She was on fire with it. That heat between her legs slick and hot and ready.

As if on cue, he put his hand there, between her thighs, rubbing at the sensitive bundle of nerves there. And she arched against him. He pushed a finger inside of her tight channel, and she winced.

Okay. Maybe the horse riding wasn't going to make this as easy as she'd hoped.

But then he pushed another finger in and kept on kissing her. And she got wetter and hotter, and if there was still pain, it didn't matter quite so much. If there was still pain, it didn't surpass the deep, throbbing need inside of her. She burned.

And he was the only thing that could possibly put out the fire. Or maybe he would simply be gasoline on a lit match. Maybe he would still get higher, and maybe that was what she wanted. To burn out of control with no end in sight.

He teased her and toyed with her until the pleasure built to unbearable heights. Until her entire world reduced to his mouth on hers and his fingers inside her.

And then she shattered. Her climax rolling over her like a wave. And when she came back to herself, he was positioned between her thighs, the protection firmly in place.

"I'm ready," she said.

And he thrust home. Deep and hard. She gasped, arching against him. She was overwhelmed by the sensation of fullness, but it wasn't bad.

No. It wasn't bad. It was him. Overwhelming and far too much, but the alternative was not having him, and that was simply something that she couldn't take. A reality that she wouldn't be happy with at all.

And then, he began to move, the fullness becoming essential rather than unbearable, the weight of him a gift that she wanted to hang on to forever. Impossibly, she felt another climax begin to build. This went deeper, more intense than the previous two. Her body tightened around his, and she arched her back, throwing her head back against the pillows, crying out her pleasure. And that was when he gave himself over to it. Lost himself in his own desire. And all the while she was still riding out the aftershocks of her desire, she was flooded by the overwhelming satisfaction of his.

She had never been with a man before. And he had been with plenty of women. But they were shaking just the same. She was clinging to him, his body sweat slicked, his desire so apparent, and she felt...

She felt more herself than she ever had in her life.

She had done it. She was no longer a virgin. But she realized that wasn't even what mattered. What mattered was him.

She pushed that realization aside as quickly as it occurred, because of all the things that could potentially ruin this, that was the worst.

This was just for the blizzard.

It was great that it could be him. Because she had always wanted him, but she didn't need him to be essential. In fact she needed him to very much not be. He was hot, and she liked him. And without feeling the need to distance him because of her attraction to him, they would probably feel like they liked each other even more.

But it could only ever be this. This cold weather thing. That would melt along with the snow.

She chose not to think about that. Instead, she snuggled against him beneath the furs. She thought about saying something. There was nothing to say. And sleep was dragging her under.

So she gave in to it. For the first time in memory Honey Cooper just didn't bother to fight. Instead, she just rested.

Chapter 9

"I told you," Jericho said when Honey's eyes finally fluttered open. "If you still had something to say then I wasn't worthy of my arrogance."

She gazed at him out of her narrowed eyes. "That is really the first thing on your mind?"

"Yes, ma'am. I'm always on hand for the 'I told you so.'"

"That is deeply, deeply petty."

"I never said I wasn't." And all right, it wasn't the most romantic thing. But they weren't romantic.

Except... She had been amazing, and he was getting impatient watching her sleep. It was the middle of the day, after all.

And you want her again.

Not that he could afford to. Not that either of them could afford this.

But hey, they were stuck here until the weather cleared, which it still hadn't done. And as long as they could make the most of it, why shouldn't they? As long as they were here...

"Well, fine. You have earned your arrogance."

"Happy to hear it."

Her stomach growled. Audibly. "I'm hungry."

He was too. But not particularly for food.

"You can have some food. After you have a bath."

"Hey," she said, as he picked her up out of the bed. "I can walk, you know. You seem to have forgotten that."

"I didn't forget. I just like carrying you."

It was true.

He liked the feeling of the soft weight in his arms. He liked feeling her in general.

"I'll get you your bird book if you want."

"I don't want the bird book."

He chuckled. "How about I take a bath with you?"

A flush covered her skin, and he was ridiculously pleased by it. That she was affected by them. By this.

You've lost your mind.

Maybe. But it didn't seem so crazy that what he wanted was to stay here, not face what was out there. Not deal with the fact that he had a long-lost family he was supposed to be spending Christmas with. Yeah, spending time with Honey was a hell of a lot nicer.

He had run the bath already, because he hadn't been totally sure that they would have enough hot water, and it had been pretty close. He'd warmed a couple pots up on the stove and added them to the deep claw-foot tub in the bathroom.

He deposited her in the warm water and watched the

way the firelight sparkled over her damp skin. She was so damned pretty. So perfect. It made him feel… Well, it made him feel a damn sight too much. "Good," he said. But she didn't move at all, and he laughed as he got into the tub and lifted her, setting her back down so that she was on his lap.

She sighed, letting her head fall back against his chest. Then she tilted her head. Looking at him as best she could. "This is very strange."

"How so?" But it made his chest tight.

"Well, just a few hours ago we were fully clothed and sitting across the room from each other talking about birds…"

"I never really talked about birds. It was mostly you talking about birds."

"Whatever," she said. "It's just that… It's very strange to now be sitting with you like this. Without clothes."

And perhaps the strangest part of all was it didn't feel strange. Because they were still them. She was still talking about birds.

"Right."

He lifted his hand from the water, let the droplets fall over her skin. Her breasts.

He was transfixed by the sight of her. By her beauty. And he hadn't gotten to where he was marinating in the strangeness of it, because he wanted her for as long as he had and now he finally had her.

She was as beautiful as he'd imagined that she might be. And that was… Well, his imagination had been pretty thorough, but it still hadn't quite managed to get the particulars. Every dip and hollow and facet of beauty that was unique to Honey.

It was strange. The rightness of it.

"Yeah. I guess," he said, even though he didn't feel the same disquiet he imagined she did. Perhaps it was experience.

Except he knew it wasn't that. Maybe it was just the way they were cocooned in this moment. The entire thing had been a little bit surreal. Maybe he had just sunk into it. Maybe he'd been sinking into it for the last month, finding out the Daltons didn't know about him—or at least Hank hadn't. That he actually wanted to get to know him.

"It's only a few days before Christmas," he said.

What was supposed to have been his first Christmas with his father.

A father. What does that even mean when you find out when you are thirty-four years old?

What did it mean at all? He hadn't been there for anything. He hadn't been there to help Jericho when everything had fallen apart.

Whether or not it was his choice didn't really matter, because the end result was the same.

And joining the family now… It was kind of the ninth inning. He didn't need their support. Not anymore.

He figured out how to get along. He figured it out on his own. That he felt compelled to go… Well, maybe it was a good thing that he hit a snowstorm.

After all, he was here, naked with Honey, rather than dealing with the awkwardness of the family situation.

"We need a Christmas tree," she whispered.

"A Christmas tree?" There was weight that came with that, baggage and pain that he didn't want to think about now.

But Honey wanted a Christmas tree, and he found that he wanted to please her. It was such a strange sensation. One lost way back in time.

"Yes, Jericho," she said, oblivious to his inner turmoil. "So that we can have a Merry Christmas."

"I didn't get you anything," he said.

She laughed. "I think you did."

"Well, I'm not the kind of man who would say that a couple of orgasms for me were a gift."

That made her howl, slapping the surface of the water. "Since when?"

"All right, I am." Something sincere rose up inside of him, and he didn't quite know what to do with it. It was just that… For her that didn't seem like enough. He wanted there to be more. He wanted to give her something, and the impulse felt strange and foreign. The impulse felt undeniable.

It was the strangest damn thing.

"All right, how about a Christmas tree then? And maybe I can find a really pretty rock to wrap up for you."

"And what will you wrap it in?" she asked, smiling sweetly.

He smiled back, but it was wicked. "Maybe some of those lace panties that you brought."

She snickered, readjusting herself, her bottom moving over his growing arousal. He really needed to give her a break. She had been a virgin. And it was very likely that she could be sore.

If you had gotten her a nice enough gift, you might not have felt so guilty about her being sore.

Well, damn. That didn't say great things about them,

but it was true. Because he wanted her again, soreness or not.

"All right," he said. "I'd rather see you in the panties. Though, I'd also rather see you out of them."

"That is something I don't really understand about lingerie," she said. "Are you supposed to dress up in another room and make a grand entrance? And then you just put it on so it gets taken off thirty seconds later."

"You could put it on in front of me right now, take it off fifteen seconds later, and I would still think the whole thing was worth it, because it was just all staring at you."

Her cheeks went red. "Really?"

"Yes. Because you're so damn hot I can hardly deal with myself."

"Wow."

"What?"

"Nothing. Just…" She looked up at him with wide, sincere eyes that damn near broke his heart. "You really *do* think I'm hot?"

That question, so artless, sat like a weight in his chest, along with Christmas trees. "I really do. I wouldn't say it if I didn't think it."

"How long?"

"Why do you need to know how long?"

She turned over, a slippery mermaid in his arms, then rested her forearms against his chest and looked up at him. "I need to know because I have had the biggest crush on you for most of my life, all the while wanting to hit you over the head with the nearest blunt object. You are both my favorite and least favorite person to be around, often during the same conversation. And I have felt like a fool for feeling that way this whole time."

That admission stole his breath. He was older, and he might not have felt that way about her back when she did, but it wasn't because she wasn't...wonderful. It was because of their age gap. "Why did you feel that way? Like you were foolish for wanting me?"

"Because I just never thought that I was all that interesting or pretty or anything of the kind. I always felt a little bit on the outside in school. And I tried not to, but... I did. Beatrix Leighton gave me a mouse once. When we were in kindergarten. I kept him as a pet for three years. I thought that was one of the nicest things anyone ever did for me. I think she was about the closest I ever got to feeling like somebody might understand me. But she was usually nursing animals back to health and not doing anything social. But I just always felt like I didn't really fit. And..."

"I think everybody feels that way sometimes."

"Yeah?"

He smiled. "There aren't a whole lot of people who look like me around here."

"No, I know," she said. She looked away.

"Hey, don't be embarrassed. It's fine that you don't just think of it. But it is true. I get it. I know what it's like to feel different. But I also know what it's like to find people who get you. Who see past the obvious surface things and know you. Understand you."

"I don't know if anyone's ever actually understood me. I mean, my dad, Creed and Jackson, they all lost my mother, just like I did. And you lost your mother. You're about the closest anyone could ever come to understanding exactly what I've been through. But I think the thing that gets me is that... Or maybe I'm

not very good at making myself understood. I'm just…
I'm upset at how much this is my fault, I guess. I was
mad at my dad, I am mad at him, but you're right. He
wouldn't hurt me on purpose. I feel all these things and
no one seems to know, and I don't know how to fix it.
Except…you I just talk to."

"I'm glad, Honey," he said. "Your dad does care
about you though. He knew I wouldn't get rid of you."
He slid his hand down her arm. "I was never going to
throw you out on the street or take your job away."

He was callous sometimes, and he knew that. His life
had made him that way. But he'd never do anything to
intentionally hurt Honey.

"But working for you isn't exactly the same as having
a real career, is it? It's not the same as what I thought I
was working toward. I guess that I somehow managed
to never really… That he never considered it… I don't
know. I just feel so desperately like maybe no one's ever
known me, and maybe I don't show who I am enough.
I've always felt like I was really honest. About who I
was and what I wanted, but you know, I hid wanting
you the whole time. Really well. Maybe I'm just hiding. Maybe it's a whole lot of hiding."

"Hey," he said. "We're all hiding. The fact of the matter is… We've been almost like family this whole time."

She wrinkled her nose. "Gross."

"Well, it's true. And for family you put on a little bit
of a performance. Because there's parts of yourself that
you gotta keep quiet. It's just…what you do. It's just
how you navigate things. At least… That's my experience of family. I never wanted my mom to know how

difficult it was for me when she was sick. So I hid that. Because I had to be strong."

He wanted to talk to her, and he didn't much ever want to talk to anyone. But maybe it was what she'd said. About being misunderstood. Maybe that was why. Maybe he wanted to find ways they could understand each other.

She nodded. "Maybe that's it. I'm so used to hiding what I want, because I wanted a lot of things that my dad couldn't give me. And I never wanted to make him sad. So I just… I kind of bump along and pretend everything is great. Even when it isn't."

"It is not too late," he said. "Obviously, there's no question of you going to see Donavan now."

"I took a job from him, Jericho. He needs at least time to find a replacement."

"You aren't touching him."

She looked shocked. "No, of course I wouldn't."

He didn't have the right to make that statement, not when they were supposed to just be…for the blizzard. But still. He couldn't stand the thought. It made him see red.

"I'm willing to sell you part of the winery."

And hell, there were layers of complications now. But this… This thing between them, it was only for the blizzard. It was only for the blizzard.

"You will?"

"Yeah," he said.

Because somewhere along the way the reason that he had wanted the winery, that desperate desire to claim his place in the valley, in the family… It had faded a little bit. Because he could see now that Honey wanted the same thing. And he didn't want to take it from her.

He would have, before this. Because what he wanted had felt more important, but it just didn't anymore.

"I'd like that. I mean, I have money. From the sale. We're just kind of passing it back and forth."

"You can make payments on a bigger part of the winery, if you want. Because otherwise you're only getting a fifth."

"I'll consider it. I'll buy a fifth, and then we'll see. If I want to pursue a bigger share, I will after that."

"That sounds a good plan."

"Can we get the Christmas tree now?"

"Yes," he said. "Bundle up. We'll go get a Christmas tree now."

By the time they got out of the tub and dressed, twilight had fallen. This single day had felt like four days. And Honey felt a little bit like she was in a daze. But the good kind.

Being with him had been... Transformative. She felt transformed.

She wasn't going to tell him that, because his ego was healthy enough without her stoking the flames, but it was true.

They didn't have to go far into the woods to find a decent tree, and Jericho chopped it down, then slung it over his shoulder to carry back. As he walked, icy little droplets fell from the tree and hit Honey in the face, but she didn't mind. She felt...renewed.

She was going to be able to buy a piece of the winery. She and Jericho were...

Something twisted in her stomach. *Nothing, you're nothing.*

Right. Of course. They weren't anything. They were just… For the blizzard.

The snow had eased up, no longer falling in large fat flakes and piling up higher and higher. Still, it was so cold it wouldn't be going anywhere for a while.

Before they went back to the cabin, Jericho walked to the truck and confirmed that it was still blocked in.

She laughed as he shook the tree out when they got to the porch, and then leaned it up against the wall in the living room, because there was no tree stand.

Honey found string and some popcorn kernels, which she popped on the stovetop in a big Dutch oven, and the two of them worked at making popcorn strings by lantern light, which then led to a contest to see who could make the most innocuous household object into a tree decoration.

In the end, their monstrous masterpiece included several ceramic figurines, a tinfoil star up on the very top and, possibly silliest of all, some perfume bottles hung from the branches by string, which ended up twinkling merrily in the lantern light and giving the entire thing a cheerfully strange effect.

"Without a doubt, the weirdest ass Christmas tree I have ever seen," Jericho said, taking a step back and putting his arm around her. The casual touch was so strange. How odd to have gone from existing in a space where it felt like there was a wall between them physically, to this moment, where they had now bathed together, and he was touching her like she was his…

She wasn't anything. She was just Honey.

She looked up at him, at his sculpted face, the fire-light illuminating his brown skin. His dark eyes glittered there, his square jaw rough with black stubble, his lips... Well, now she knew what they tasted like. And what they felt like when they tasted her.

How could she ever go back to a time when she didn't know that? Where he wasn't hers anymore? To touch and do with as she pleased. How could she ever bear it?

You've borne a lot of things. You'll just have to bear this too.

She had more than she had when she'd first set out on this trip. She lost her virginity and she secured a job. It just wasn't what she'd been planning.

It was better.

She'd gotten what she wanted.

She wanted him physically, and nothing more.

And if the thought of that made her ache now... That was her own problem. It certainly wasn't his.

"It is indeed. But it's nice."

They lit a fire in the hearth there, and Jericho brought furs down from upstairs and spread them over the floor while Honey gathered together some cheeses, cured meats and crackers for a cheese board. There was even a glass of wine, and all up, the entire thing felt nearly sophisticated.

"I didn't imagine that being off-grid could be so glamorous."

"Helped very much by the fact that the generator runs some indoor plumbing," he pointed out.

"Well. There is that." She wrinkled her nose. "Not much glamour to be had with an outhouse."

"No indeed."

They settled into each other, into the moment. The furs soft and warm, the fire crackling in the hearth. It felt safe, right. She felt safe. To say what she needed to. To feel what she needed to.

The thought made her heart feel pierced, because her emotions had felt too big and wrong from the time she was a girl.

From back when her father had been so upset with her grief, and she had nearly drowned in it. And she'd learned to put it away because she'd had to.

"I never knew what to do about you," she said, her chest feeling tender. She shouldn't talk about this. Except, maybe it would help. Maybe it would explain things. Because she wasn't foolish enough to believe that she had a future with Jericho, and she never had been. It was just that… She knew him. And there was something about desiring him that had felt both dangerous and safe at the same time. And maybe that was it. Maybe that was all it was. Because she hadn't had a mother to talk to her about those things…

"You were this…teenage boy that came into the house and you weren't my brother. And you made me feel all kinds of things and they were scary. I've never really had anyone I could talk to about this. Some casual friends at school when I was kind of on the outskirts of a couple of different groups. But I never really felt like I could share with them. I never really wanted to. It felt too… Precarious, I guess. I didn't know how I was going to explain to the girls in my class that I was more interested in a boy in his twenties than a boy my age. And I didn't really want to… I don't know. Maybe it's just that you've always felt safe."

"Safe?" he questioned, lifting his brows.

"You know. Not in a beige kind of way, but in a… I've always had a lot of feelings, and I've always been around men. And the way that men do feelings. And so I've always had to be really careful… Or I felt like I did. Because I wanted to fit in and I wanted to be understood, but at the same time I didn't want my brothers or my dad to think that I was dramatic. And I didn't… I dunno, maybe keeping my sexual attraction type feelings down to somebody like you was… Because I could talk to you, always. Even with all of that. Because our relationship has always been… Sure, we fight and things like that, but it's always been important. And kinda special. And…"

"You've been lonely for a long time, haven't you?"

The words were far too incisive, and they hit Honey right where she lived.

"Yeah," she said. "I guess so."

"Well, we can talk."

"We've always been able to talk," she said. "I mean, that's what I'm saying."

"You did not tell me about the way you felt about the winery."

"Yes, I did. I just waited too long to do it. But you were still the first person that I told."

He shook his head. "Honey, you should've talked to me sooner."

"And what would you have said?"

He looked at her, long and hard. "That I was buying it. And you were out of luck."

"Yeah, I thought so."

"I feel differently about it now though."

"Oh please don't… Please don't be trading my virginity for a fifth of the winery."

He recoiled. "No," he said. "That's not it. It's talking to you. It's talking to you and understanding where you're coming from. What you want. It's actually listening. Which, I'm embarrassed to say, hasn't always been my strong point."

"Well, mine either. Which you know."

"Here we are. Listening."

She looked up at him, and her happiness suddenly felt so big that it threatened to overflow, and with that came a sense of wonder so big it threatened to burst from her mouth in the form of a song or a laugh or… Declarations that she wouldn't even really mean.

She didn't know if it was the wine making her a little bit tipsy or if it was just…him.

"This is the Maxfield label," she said. She shook her head. "So basic."

"The wine or the fact that they have it?"

"Regrettably, the wine is complex and lovely," she said.

"It is," Jericho said. "Not like my wine. Our wine." He shook his head. "This is some surreal stuff."

"What is?"

"I guess it's the same moment that you had up in the tub earlier. Us. Sitting here together. Drinking wine. I own a winery. Same as I don't know how I got from that boy to here."

"I do," she said. "You worked hard. I mean, you more than worked hard. You worked like there was a demon on your back."

"Yeah. I guess I did."

"And this is what you've earned. You know, less my fifth."

"True."

And suddenly, this wasn't enough. The joy that she had felt a moment ago was still there, but it had taken on a strange, sharp sensation. It made her feel like she was suffocating. Like she couldn't breathe.

There was a desperation with it. A hunger. And she didn't know how to satisfy it. Because it wasn't enough just to sit here with him. Wasn't enough just to talk to him. Suddenly, they weren't close enough. And much like what he'd said just a moment ago, she couldn't reconcile where they were right now with where they had been two days ago. The Honey and Jericho that had walked through the snow to this cabin were not the same two people that sat here now.

Or maybe they were. And that was the strangest part. That the transformation was so real. That it had actually just reshaped everything that she had believed about him, about herself. About her feelings. Or perhaps it had simply exposed what was already there. He had wanted her before. And she wanted him. It was just that they hadn't been able to be honest enough about it because their worries about what other people might think got in the way.

And there was none of that here.

This was like a snow globe, its own separate world with a beautiful glass dome that kept the bad parts away. Their trauma, their pasts. All the people they might disappoint, the future, and what they could or couldn't have in it. All of that. It was as if only they and this moment truly existed. Encircled by snow and magic and firelight. By an improbable Christmas tree and an improbable desire. Because outside of the space they were both…too them to ever make something work. That was just a fact. But here… Here it all seemed possible. And she wanted to seize hold of it. Wanted to grab it and hold it to her chest, claim it for herself, only for herself.

She felt wild with it. Selfish. And utterly and completely at peace with it.

Because he was hers. And this moment was hers.

And she wanted it to be naked.

She wanted him skin to skin. She wanted him inside of her.

She wrapped her arms around his neck and kissed him then. The flavor of the wine lingering on his lips, and the desperation of her desire creating a palpable need that drove her. Made her feel wild.

She clung to him, and she didn't know if she wanted him to feel what was inside of her, or if she never wanted him to know. If she didn't even want him to get a peek at the profound, forever changing sensations that were rolling through her. Her desire was so deep. So raw and real that it touched places in her own soul that she had never seen before, and the idea of sharing it was terrifying. So all she did was kiss him. All she did was kiss him, because it was all that could be done. Because everything else felt uncertain. Because she didn't even know what she wanted. Because she didn't have names for the feelings that ebbed and flowed and grew and snaked themselves around her like vines or glitter, magic or a curse, she didn't know. She took her shirt off and cast it to the side, then pushed her hand beneath the waist of his. His body was solid, hard and well muscled, and her heart nearly leaped out of her chest when her fingertips grazed over his abs.

Because she had spent a lot of years fantasizing about this. About him, and emotion aside, there was just so much pent-up desire there.

No. There was no emotion aside, there never could be. And that had been her biggest mistake. Thinking that desire and emotion did not have to exist together. Thinking that she could simply ignore emotion. That she did not have to take it on board. Believing that she could have sex and go back to seeing him as she had done before, or maybe even with her attraction to him neatly removed, having been explored.

No. Instead, everything had gotten tangled together, and there was no going back to seeing him any other way besides this. Because it wasn't separate.

This need inside of her, the ache in her chest, the man that he was. It wasn't separate. And it never could be.

She had been a fool for thinking so. For thinking that common sense and bird field guides and a hard limit on time could fix this thing. Could help them make sense of it and be sensible with it.

But there was no sense to be found here. It was only need.

It was only this.

But she tried to focus on the feel of him beneath her hands, tried to focus on his body, because at least while that overwhelmed, it was not as sharp as the rest.

She pushed his shirt up and off, moving her hands over his chest, down his stomach and back up again. Then she wrapped her arms around his neck and kissed him. Ran her hands over his short hair, down his muscled back as she tasted him. As she angled her head and took a deep breath, meeting the thrust of his tongue with enthusiasm.

He had taken her bra off and she hadn't even noticed, not until one large hand came up to palm her naked breasts.

She shivered.

And she arched into him, wanting more. Craving more.

She found herself laid back against the soft furs, and he was over her, and she loved the feel of his body against hers. Luxuriating in it as he removed the rest of their clothes. And then suddenly, she got that feeling of being overwhelmed again. Of deep need that demolished her sanity. All the energy building inside of her propelled her forward, and she sat up, pressing her hands against his shoulders and pushing him back.

She moved so that she was over him, leaning over and kissing him hard, her heart hammering, threatening to beat right outside her chest. She ached between her legs. Felt hollow with her need for him. She reached over for his jeans and happily found his wallet and a condom inside.

She tore it open, then with shaking and uncertain fingers, wrapped her hand around the base of his arousal as she rolled the protection over him with deep concentration.

Then she positioned herself over his body, taking him in slowly, a moan of satisfaction rising in her throat as she did.

"Jericho," she whispered.

His hands came up and gripped her hips, his hold bruising, but she loved it.

She began to ride him. Establishing a rhythm that

pleased them both, watching as the cords in his neck went tight with his need for her. She shivered. And nearly came right then, just from watching his pleasure.

From watching the effect that she had on him. He arched up into her, thrusting up, changing the tempo, the pace and the strength of it. She bowed over, grabbing hold of his face and kissing him on the mouth, shattering as her orgasm overtook her, wave after wave of pleasure that blended into his as he shouted his release, the two of them shaking and trembling in the aftermath.

Then he gathered her close, swept the cheese platter to the side and wrapped them up in the furs.

She reached out and grabbed a cracker, chewing on the end as he held her close.

Because hopefully focusing on that would keep the tears at bay. Would keep her from dissolving completely.

How could they ever go back?

There was no going back, that much she knew. But maybe they could go forward and find a new shape. A new evolution. That was what this was, after all. A different sort of shape than what they'd been before. So no, they would never be able to be the exact thing they had been previously. But maybe they could find what Honey and Jericho after sex looked like. After baths and cheese platters and sharing secrets.

They had to. There was no other choice. She owned part of the winery now.

She had what she wanted.

Yet she felt hollow. A winery and a saltine cracker were not going to fix that.

Chapter 10

When Jericho woke up the next morning, he could see that the sky was clear outside the window.

He was lying on the floor wrapped up in fur and Honey, still feeling the aftereffects of the night before. But he was going to have to check the weather.

He got up and put his pants on, then went out for his coat. He did his best to get out of the house without disturbing Honey. Outside it was completely quiet. Still. The sun was shining now, making it look like diamonds had been scattered across the surface of the undisturbed snow. The only dents had been made by their footprints last night when they went to get the Christmas tree.

It was bright today, and likely it would bring a little bit of snowmelt along with it.

It was Christmas Eve. He wondered if that meant there would be people coming to plow the roads or not.

He hiked out to the road, and there was a snowplow. There were also a few ODOT workers standing around.

"Hey," Jericho said to the first man, who was wearing a heavy coat and a bright yellow vest. "This is my truck," he said. "What are the odds that he gets out today?"

"We'll have this cleared within a couple of hours," the guy said.

"Thanks. It doesn't start well. Would I be able to get a tow truck out here you think?"

"Everything is eased up so much, and we're expecting highs to hit the fifties today. So this should be your window."

"Thanks," Jericho said.

He hiked back over to the house, where Honey was just beginning to stir.

"Looks like we'll be leaving today," he said.

She looked… Well, she looked stricken. But she didn't say anything. They started the task of putting everything in the house back the way they'd found it.

Jericho wrote a note with his contact information, asking that the owners tabulate the cost of what they had used and send him a bill. Plus charge whatever occupancy fees they normally did.

They looked at the tree.

"I guess we have to take it down. And put everything back."

It was a lot less festive than putting it up had been.

But they had everything restored to its rightful place, and he walked back up to the road to find his truck had had the snow cleared out from around it.

They could go.

"You ready?"

She nodded slowly. "Jericho… I'm not going to Lake Oswego."

He froze.

"All right."

"I think you already knew that. You know, what with the offer of the winery and all."

"Well, yeah."

"But I would like to go to Christmas with you. For… For the Daltons and all that."

"Oh," he said. "Well, that's…good of you."

"It's not good of me. I want to go with you. This is going to be super… Super weird for you. Wouldn't you like to have a friend with you?"

"Yeah," he said. "A friend."

Honey was his friend. But the word felt limp in comparison to what they'd been here. Where they were snowbound and hot as fire anyway. Where they'd talked and made love and decorated the first Christmas tree he'd touched since he was sixteen.

A friend.

He supposed that's how it would have to be explained to Jackson and Creed when it came up. Because it would come up.

As soon as they hit civilization, their phones were going to go crazy.

They'd been out of communication for nearly three days.

It suddenly felt like longer, and a lot less time all at once. It would be like walking through a veil. Where everything changed when they got back to civilization. And she wanted to go with him to see the Daltons.

He helped her carry her bags through the woods, back to the truck.

And when they climbed inside, it all felt a little bit too modern.

She laughed. "I'm not going to know what to do when a heater just comes on."

It was funny the way her mind tracked with his. For a minute, he wondered if the engine would even turn over, but it did. And it was a strange little string of miracles, if he was honest. From the vacation rental down to this.

I mean, it made him question why they had to be caught in the snowstorm in the first place, but everything that had happened since had a strange sort of charmed feeling to it. He would've called it fate if he believed in things like that.

Hell, he couldn't actually fathom that fate had led him to cozy up with his friends' sister for a few nights of pleasure. Hell, one night. Hadn't been enough. But it was done now. It was done now because it had to be.

The heater got going and the only sound was the air, the tires on the newly plowed and graveled road and the engine.

They had talked easily at the vacation rental, but neither of them seemed to know what to say now.

Now it seemed like...

"When do you think we will have service?" She was looking down at her phone.

"I have no idea. I didn't know there was as big of a dead zone out here as there is."

"Oh," she said, tapping her fingers on the door.

"Right."

"So."

They said nothing for another whole minute.

"What if… What if we kept on doing it. You know, just while we're away," she continued.

He looked over at her, and she was staring fixedly out the window.

"Are you looking for birds out there?"

"No," she said, looking back at him. "I just… Yeah I… Maybe we should… Keep doing it. Yeah. Don't you think that would be fun?"

"Fun," he echoed.

"Yeah. Fun. Real fun."

"Look," she said. "If you don't want to do it."

"No. I don't want to make a bigger mess out of this than we already have. At least before we came to the cabin, we would fight when we were sitting together in a car. Now we can barely speak a sentence to each other."

"That's a very coherent sentence," she said.

"Thanks," he said.

"I mean… I just can't see being at the Dalton place and not doing it."

"We should have just gone back."

"No. Let's do this." She slapped her hand on her thighs. "We're survivalists."

"Right."

"We are. And… I still feel bad that I never really… That I didn't realize what a big thing it was. You finding out that Hank never knew about you. I didn't really think about it. And I'm embarrassed. And if I can help you through it any way, I want to do that."

"And you want to get laid," he said, unable to keep the smile from curving his lips, even though mostly the entire topic wasn't that amusing to him.

"Well, I'm not dead below the waist. Or anywhere, for that matter. So all right. Maybe I want more."

More.

More.

He tried not to let that word resonate too much inside of him. Because she meant more sex, and more sex was all it could be. More sex wasn't what it should be, but still.

More.

More people in his family. And with that, just more complication in general. Yeah, initially he thought he'd show up and flaunt his wealth. His success. And now he was...bringing a girl home to meet his folks. Well, his dad anyway. His father.

Tammy Dalton was not his mother. Tammy Dalton was the reason his life had gone the way that it had.

He wasn't going to let himself get too bitter about it. Mostly because, even though what Tammy had done was wrong, Hank had committed the first wrong, and he didn't know if a person was responsible for being perfect in response to something like that.

Still. She was just the woman who had paid his mother off and made her go away. Who had lied to her husband about the extent of his misdeeds for all those years.

"Looks like we'll make it in time for Christmas Eve dinner."

The rest... He wasn't going to think about.

It took another couple of hours to get up to the compound, and by the time they did, they had cell service. He could call and let the Daltons know he was coming, but the idea of speaking to them on the phone felt...

wrong somehow. He didn't want to answer questions about where he'd been. He had directions to the cabin that was his for the next couple of days, and he went straight there.

"I guess dinner is kind of a formal affair," he said. "I don't think your lingerie is going to cut it."

"Oh, I have something," she said. "I was prepared for the fanciness of Lake Oswego."

She was a dark horse, was Honey Cooper. And that was for certain.

The cabin itself was small but luxurious compared to where they'd just been. It had all the modern amenities, hypermodern even. A steam shower, not a wood sauna, and towel warmers and lights. There were lights. He may have stopped and flipped the switch off and on a couple of times.

"What are you doing?" Honey asked.

"Aren't you amazed by the electricity?"

"I'm not that far gone," she said.

"Have you looked at your phone yet?"

"No," she said, wincing. "I was expecting to get chewed out by my dad and my brothers for my disappearing act, and that was when I just thought I was going up to Lake Oswego and would be able to contact them that same day. Though I guess… At least… At least I'm not moving."

"Should we get dressed for dinner?" he asked.

"Yeah," she replied.

She disappeared off into one of the other bedrooms, which he thought was interesting, considering she was the one who had suggested they keep things up. Not that he was complaining. And he couldn't stop himself from imagining her getting undressed now. Peeling her clothes off, revealing her beautiful body.

He gritted his teeth, then went to the other bedroom with his suitcase and took out the suit that he brought for the occasion. He dressed and put a black cowboy hat on his head. And he figured he probably looked more rodeo royalty than Hank Dalton did on a good day.

He went out to the living room, and Honey still hadn't appeared. He checked his watch, waiting.

And then she emerged, wearing a figure-hugging red dress, her hair spilling over her shoulders in a curled cascade. He couldn't remember ever seeing Honey in makeup, the effect dramatically highlighting all the things about her that were already beautiful.

"Damn," he said.

"Do I meet with your approval?"

"Hell yeah," he responded.

She smiled.

"Is that why you hid from me?"

"Well, yes. I wanted there to be a little bit of a surprise."

"You are a surprise, Honey. Every day. In a thousand different ways."

He linked arms with her, and led her out of the cabin. It was dark out, but it was easy to navigate their way from there to the main house, which he knew Hank and the rest of the family were in.

He had been told to just come in when they arrived, so he did. Pushing the door open and revealing a glittering Christmas scene. A huge tree that had to be eighteen feet high at least, stretching up to the top ceiling beam, casting a warm glow over the room. There were garlands and big velvet bows. On the big mezzanine floor that overlooked the living area. No one was here, but he could hear voices coming from what he assumed might be the dining room.

He took Honey's hand. Without even thinking.

They walked down the short hallway and went to the left, and there it was. There everyone was. The table was massive, laden with food, huge candelabras in the center, along with tiered trays of meats and desserts. It was the gaudiest, tackiest thing he'd ever seen this side of the *Harry Potter* movies, and it was incredible.

And around that table was… Everyone.

Hank at the head, wearing a white cowboy hat and suit, along with a bolero tie. Tammy at the foot of the table with big hair and a big smile.

And filling in the middle part… His half siblings and their spouses. Everyone went around the table for a quick intro.

West, who he'd met, and his wife, Pansy. Gabe, Jacob and Caleb, with their wives and kids. Logan and his wife, and McKenna, the lone sister, and her husband.

He knew who they all were, but he hadn't… Had never really thought that he'd be part of the family. Not ever.

But here they were. And here he was.

At a crowded table, and he had the strangest ache at the center of his chest that he ever felt.

"Jericho," Hank said. "We thought you decided not to come."

"I got waylaid by the snowstorm. We had to wait it out in a cabin on the way here."

"No shit," Hank said, laughing. "That must be quite a story. Pull up a chair. Who is this?"

"Honey," he said. "She's a...a family friend."

"He's not calling me *honey*," she said. "My first name is Honey."

Hank laughed at that too. "I love it."

"My parents are...were...are eccentric," Honey said.

"Eccentric," he said. "I like it. I can definitely understand eccentric."

It was Tammy, though, who stood.

There was a strange, soft note in her eyes, and Jericho couldn't say that he liked it much.

It was too much like pity. Or sorrow.

"I'm glad you could come," she said, walking forward and reaching her hand out.

It was Honey took it. "Thank you," she said.

And he realized that Honey was protecting him. That she had sensed his hesitance and put herself right in Tammy's path.

"Have a seat," Hank said. "The food's getting cold."

"Thanks," Jericho said.

They added another chair for Honey quickly, and they sat down beside each other. Honey made quick work of putting her plate together, then jumped right into the chatting.

And he had never been more grateful to have someone he knew at his side than he was right at this moment.

Because she was covering the awkwardness with ease, and he had never really thought that Honey was the kind of person who would do that.

"So what is it you do?" This question came from Grant, who he supposed was his half brother-in-law.

"I own Cowboy Wines."

"Are you familiar with Grassroots Winery?"

"Yeah," Jericho said.

"That's my sister-in-law's. She's great. If you like to do any kind of collaborating, you should have a chat with Lindy."

The family connections just kept growing. But he supposed that was the nature of something like this.

He wasn't clear on everyone's stories or circumstances, but as the evening wore on, he began to get filled in with bits and pieces of conversation. Grant and McKenna had met and married several years ago when she had come to town looking for Hank. Grant had lost his wife several years before and had never really thought about getting married again.

West was an ex-convict, and as opposite to his wife—a good girl police officer—as it was possible to get.

But they seemed completely crazy about each other.

Gabe Dalton's wife was a total horse girl, and had plenty in common with Honey, who took up easy chatting with her over dessert.

Jacob and Caleb were married to teachers—who taught at the school for troubled kids that was apparently now on Dalton land. Logan and his wife were ranchers.

They were an interesting group, all with completely different stories. Though loss was something most of them had dealt with in one form or another. McKenna had been abandoned by her mother, while Logan's had died.

He felt an immediate kinship to him.

He vaguely remembered Logan from high school, though they weren't in the same year. And he'd been too caught up in his own grief to think about a kid younger than him dealing with anything similar.

The fact was, tragedy was more commonplace than anybody really liked to think.

It made your aches and pains feel like garden-variety stuff, when it felt absolutely significant to you.

He wasn't sure if it made it worse or better. He had lived in a cloistered version of this experience for most of his life. What he wasn't used to was having casual conversations about things like this with people he didn't even really know all that well.

"So she's a friend?" West asked, looking at him pointedly, then over at Honey, who was chatting with Jamie and Rose.

"Yeah," he said. "Actually, my friends' sister…"

At that, Gabe and Logan laughed. They laughed.

"What?"

"Been there," Logan said.

"Married that," Gabe added.

"Well, I'm not getting married."

"Why not?" West asked. "I recommend the institution, actually, and I never did think that I would."

"Nice for you," Jericho said. "But…"

"Oh, have you had a hard life?" West asked.

"Too bad," Logan said.

"Are we talking about hard lives?" McKenna came over to them, hands on her hips. "I'd like to play. Who had ten homes in four years?"

"You win that game," West said. "I had way less. Well, not way less."

"But who has the most half siblings?"

"I wouldn't know," McKenna said. "Because I don't know my mom."

"I only have the one other half sibling that I know of." West looked at Jericho. "No relation to us. My mom's kid."

"Just you people," Gabe said.

"Same," Logan added.

"You all seem pretty…relaxed about this."

"No point getting wound up about it at this point," Gabe said. "Now, that wasn't true back when it all first… Back when it all first happened."

"Yeah, it was not the best when I showed up," McKenna said. "Everyone was trying to put all the unpleasantness of the past behind them, and there I was, a big reminder of the way things had been before."

"No one blames you for that," Gabe said.

"I know you don't," McKenna said. "And I'm glad that I came here. If I hadn't… I wouldn't have all of you. Or Grant."

"I think you like Grant best," Logan said.

"I do," McKenna said. And that made her brothers laugh.

Her brothers. He supposed they were his brothers. And he was her brother.

Growing up an only child, that was a strange thing to wrap his head around. Sure, he had been brought into the Cooper family, but it wasn't quite the same. And he'd been sixteen when he had been.

Of course, he was thirty-four now.

"I think you like her," McKenna said.

"Well, you don't know me," Jericho answered.

"Oh good," McKenna said, smiling. "You have a chip on your shoulder. You really will fit in nicely. I was feral when I first came here."

"I'm not exactly feral," he said.

"But not exactly not," McKenna said.

All right, that was a fair enough characterization of him in the entire situation. But he wasn't going to let her know.

"Well, it's getting late."

"You have to make sure you get back here bright and early," McKenna said. "They take the present opening very seriously."

"We do," said his brother Caleb's wife, Ellie, holding a baby and hanging on to her seven-year-old, who was looking terribly sleepy.

"Yeah, and Amelia isn't going to wait," Caleb said, indicating the child.

He stood up, and Honey stiffened. She wasn't even looking at him, but she seemed to sense his move to leave. He couldn't begin to figure out how she was so in tune with him. It was just the strangest thing. The way she seemed to know what he felt. The fact that she was here at all.

"I'm going to head back to the cabin," Honey said. "I need to call my dad. I'll see you in, like, ten minutes."

That surprised him. Because he thought that she had sensed his readiness to leave. But then she was scampering out, saying good-night to everybody, and Hank was looking at him. And he realized she had done that on purpose.

She was sensing things, but she wasn't on his team.

"Hey there, son," Hank said. "I wanted to have a talk with you."

"You don't have to do that."

"I don't have to do what?"

"Call me *son*."

"Maybe I don't have to. But I want to."

Maybe I don't want you to. But he didn't say that. Because he was here to see Hank, after all, so what was the point of being hostile. At least overtly.

Hank stood, and he followed him out of the room, back into the grand dining room, which was now empty. "Thank you for coming," he said. "I didn't think you would. But you know… Whether you believe it or not, I've known you were out there for a while. I just didn't know your name. And her last name made it tricky to track you down. I had never gotten your first name, and your mother, Letty Smith, it was a common name. And when I finally did find her… And I found out she was gone…"

"Yeah. She died when I was sixteen."

"I'm sorry. I didn't know."

"I know you didn't, Hank."

"You thought I did though. For your whole life, didn't you?"

"Yeah. But you know… It's good to have an enemy. Good to have a bad object that you can fight against. It's probably why I have been so successful." There he was, giving him credit for something that he had been bound and determined not to give him credit for. Even if he had said it as a joke, it was closer to acknowledging the role that Hank had played in his life than he wanted.

"Sure," Hank said. "I know a little something about that. I ran from my demons for a long time. And they took me to dark places. I wasn't a good husband to Tammy. And I failed a lot of other women as a result too. McKenna is working on teaching me about feminism."

"Is she?" Jericho asked, and that was truly the funniest thing he'd ever heard.

"Yeah," he said. "Because of the patriarchy and power imbalances and things, what I did was especially wrong. But at the time it just felt like… I didn't feel particularly powerful. I felt like a dumb kid that was out of control. I felt like a fool. Someone who didn't deserve any of the things that he had. Who was just trying to feel alive. But at some point, you have to feel more than alive, and you have to work at feeling more than good. What you have to do is learn to sit on your bad feelings. That's a hell of a thing."

"Yeah, I've had enough bad feelings to get me through for a long time."

"I'm not meaning to lecture you. I'm just… I'm glad that you're here, I hope that I'll see you past Christmas. I hope that you give this family thing a chance."

"Then that would give you a happy ending, wouldn't it? It would make all of it seem like it had a meaning? If you could get all of your wayward kids here and happy to be with you. Everybody forgiving everybody else and getting along. I guess that would go a long way in soothing your guilt."

Guilt.

He was more familiar with the concept than he'd like. Especially in regards to Honey.

Not touching her. He couldn't feel guilty about that. But because of all he could never give her.

"Sure," he said. "But you know, it's a lot of guilt, Jericho. Because McKenna was in foster care for all of her life. And Logan lost his mother. And you lost yours. And you boys were alone. McKenna was alone. There's a lot of guilt with that. It's not easy to live with."

"Well, we'll see what happens. But whatever happens, I'm not making the decision for the purpose of saving your soul. I enjoyed tonight. But I have a life. I have family." The Coopers, whom he was drastically betraying with his dalliance with Honey. But he wasn't going to think about that.

"I wouldn't ask you to," Hank said. "I wouldn't ask you to do anything for the purpose of appeasing me. But sure, the side effect is that it probably will. If that stops you then… Not much I can do about it."

"Sorry," Jericho said. "It's been a hell of a trip up here. It's been a hell of a few days. I don't know if I'm coming or going. But I'll be here for Christmas morning."

"Merry Christmas," Hank said. Then as Jericho turned to go, he added, "Son."

Hank was pushing. Jericho should be furious and yet…

He'd been a boy with no one. When he'd been sixteen and people had complained about annoying parents… He'd been nothing but jealous.

Something in him… Something in him wanted this and he couldn't deny it, even as the wounded part of him wanted to pull away from it.

Jericho turned. "You couldn't resist."

"I couldn't."

"You did it because I told you not to."

"Maybe. Look. I might've tried to better myself, but I'm still a no-good jackass. I just keep it managed now."

"Well, see that you do."

"Also, I'm going to have to build the bridge between us," Hank said, his voice full of gravity. "No matter how wide the valley is, I'm committed to it, Jericho, I promise you. But I'm the one that should have to work for it. I'm the one who messed up. I just hope you'll stick out waiting for me to get to the other side."

Jericho's throat went tight. "Yeah. Sure."

Which wasn't enough, but there were no other words.

He turned and walked down the long hall, out the front door, managing to slide by everybody without having to say a string of long messy good-nights.

He didn't think he could face that level of family.

Outside it was crisp and cold and the sky was clear, the stars twinkling above, the trees inky black with spots of white snow a shout in the dark.

He had a family back in that house. A family.

And a woman waiting for him at his cabin.

And suddenly, his life felt fuller than it ever had.

Chapter 11

"I'm okay, Dad," she said, pacing back and forth in the living room. It was a little bit dastardly that she had left Jericho to talk to Hank. She had realized at some point that Hank was itching to do it, and she knew that unless she did something like this, Jericho was going to come back to the cabin with her.

But, she needed to talk to her dad. He needed to talk to his.

"I wish you would've talked to me about leaving in the first place. By the time I found out you'd gone up north, you were already gone, and then I had no way of knowing that you were trapped in a snowstorm."

"Jericho found me," she said. "We found a vacation rental. We hunkered down there." And the less she said about it the better. "And then I decided to come up with him to support him while he met with his dad."

"You're not usually all that friendly with him."

"Well, he saved my life. I mean, really, if I hadn't been with him I don't know what would've happened. And I'm not moving. I changed my mind."

She'd left it all in her note. Well, nothing about her virginity of course.

"Really?" her dad said.

"Yeah. Really. I talked to Jericho, and he said that he's going to sell me a portion of the vineyard back."

"Did you... Did you want some of the vineyard?"

"Yes, Dad. I wanted it desperately. It's why I've been furious for the last few months."

"You've been furious?"

She'd been so honest with Jericho. And the walls she'd always felt existed between herself and the world felt thinner now. And she liked it that way.

So why not speak?

Why not now?

She'd been ready to leave. Which was so extreme in hindsight. More ready to run than have a conversation.

But being with him had changed her.

And this was her moment to live in that change.

"Yes. Furious. Absolutely incensed that you would do that to me. That you would sell the winery out from under me without talking to me first. It's why I decided to move away. But, Jericho saved me from the snowstorm, and we talked about my future."

There. Now Jericho sounded like a hero.

She heard female voices in the background. "Are you at the Maxfields'?"

"Yes," he said.

"Are you and..."

"I really do love her, Honey."

"Right. You love her and… I guess you're going to marry her and close this big strange circle of our families?"

"Well, that depends. She ended up getting so much of the winery. She's a very rich woman. I'm not sure that she's interested in getting hitched. We might just live in sin."

"Oh, for heaven's sake, Dad. I don't want to know that."

"You should be happy for me. I've been miserable for a long time."

"I am happy for you. Only if you can be happy for me too. And realize that for me the winery is happiness."

"Of course, Honey. I only want what's best for you. I'm sorry if I didn't see it. I just… I was never very good at having a daughter."

"I don't know, sometimes I wonder if I was any good at being one. I just wanted to be like the boys. But I'm not. They're outspoken and they know how to tell you what they want. And they do it without emotions. But I have feelings. A lot of them, and I just spent a lot of time shoving them down deep. I didn't want to cause trouble. I know how much it upset you… The way I was at Mom's funeral."

It was a memory that lodged deep inside of her. One that she didn't like to talk about.

"It was an upsetting time."

"I just didn't want to upset you. Not again."

"I love you, Honey. You don't upset me. I think sometimes I just don't look at you and know immediately what you want."

She thought of Jackson and Creed and the different things they'd been through, and honestly, she didn't think her dad knew anymore what they wanted. Hell, they hadn't known what they wanted until they'd gotten with Wren and Cricket. So maybe that was just it. Maybe everybody was always learning, and they needed to do a better job of talking.

"I love you, Dad," she said. "I'll be home in a couple of days."

"Tell Jericho no funny business."

And then her dad laughed, as her heart shimmered down into her stomach. And she realized he thought it was a hilarious joke.

"I think I'll let him have his way with me," she said.

"You do that," her dad said.

"Merry Christmas," she said.

And then got off the phone, happy that the idea of Jericho touching her was just such a joke.

She frowned furiously, and was still frowning at the front door when it opened and Jericho came in.

"Hey," he said. "What's up?"

"I told my dad I was going to let you have your way with me, and he literally laughed."

"Oh, don't take offense to that," Jericho said, shrugging out of his jacket. And she couldn't help but admire the muscles in his body as he moved. In fact, she just went ahead and ogled him, because she was out of sorts, and she felt owed.

"Why should I not take offense?"

"Because it's to do with it being you and me. It's not you."

"Well, why do people think we're so incompatible?"

"Because we bicker."

"So what?"

"Well, we bicker quite a bit."

"Clearly unresolved sexual tension. Haven't they ever seen a romantic comedy?"

He crossed the room, wrapped his arm around her waist and drew her up against him. He gripped her chin between his thumb and forefinger, his dark eyes intense. "Honey, we are not a romantic comedy." And she could feel the evidence of his desire pressing against her body. And no. They were not a comedy. There was nothing funny about this.

"Okay," she said.

And what she meant was, *I trust you.* What she meant was, *you matter to me.*

And he seemed to know that, because he leaned in and kissed her on the lips.

"It's Christmas Eve," she said.

"It's Christmas Eve."

"Did you like Christmas when you were a kid?"

"No," he said, his voice hoarse. "I hated it. I always had to figure out ways to get Christmas decorations up. Get a tree. Get a meal from the local church, so that we had something nice, even though in the end my mom didn't want to eat. But somebody had to make Christmas happen. And she didn't have the energy to do it. So I always did. After she died, I just didn't do it. I mean, I would go be with your family, but I haven't put up a decoration in my own house… Ever."

"Jericho," she whispered. "I'm so sorry." Because for all that she had felt like she had to do something to hide her emotions, there had always been people there taking care of her. It might not have been perfect, but she wasn't alone. She might've had moments of loneliness, but that was different than being alone. It was different than being a child who was expected to be an adult. Different than being forced to be the one that brought the Christmas magic into the house when people should've been making it happen for you.

"You never believed in Santa Claus, did you?"

He shook his head. "No. Because I figured I was about as good as a kid could be. So if I was going to magically get gifts… No. I didn't. I wanted to believe in Jesus though. Because that made me feel less alone. So that was about…the only point of Christmas as far as I could see. Well, and Christmas dinners made by church ladies."

"I'm so sorry."

"It's okay. I've made it okay."

But when he smiled, it didn't reach his eyes, and she wondered how she hadn't realized that before.

And she knew what it was like. To carry things that were absolutely not okay, but to also realize there was no point mourning what you should've had, because none of it was going to bring it back to you. But her heart ached for the little boy who had made sure there was Christmas for his mother. Who probably needed there to be Christmas so that she didn't feel quite like she was failing him so badly, but it had rebounded and turned into something he had to perform. And it made her feel so… So desperately sad.

And for the first time, she wanted to tell the story of what happened at her mother's funeral. She had never talked about it with anyone. Until she had mentioned it with her dad a few moments ago, they had never even brought it up to each other.

"I was so sad when my mother died," she said. "I couldn't stop crying. I thought I was going to die myself. I was gasping for air, gulping. It lasted…days, Jericho. Days. Then I stopped. And it was just sort of a horrible silence. But then at the funeral it all came back. And I just… I screamed. And I cried. My father was so distressed, he did't know what to do with me. He was stoic, and the boys were stoic. And…"

"You were a little girl."

"I know," she said. "I was a little girl who really really missed her mother. And… My father found it so upsetting. He didn't know what to do with me. He told me to be quiet. And he told me to stop crying. He told me to wait outside the church until I could get my emotions together."

"Honey…"

"So I just sat there and I bit my tongue through the whole thing. And eventually, the pain did something to block out my sadness. The tears. I just tried after that. Every day. To be a little bit stronger. Because I realized that…on top of everything else my dad couldn't handle my sorrow."

"Dammit," Jericho said. He put his hand up to her cheek. "That's wrong."

"He was just trying his best. It's like Christmases that you have to throw yourself when you're a child. Yeah, it's sad. But… There's nothing you can do about it. We just got stronger. We just did the best we could."

"You don't have to hide yourself. Not now."

She could tell he hadn't meant to say it.

"You don't have to hide yourself either."

And then he was kissing her. When she thought they might both be consumed by it. By the flames of their desire. The fire of this need between them that could no longer be controlled. And she couldn't quite wrap her mind around this Jericho. Vulnerable, strong. Sexy. So much more than the man she'd always seen. The man she'd wanted, but the man she hadn't really known.

He was... He was brilliant and wonderful and everything. And so strong, so amazingly resilient, having been through so much.

And she wondered how she had ever believed that it was a crush. How she had ever thought that all that they were could be reduced to something so basic, so...juvenile.

Because it was easier. Because it was then. But all it had taken was a few honest conversations, and it was different. She was different. And she saw the ways that he was different.

And that they were the same. All the ways that he was able to fill the gaps in who she was, and who they both were. And the way that she was able to do the same for him.

And she kissed him. Because she wanted him. Because he was the man she'd always known, and this man she had gotten to know over the past few days. Because he was her brothers' friend, but most importantly he was her friend. Because they were business partners and they had known each other half their lives. Because... Well, quite simply because she loved him.

And it was a truth that rang out as clear and lovely inside of her as anything ever could have. It was a truth that reverberated across her soul. She loved him. And she was in love with him. It was every layer, every piece of all the ways she'd seen him bonded together in one strong undeniable feeling. Because she saw the truth of who he was now. The whole of him. All of him. And because of that she saw the whole of herself, as well. The woman that she was. The woman that she wanted to be.

The ways that she had been hurt and the way that she had overcome. And the way that she wanted him. The way that she loved him. She was no longer protecting herself, because that was what it had been. Telling herself it was a crush. Pushing herself to find a way to get over him. To be with someone else, because of course being with someone else would've been easy. The easiest thing.

Because Donovan might have taken her clothes off her, but he would never have stripped her bare. And Jericho had brought her down to the truth of who she was.

Jericho was… He was the only man for her. The only one that she could ever love. And she did. She had told him… Oh, foolish her, she had told him that she didn't expect them to get married or be in a relationship, or be anything. And she had been wrong. She had lied, even though she hadn't meant to. Because she had hoped. She had always hoped. And in a life that had given her so few reasons to hope, this one last bit of light had existed in the very corner of her soul, reserved for him, reserved for this. For all that she wished they could be.

And she kissed him with that truth. All of it, resonating inside of her.

And when he picked her up and carried her to his bedroom, she didn't make any comments about his carrying her, didn't try to defuse the tension with a joke.

No. She was there. Completely. Doing nothing to block out the intensity of her need for him. The intensity of their desire for one another.

It was raw and real, and she would do nothing to make it less.

She wrenched his black tie loose, slid it through the collar of his shirt and cast it down to the floor. Pushed his jacket from his shoulders and unbuttoned his white shirt, revealing a wedge of tan skin. He was so beautiful.

Utterly brilliant in all of his glory. Whether he was in a T-shirt and jeans or a suit. Naked, which was how she preferred him most of all.

She stripped him bare, like it might give her access to the deepest parts of him. Like it might give her a part of his soul, that part of him that she so desperately craved.

She stripped him bare, as if she was dependent upon it.

And then he was naked before her, his eyes shining with the light of intensity that ignited her from within.

She reached behind her back and grabbed the zipper pull on her dress and let it fall free, let it pool at her feet. She was wearing some of the lingerie. Lacy and white, bridal, it could be said.

And the way that he looked at her, as if he wanted to devour her, satisfied her. Made her feel utterly and completely captured. By a look. By the promise of his touch. By the desperate hope of his love.

And when they were finally joined together, laid out on the bed, she wrapped her arms around his neck and kissed him. Poured out every ounce of her love—her love because she would name it now—into that kiss.

She had been afraid before, of all the things rising up inside of her.

Because she had been afraid of her feelings for so long. For too long.

But they were here, and they were big. Bigger than she was. Maybe bigger than the both of them. Maybe they would consume her. Maybe they would swallow them both. Maybe it would leave her with desperate, sad scars, but she could no longer live a life where she denied all that she was for the sake of safety. For the sake of making everyone else comfortable.

She had to do this. She had to step into who she was. Into who she hoped to be. Because the only reason she had ever been unhappy was because of her own self. Because she had kept too many things to herself. Whether it be her feelings about the winery or her feelings about Jericho. The way that she felt disconnected from her family sometimes… She was the one that had chosen to keep them locked down deep, and it might've been for other people, but no one had ever outright asked for it. And even if they had… Why did she have to give everybody what they wanted?

Couldn't she have something for herself?

Perhaps this was growth, and other people needed to grow right along with her.

Perhaps, she wasn't the one who was broken.

"I love you," she whispered.

And then they both went over the edge together.

Jericho was shaking. The aftermath of the pleasure he just experienced roared in his blood, in his head, along with Honey's words.

"I love you."

His chest felt like it had been rent. With sharp claws and sweet words, and everything Honey.

"Honey... Don't do this."

"Don't do what?"

She rolled away from him, all soft and naked, and he wanted to bring her back into his arms, because what he wanted to do was hold her all night. He didn't want her to do this. They were supposed to have this thing until they all went back to their real lives. It was still Christmas. He was still supposed to get to have this.

"Don't do what?" she repeated.

"Don't make this into something that it isn't supposed to be," he said.

"Who gets to say?"

"We already said."

"Yeah. Things change. Life is not fair. You and I both know that. Why are you acting like just because we decided on something doesn't mean we can't change our minds."

"Because I can't," he said, looking at her earnest face, feeling his heart beating so hard he thought it might tear through his chest and land bloody on the bed in front of them.

"So I was just supposed to keep my feelings to myself again. How is that any different than what my dad wanted me to do when he made me sit outside of my mother's funeral."

"Because that was real," he said. "Those feelings were real. But this... This is just you having your first sex partner."

He felt like he was standing on the edge of a dark, endless well and all that was down there was…grief.

All-consuming, terrifying.

It was the only path love led to.

It took and took and took, until in the end, love took itself away too and you were cut off at the knees.

He couldn't.

He *couldn't*.

"Don't do that to me," she said. "Do not be condescending to me. I am not a child. I am a woman. And what life has thrown at you it's thrown at me too. I know what it's like to lose somebody that I love. I know it. Deep in my soul. To miss someone all the time that you can never see again. To feel so isolated in your grief, even though there are people around you who should understand. To feel the way that it burns when you just need this person who's gone forever. I know. I had to grow up early too. I get it."

"You didn't have to throw your own Christmas."

"No. I'm not saying I had every hardship you did, but I am not a baby. Don't treat me like one. Don't you dare."

"I'm not treating you like a baby, but I am treating you like what you are. A woman with vastly less experience than I have. And I think you want to listen to me when I tell you that you're probably just putting too much weight on this."

"As if you don't put any weight on it," she said. "As if it doesn't matter to you at all that we had sex."

"I'm not saying it doesn't matter."

"What are you saying then?"

"I don't want love. Not yours, not anyone's. It is too much work, Honey. And I am not worth the struggle."

"That isn't true."

"Fine then. I don't think it's worth the struggle. I don't want it. I don't want to do it. I don't want your love. I don't want to love you back. I just wanted to fuck. That's it. I think you're hot—I have for a long time. You told me you were going to go give your virginity to some other guy, and it pissed me off. Because I'm a guy. But that's it. It's the beginning and end of the story."

Tears were running down her face, and he felt like… He was the worst. He was the absolute worst person. He hated himself just then. But all he could think of was that horrific, weighted feeling when Christmas rolled around. When he had to do everything and make things merry and bright and pretend that he wasn't living in some damned horror show in his heart, where he knew that the end of his mother's life was coming, and he knew that he was facing a future by himself, and it was just spinning out slowly and terribly, and he was putting on a grim performance in the meantime. He couldn't stand it. He simply couldn't stand it. The expectation. The certain feeling that no matter what, no matter how much he loved, no matter what he did, he was hurtling toward an inevitable end, something that would never be fixed or satisfied.

And he couldn't. He just couldn't.

"Honey… No. We can't do this."

And her face crumpled. And he felt like an absolute ass.

But there was nothing he could do about it. Sitting there, lost in every bad feeling that he'd ever had in his life, every grief that he never contended with, he simply couldn't do it. She got up, and she walked out of the room.

And it took him a few minutes to realize that she wasn't just leaving the room. She was leaving.

A car pulled up to get her some fifteen minutes later. And then she was gone. And he was left. Crushed beneath the weight of damn near everything.

He looked outside the cabin window and he saw the Christmas tree shining through the window of the main house. And he nearly choked.

Merry Christmas.

This was what Christmas was all about. At least what it always had been for him.

Being given a taste of something, something brilliant and beautiful and hopeful, the light of the damned world.

Knowing that darkness hovered around the edges, knowing that this feeling could never really be his.

That was what Christmas was to him.

Apparently, it was what it always would be.

Chapter 12

Honey didn't collapse until she got home and climbed into bed.

Then she wept like she was dying.

It was two o'clock in the morning by the time she got back to Gold Valley, and she was a whole disaster mess.

She cried and cried, and then slept for about two hours before climbing out of bed and putting on clothes to go to the Maxfields. Because even though she didn't want to see anybody, she figured she had to go do it. Because it was Christmas.

But she felt devastated. Horrendously.

And she hoped that she could pull it together for the celebrations.

But what if you didn't? What if you let them know that you were hurt?

The idea made her shiver slightly.

But still, she got dressed and went into the house.

"Honey," Emerson said. "We weren't expecting you."

"I'm here," she said, looking around the Tuscan-style villa, feeling as hideously out of place there as she always did.

The Maxfields were fancy. Fancy fancy, and she had never really felt comfortable with it.

But why? She supposed it was because she was afraid of what they might think. That she might not blend.

That she might stand out.

Well, who cared.

She wasn't fancy.

Neither was Cricket.

And all the worries that she had about connecting with Cricket were based around what Cricket might think too. Because she was just so... She was so consumed by that. By making everybody comfortable, and not exposing them to her weirdness.

Except Jericho. She had been 100 percent herself with him, and it had not gone well.

But who cared.

She was done. She was tired.

"I figured I should spend Christmas with all of you. So here I am."

"You don't have any presents here," her dad said. "I was planning on mailing them."

"It's fine, Dad. I don't really need any presents. And you won't have to mail them, because I'm not leaving."

"Well, that's a good thing."

She looked awkwardly at her dad's girlfriend.

Lucinda Maxfield was supernaturally beautiful. But smooth like a doll, and a bit unapproachable in Honey's opinion. Though the other woman had warmed a lot recently.

"It's good to have you here, Honey," she said.

"Thanks."

She still didn't really know how to interact with her.

It was Jackson who looked at her with the hardest eyes.

And she chose to ignore him.

Instead, she helped herself to the pastries that were set out and took her position around the tree while the others began to open gifts.

"And do you care to give a full accounting for your whereabouts?" Jackson said, succumbing to sit beside her.

"No," she said.

"You were going to leave?"

"I was," she said.

But you didn't. "I didn't."

"But you've been gone."

"Well, I got stuck in the snow."

"Dad mentioned something about that. He mentioned that you and Jericho stayed in…a cabin?"

"I mean, it was a massive vacation rental. But yes."

"I see," he said.

"But I also heard that you were staying with Jericho while he dealt with the Daltons."

"Things change." She sniffed.

"What exactly changed?"

"I didn't want to stay with him anymore?"

"Why?"

"I don't see how that's any of your business," she said.

"You have had the biggest crush on him for as long as I can remember," Jackson said.

Honey's mouth dropped open as a mortified blush spread over her face. She had been prepared to own this and shock them all, and they'd known she had feelings for him! "Now that's not fair…"

"Look, just tell me if I have to go kill him or not."

"I don't want you to kill him," she said, stamping her foot.

"Who are we killing?" Creed asked.

That seemed to get her father's attention too.

"I'm trying to find out about killing Jericho."

"You are not killing him," Honey said.

"Why?" Creed asked.

"Because she's upset about something," Jackson said.

"And?" Creed asked, his tone getting dangerous.

Cricket punched Jackson in the arm. "What is your problem? If you're going to interrogate your sister, at least do it privately. Don't make a dick out of yourself in public."

It was especially funny coming from a woman who was roundly pregnant.

"I'm not being a dick," Jackson said. "I'm trying to figure out if my best friend did something to her. Because I will kill him."

"On what grounds?" Cricket asked, eyeing him closely.

"She's twenty-two."

"And?" Cricket asked, squarely in the same age bracket.

"She's…inexperienced."

Cricket narrowed her eyes. "And?"

"He's my best friend," Jackson said, pointing at Cricket as if that ended things completely.

"Fine. Something happened between myself and Jericho."

That earned her a shocked gasp, and she decided that was pretty satisfying. "And I'm upset about it. But so what? I'm allowed to be upset. You can't protect me from every bad feeling, any more than you can just order me not to have them. I'm going to live life."

"He didn't need to help you do it," Creed said.

"I wanted him to," Honey said. "Because I love him. Okay?" She was saying it. Saying it all. If she'd gotten one gift from Jericho over this time, it hadn't been losing her virginity or the winery. It had been this. This path to honesty. To figuring out that she wanted to share her emotions, whether it made others comfortable or not. To having the confidence to be true to herself, no matter what.

"I don't have a crush on him. I am in love with him. And he can't handle it. That's fine, it wouldn't be my problem, except that I'm in love with him, so it de facto becomes my problem, because he hasn't sorted his shit out yet. But I love him. And that's just... It's the way it is. I don't need any of you getting up in my grill and meddling. I don't need any of you to tell me not to be upset. Because I am. I'm upset. And I'm just... I'm going to be upset for a while. That's how it is."

"Honey, he should never have..."

"He should never what? No, I'm part of this. It wasn't him. It was me too. I wanted it. I want him. And everybody needs to listen to me and to what I want for a minute. Because I have done a pretty terrible job of making myself seen these last few years of my life, and I'm over it. I want him. I want to own the winery. I'm not a kid. I'm a woman. And I want to be treated like one."

"Nobody means to treat you like a kid…"

"No, you do. Because it makes you more comfortable. And I have been all about making sure that you guys are as comfortable as possible. And I'm done with it. So yeah, I'm hurt. And I'm going to be hurt for a little while. And maybe I'm going to have to navigate working with Jericho while I also sort through dealing with the fact that he broke my heart. But I have to deal with it. Not you. You don't get to go and punch him in the face just to make yourselves feel better. Because that's all it would be."

"I aim to kill him," Jackson said, which earned him another slug from his wife.

"Your sister just told you not to. So who would you be doing it for?"

"Me," Creed and Jackson said together.

"I am sorry," her dad said slowly, shaking his head. "I haven't stopped thinking about what you said about your mother's funeral. Not since you mentioned that to me last night. I knew I'd handled that badly, but honestly… I had not been able to remember it. So much of those days are a blur."

"It affected us all," Creed said, taking a step closer to her. "We should have recognized you needed more."

"No, you were grieving too," Honey said.

"Yeah, of course we were," Jackson said. "None of us were ready to lose her. But you were thirteen."

"I didn't handle it well, Honey, and I'm just so sorry," her dad said.

"Dad, I don't need you to apologize to me."

"But I need to," he said. "Your tears hurt me, Honey. And I couldn't stand them. I tried to make myself comfortable, you're right. And I never meant to teach you to do that for the whole rest of your life. That's not what I wanted. I don't want you to be hurt by Jericho. It makes me angry enough to go ask him how the hell he could betray me after I did so much for him. But you're right. It was your choice. And it's your choice what you do going forward. Because heartbreak happens. It just does. And there's nothing anyone can do to shield us from it. I wish I could, but I didn't protect you when it mattered most, so I have no right to go meddling in your business now."

"But you did protect me, Dad. You loved me, and you gave me a place to live. You didn't fail me across the board just because I have some issues. We all have issues."

At this, Lucinda laughed. "Yes, we really do."

Emerson raised her glass, and next to her, so did her husband Holden. "Amen," Emerson said.

"I don't know what any of you are talking about," Wren said. "I am a shining example of being perfectly adjusted."

"Yeah, your choice of husband says otherwise," Emerson pointed out.

"What's wrong with Creed?"

"It's not Creed himself," Emerson said. "It's the fact that you literally thought you hated him so much you wanted to tear his throat out with your teeth before you hooked up with him."

Creed shrugged. "She does have a point. That's not exactly the act of a well-balanced person."

"You're all terrible."

But they weren't. They were her family. And it was a little bit of a strange mess. And so was she. And she wasn't entirely comfortable here still. But... She would be. Because she would figure it out. She wasn't afraid of trying and failing. She wasn't afraid to ask for what she wanted.

She had done it, and it had backfired spectacularly. But now there was basically nowhere left to go.

She was just going to survive it, because she had to.

And that was—in the middle of a very bad Christmas—perhaps the brightest revelation of all.

When he arrived at Christmas breakfast without Honey, he got a lot of follow-up questions.

"She had to go back home," he said.

And that was how he fended off every single one of them.

They had only been his family for two seconds. They didn't get to ask questions. They didn't get to pass judgment on him. Even though he was neck-deep in passing judgment on himself. He just kept seeing Honey's face in his mind's eye. The way that she was crying.

Yeah. He was a total dick.

"How are you finding the family?"

McKenna sidled up beside him, a big gooey cinnamon roll in hand.

"Just fine."

"You seem...like you aren't sure about all this."

"I'm not," he said.

She nodded. "I get that. I do. You know, I was just going to try to get money out of Hank." She tore a strip off the cinnamon roll and took a bite of it.

"I don't need his money."

"Well, nice for you. I sure did. I was homeless when I came here. Pretty much hated everyone and everything. I did a lot of rough living. I was just… I was really angry at the world. And it was really something meeting Grant, who experienced… Just such a sad loss. And yet he was him. Just unfailingly him. He's a really good man. I don't know that I was a good person when I showed up. I just wanted to get what I felt like Hank owed me. And go on my way. But in the end I got something a lot more."

"You sound like a holiday commercial for plastic wrap."

"Are they particularly sappy?"

"Every holiday commercial is particularly sappy."

"Well, sorry I sound like an ad. I don't intend to. But I don't want you to just never come back."

"Why?"

"Because we all need somebody. I really needed this family. I didn't know it. And I really needed Grant."

"And why mention that?"

"Because I don't want you to let Honey get away either. I think you love her."

"Yeah, because you've known me for twelve hours?"

"Maybe that's how being your sister works. I don't know. Maybe I just sense it."

"So, you're psychic?"

"Maybe I'm just not a dumbass."

"Right. Okay." He started to move away from her, but she followed him. Was this what having a little sister was like? He couldn't say that he loved it.

"I think you love her, and I think you're letting your

baggage get in the way. I don't think she just randomly left."

"So what? So what if something happened?"

"I think it's sad. Because I think she's a sweetheart. And I think you're probably a decent guy underneath all your rage at the unfairness of life."

"Look, you've been through some stuff," he said. "Haven't you ever just felt like love was too hard? Like it was too much work?" He shouldn't have asked for that. Because it pushed at tender places inside of his soul that he didn't want to acknowledge. Things he never wanted to deal with.

"Sure," she said. "And loving Grant wasn't simple. Because he had to make room in his heart for me, because he… He'd been in love with someone else before. And she was a really neat woman. She changed him. Into the man who I needed. The man who could love me. Always be grateful to her for that. But that didn't make our road easy, and yeah, I wondered if it was worth it. And why I had to work so hard for love. But you know… In the end, it's worth it. In the end it gives more than it takes."

"Unless it takes everything."

"Are you really afraid of love being hard work? Or are you afraid of losing it? Because I have to tell you, I'm pretty sure it's the second one. And it seems to me that you've already lost her."

"I…"

"The fact that it's on your terms doesn't make it any different."

And he didn't know how to argue with that. Didn't

know what to say. Because yeah, he was sitting there, and he didn't have Honey.

He didn't have her.

The realization hit him with the force of a ton of bricks.

She had said that she loved him and he chased her away.

And she was...

He never wanted that. That domestic life, because it reminded him of dark houses and struggle. Of illness.

But not Honey.

She was something else. She was a generic imagining of what marriage might be like. Of what love might be like. She was her. Utterly and uniquely her, and she had been brave enough to tell him how she felt and he had pushed her away.

Did he love her?

Yeah, he already did. He had for a long time, and he hadn't known what to do about it. And he could see himself suddenly, clearly. A man at the top of his game, at the top of the world. Rich as fuck, but poor where it counted. He had come to his family to prove how together he was, but he wasn't together. He just happened to own a lot of shit. That wasn't the same as being successful. He didn't know how to love.

He didn't know how to accept the love of the beautiful woman he had taken to bed last night. He didn't know... You know how. You just got too selfish. Too scared to do it.

The truth stretched before him, undeniable, like the clear harsh light of the sun. And he didn't want to look directly at it. Because it burned him, that truth. That he was nothing. That he had nothing. That he would trade every ounce of success for a week in a cabin with her. No electricity, just Honey to keep him warm.

Right then he felt bankrupt. As rich and successful as he'd ever been, and useless with it.

"Are you having a revelation?" McKenna asked.

"You know," he said. "Having a sister really is overrated."

"It's a weird thing, to go from looking out for yourself to having a whole bunch of people look out for you. Believe me, I get it. But in the end it's worth it."

"So what do I do?"

"It's not easy. But something my husband did… All those years ago and we were working out our stuff, it has stuck with me ever since. It's informed a lot of what I've done, and the ways that I worked out my own issues. Because it's ongoing. I love Grant more than anything in the world, but I'm still scarred from the way that I grew up. And sometimes I lash out. Sometimes I'm not the best to be around. Sometimes I'm insecure. He used to wear this wedding ring. Around his neck. And it was a symbol. Of his grief more than anything else. And one that he chose to set down. He left it at her grave. And it doesn't mean that all the feelings went away. But it's just that… The act of it. Putting it down. Rather than carrying it. That has stuck with me. So every time an issue from my past comes up, I ask myself… McKenna are you just carrying this around? Are you still holding on to it? Why don't you put it down?"

"And that works?"

"Like I said. Not perfectly. But I can picture myself doing it. And walking away. And being happier for it.

Just because the world gave you grief doesn't mean you're obligated to carry it on your back forever."

"I don't want to."

"Then don't. I choose to carry around love in the greater measure. And my arms aren't big enough to hold everything. So, mostly, I try to make room to hold that."

"Still sounds like it's work."

She shrugged. "So is being miserable."

And she had a damn good point. She really did.

"What do I do?"

She smiled and took another bite of that cinnamon roll. "Grovel."

Chapter 13

By the time Honey got back to the winery that night, she felt gritty. Tired. She was glad she had persevered through the entire holiday, but she hadn't always been the best company, and… She hadn't minded.

She had spoken her piece. And she had been honest about how she felt, and from her perspective that was some pretty decent growth.

Good for her. She had emotional growth. She did not, however, have the love of her life.

She saw headlights, and her heart stopped. She looked out the window of her little house, and she stared.

Was it Jericho?

It was a big ass truck.

He would go to the house. He wouldn't come talk to her.

Except he pulled right up out front, and he turned the engine off.

Like he intended to stay a bit.

She paced back and forth for a second, and then she decided to take action.

She flung the door open. "Have you come to cause more damage? Because I warn you, I am not in a space to make stupid men comfortable by minimizing my feelings."

"You sound like my sister," he said.

"Your sister?"

"Yeah. McKenna."

That made something in her chest tighten. "Oh. So that went well."

"Yeah. I'm going to have to see them again another time. Because I realized that I needed to get back here."

"Why?"

"I realized I needed to get back to you."

"Back to me?"

"Yeah," he said. "Because I realized that I was being a coward. You said that you love me and I couldn't handle it. Because it reminded me of grief. You know why I hated Christmas so much? Because it almost made me feel happy. And it gave me this terrible sense that there was joy out there in the world, and all these people were feeling it. And I felt like I was standing on the outside of it. Able to feel just the edges of it. But never the whole thing. Like I could see the light in this dark winter, but I could never really... I can never really stand in it. It reminded me of that. You offering me your love. Like I was standing on the edge of something beautiful but I didn't know how to take it."

"Jericho…"

"I want it. I want all of it. I want you and me and I want to love you. And I want you to show me. And I need you to have all your emotions, Honey. I need them to be as big and bright as Christmas Day. I need them to be bigger and brighter than the sun, because I need to feel them. Because I need… I need that joy. I need more than the darkness."

Her heart expanded, full to bursting. "I need it too," she said, flinging herself into his arms. "I love you."

"You're not even going to make me suffer?"

"We've both suffered enough," she said.

And that was the damned truth. It truly was. They had both suffered enough.

And what he found was that even though it filled his chest, love wasn't heavy. Not really. It wasn't light, but it didn't weigh them down. And it lit up the dark corners of his soul with all the brilliance of midday.

With the promise of Christmas. And joy to the world. But most especially and finally, to him.

They had been caught in the storm, but the biggest storm had been raging inside of him all this time. And now it was like the sun had come out from behind the clouds. And everything was gold.

Gold like Honey.

"I love you," he said. And while he did, he imagined himself setting his fear down on the floor and leaving it there. Dropping bits and pieces of grief, of doubt. Because all he wanted to carry was her. He wanted to fill his arms with her, fill his chest with her. Forever.

"I love you too," she said. "I'm really glad I didn't burn this place to the ground."

"What?"

"You know, just something I considered. When I was furious at you and convinced that I couldn't have everything that I wanted."

"And what do you think now?"

"That I'll take everything I want and then some. Because why should we settle? That's what we've been doing. Deciding that people like us—who have experienced a measure of tragedy—that we don't get to have the full measure of happiness. But I say we do it. I say we claim it."

"That sounds like a great idea."

And he kissed her. With no doubt or shame, and a whole lot of love.

And he knew that he would be doing it for the rest of his life.

Epilogue

Their whole family was practically a town gathering. Between the Daltons, the Maxfields and the Coopers, Cowboy Wines was absolutely full tonight for Christmas. They had decided in the end to rotate around the Christmas festivities, because it allowed everybody to have the kind of Christmas they loved the most. And no, they didn't do it once a year, they had three Christmases. And everyone was invited.

And when the Daltons hosted, the festivities included the Dodges, Luke and Olivia Hollister, and hell, they might as well just have invited the whole town.

If there was one thing Honey had learned, really learned in the last few years, it was that love grew to accommodate. To expand around all your joy, all your sorrow. And she was sure that their joy was only going to expand more as they added to their family. She hadn't told Jericho yet.

But she would. Christmas morning.

She smiled thinking of the onesie wrapped beneath the tree.

And she felt tears sting her eyes. Just for a moment.

As she thought of the ones they wouldn't have with them for the birth of their first child.

And then she realized, with absolute certainty. But they did have them. In their hearts. Always. Because all the people they'd lost, whether it was her and Jericho or even the members of the Dalton family... Their losses had brought them to this place. Of loving with fierce abandon. Of loving as if it was the most important thing on earth. The only thing on earth.

Because it was.

She looked over at her husband, and she smiled.

She was quite certain that their love was the biggest and brightest of all.

And the next morning when he took that small box from beneath the tree and unwrapped it, it was a moment shared just between the two of them.

"You're kidding me," he said, his eyes filled with wonder. Joy. And she realized that all those years before, she had never seen him look quite like that.

"I'm very serious. And very happy. I hope you are too."

"I didn't have a father growing up," he said, his voice sounding strangled. "And I never imagined I'd be one. I didn't think that I would ever get to be so damned blessed."

"We both are. We both are."

And he kissed her. In that way that she had grown to love so very much. That way that meant forever. That way that always reminded her of Christmas and field guides to birds and love.

Always and forever love.

* * * * *

SEDUCE ME, COWBOY

Chapter 1

Hayley Thompson was a good girl. In all the ways that phrase applied. The kind of girl every mother wished her son would bring home for Sunday dinner.

Of course, the mothers of Copper Ridge were much more enthusiastic about Hayley than their sons were, but that had never been a problem. She had never really tried dating, anyway. Dates were the least of her problems.

She was more worried about the constant feeling that she was under a microscope. That she was a trained seal, sitting behind the desk in the church office exactly as one might expect from a small-town pastor's daughter—who also happened to be the church secretary.

And what did she have to show for being so good? Absolutely nothing.

Meanwhile, her older brother had gone out into the world and done whatever he wanted. He'd broken every rule. Run away from home. Gotten married, gotten divorced. Come back home and opened a bar in the same town where his father preached sermons. All while Hayley had stayed and behaved herself. Done everything that was expected of her.

Ace was the prodigal son. He hadn't just received forgiveness for his transgressions. He'd been rewarded. He had so many things well-behaved Hayley wanted and didn't have.

He'd found love again in his wife, Sierra. They had children. The doting attention of Hayley's parents—a side effect of being the first to supply grandchildren, she felt—while Hayley had...

Well, nothing.

Nothing but a future as a very well-behaved spinster.

That was why she was here now. Clutching a newspaper in her hand until it was wrinkled tight. She hadn't even known people still put ads in the paper for job listings, but while she'd been sitting in The Grind yesterday on Copper Ridge's main street, watching people go by and feeling a strange sense of being untethered, she'd grabbed the local paper.

That had led her to the job listings. And seeing as she was unemployed for the first time since she was sixteen years old, she'd read them.

Every single one of them had been submitted by people she knew. Businesses she'd grown up patronizing, or businesses owned by people she knew from her dad's congregation. And if she got a job somewhere like that, she might as well have stayed on at the church.

Except for one listing. Assistant to Jonathan Bear, owner of Gray Bear Construction. The job was for him personally, but would also entail clerical work for his company and some work around his home.

She didn't know anything about the company. She'd never had a house built, after all. Neither had her mother and father. And she'd never heard his name before, and was reasonably sure she'd never seen him at church.

She wanted that distance.

Familiar, nagging guilt gnawed at the edges of her heart. Her parents were good people. They loved her very much. And she loved them. But she felt like a beloved goldfish. With people watching her every move and tapping on the glass. Plus, the bowl was restricting, when she was well aware there was an entire ocean out there.

Step one in her plan for independence had been to acquire her own apartment. Cassie Caldwell, owner of The Grind, and her husband, Jake, had moved out of the space above the coffee shop a while ago. Happily, it had been vacant and ready to rent, and Hayley had taken advantage of that. So, with the money she'd saved up, she'd moved into that place. And then, after hoarding a few months' worth of rent, she had finally worked up the courage to quit.

Her father had been... She wouldn't go so far as to say he'd been disappointed. John Thompson never had a harsh word for anyone. He was all kind eyes and deep conviction. The type of goodness Hayley could only marvel at, that made her feel as though she could never quite measure up.

But she could tell her father had been confused. And she hadn't been able to explain herself, not fully. Because she didn't want either of her parents to know that ultimately, this little journey of independence would lead straight out of Copper Ridge.

She had to get out of the fishbowl. She needed people to stop tapping on her glass.

Virtue wasn't its own reward. For years she'd believed it would be. But then…suddenly, watching Ace at the dinner table at her parents' house, with his family, she'd realized the strange knot in her stomach wasn't anger over his abandonment, over the way he'd embarrassed their parents with his behavior.

It was envy.

Envy of all he had, of his freedom. Well, this was her chance to have some of that for herself, and she couldn't do it with everyone watching.

She took a deep breath and regarded the house in front of her. If she didn't know it was the home and office of the owner of Gray Bear Construction, she would be tempted to assume it was some kind of resort.

The expansive front porch was made entirely out of logs, stained with a glossy, honey-colored sheen that caught the light and made the place look like it was glowing. The green metal roof was designed to withstand harsh weather—which down in town by the beach wasn't much of an issue. But a few miles inland, here in the mountains, she could imagine there was snow in winter.

She wondered if she would need chains for her car. But she supposed she'd cross that bridge when she came to it. It was early spring, and she didn't even have the job yet.

Getting the job, and keeping it through winter, was only a pipe dream at this point.

She took a deep breath and started up the path, the bark-laden ground soft beneath her feet. She inhaled deeply, the sharp scent of pine filling her lungs. It was cool beneath the trees, and she wrapped her arms around herself as she walked up the steps and made her way to the front door.

She knocked before she had a chance to rethink her actions, and then she waited.

She was just about to knock again when she heard footsteps. She quickly put her hand down at her side. Then lifted it again, brushing her hair out of her face. Then she clasped her hands in front of her, then put them back at her sides again. Then she decided to hold them in front of her again.

She had just settled on that position when the door jerked open.

She had rehearsed her opening remarks. Had practiced making a natural smile in the mirror—which was easy after so many years manning the front desk of a church—but all that disappeared completely when she looked at the man standing in front of her.

He was… Well, he was nothing like she'd expected, which left her grappling for what exactly she had been expecting. Somebody older. Certainly not somebody who towered over her like a redwood.

Jonathan Bear wasn't someone you could anticipate.

His dark, glittering eyes assessed her; his mouth pressed into a thin line. His black hair was tied back, but it was impossible for her to tell just how long it was from where she stood.

"Who are you?" he asked, his tone uncompromising.

"I'm here to interview for the assistant position. Were

you expecting someone else?" Her stomach twisted with anxiety. He wasn't what she had expected, and now she was wondering if she was what *he* had expected. Maybe he wanted somebody older, with more qualifications. Or somebody more… Well, sexy secretary than former church secretary.

Though, she looked very nice in this twin set and pencil skirt, if she said so herself.

"No," he said, moving away from the door. "Come in."

"Oh," she said, scampering to follow his direction.

"The office is upstairs," he said, taking great strides through the entryway and heading toward a massive curved staircase.

She found herself taking very quick steps to try and keep up with him. And it was difficult to do that when she was distracted by the beauty of the house. She was trying to take in all the details as she trailed behind him up the stairs, her low heels clicking on the hardwood.

"I'm Hayley Thompson," she said, "which I know the résumé said, but you didn't know who I was… So…"

"We're the only two people here," he said, looking back at her, lifting one dark brow. "So knowing your name isn't really that important, is it?"

She couldn't tell if he was joking. She laughed nervously, and it got her no response at all. So then she was concerned she had miscalculated.

They reached the top of the stairs, and she followed him down a long hallway, the sound of her steps dampened now by a long carpet runner the colors of the nature that surrounded them. Brown, forest green and a red that reminded her of cranberries.

The house smelled new. Which was maybe a strange observation to make, but the scent of wood lingered in the air, and something that reminded her of paint.

"How long have you lived here?" she asked, more comfortable with polite conversation than contending with silence.

"Just moved in last month," he said. "One of our designs. You might have guessed, this is what Gray Bear does. Custom homes. That's our specialty. And since my construction company merged with Grayson Design, we're doing design as well as construction."

"How many people can buy places like this?" she asked, turning in a circle while she walked, daunted by the amount of house they had left behind them, and the amount that was still before them.

"You would be surprised. For a lot of our clients these are only vacation homes. Escapes to the coast and to the mountains. Mostly, we work on the Oregon coast, but we make exceptions for some of the higher-paying clientele."

"That's…kind of amazing. I mean, something of this scale right here in Copper Ridge. Or I guess, technically, we're outside the city limits."

"Still the same zip code," he said, lifting a shoulder.

He took hold of two sliding double doors fashioned to look like barn doors and slid them open, revealing a huge office space with floor-to-ceiling windows and a view that made her jaw drop.

The sheer immensity of the mountains spread before them was incredible on its own. But beyond that, she could make out the faint gray of the ocean, white-capped waves and jagged rocks rising out of the surf.

"The best of everything," he said. "Sky, mountains, ocean. That kind of sums up the company. Now that you know about us, you can tell me why I should hire you."

"I want the job," she said, her tone hesitant. As soon as she said the words, she realized how ridiculous they were. Everybody who interviewed for this position would want the job. "I was working as a secretary for my father's…business," she said, feeling guilty about fudging a little bit on her résumé. But she hadn't really wanted to say she was working at her father's church, because… Well, she just wanted to come in at a slightly more neutral position.

"You were working for your family?"

"Yes," she said.

He crossed his arms, and she felt slightly intimidated. He was the largest man she'd ever seen. At least, he felt large. Something about all the height and muscles and presence combined.

"We're going to have to get one thing straight right now, Hayley. I'm not your daddy. So if you're used to a kind and gentle working environment where you get a lot of chances because firing you would make it awkward around the holidays, this might take some adjustment for you. I'm damned hard to please. And I'm not a very nice boss. There's a lot of work to do around here. I hate paperwork, and I don't want to have to do any form twice. If you make mistakes and I have to sit at that desk longer as a result, you're fired. If I've hired you to make things easier between myself and my clients, and something you do makes it harder, you're fired. If you pass on a call to me that I shouldn't have to take, you're fired."

She nodded, wishing she had a notepad, not because she was ever going to forget what he'd said, but so she could underscore the fact that she was paying attention. "Anything else?"

"Yeah," he said, a slight smile curving his lips. "You're also fired if you fuck up my coffee."

This was a mistake. Jonathan Bear was absolutely certain of it. But he had earned millions making mistakes, so what was one more? Nobody else had responded to his ad.

Except for this pale, strange little creature who looked barely twenty and wore the outfit of an eighty-year-old woman.

She was… Well, she wasn't the kind of formidable woman who could stand up to the rigors of working with him.

His sister, Rebecca, would say—with absolutely no tact at all—that he sucked as a boss. And maybe she was right, but he didn't really care. He was busy, and right now he hated most of what he was busy with.

There was irony in that, he knew. He had worked hard all his life. While a lot of his friends had sought solace and oblivion in drugs and alcohol, Jonathan had figured it was best to sweat the poison right out.

He'd gotten a job on a construction site when he was fifteen, and learned his trade. He'd gotten to where he was faster, better than most of the men around him. By the time he was twenty, he had been doing serious custom work on the more upscale custom homes he'd built with West Construction.

But he wanted more. There was a cap on what he

could make with that company, and he didn't like a ceiling. He wanted open skies and the freedom to go as high, as fast as he wanted. So he could amass so much it could never be taken from him.

So he'd risked striking out on his own. No one had believed a kid from the wrong side of the tracks could compete with West. But Jonathan had courted business across city and county lines. And created a reputation beyond Copper Ridge so that when people came looking to build retirement homes or vacation properties, his was the name they knew.

He had built everything he had, brick by brick. In a strictly literal sense in some cases.

And every brick built a stronger wall against all the things he had left behind. Poverty, uncertainty, the lack of respect paid to a man in his circumstances.

Then six months ago, Joshua Grayson had approached him. Originally from Copper Ridge, the man had been looking for a foothold back in town after years in Seattle. Faith Grayson, Joshua's sister was quickly becoming the most sought after architect in the Pacific Northwest. But the siblings had decided it was time to bring the business back home in order to be closer to their parents.

And so Joshua asked Jonathan if he would consider bringing design in-house, making Bear Construction into Gray Bear.

This gave Jonathan reach into urban areas, into Seattle. Had him managing remote crews and dealing with many projects at one time. And it had pushed him straight out of the building game in many ways. He had turned into a desk drone. And while his bank account had grown astronomically, he was quite a ways from the life he thought he'd live after reaching this point.

Except the house. The house was finally finished. Finally, he was living in one of the places he'd built.

Finally, Jonathan Bear, that poor Indian kid who wasn't worth anything to anyone, bastard son of the biggest bastard in town, had his house on the side of the mountain and more money than he would ever be able to spend.

And he was bored out of his mind.

Boredom, it turned out, worked him into a hell of a temper. He had a feeling Hayley Thompson wasn't strong enough to stand up to that. But he expected to go through a few assistants before he found one who could handle it. She might as well be number one.

"You've got the job," he said. "You can start tomorrow."

Her eyes widened, and he noticed they were a strange shade of blue. Gray in some lights, shot through with a dark, velvet navy that reminded him of the ocean before a storm. It made him wonder if there was some hidden strength there.

They would both find out.

"I got the job? Just like that?"

"Getting the job was always going to be the easy part. It's keeping the job that might be tricky. My list of reasons to hire you are short—you showed up. The list of reasons I have for why I might fire you is much longer."

"You're not very reassuring," she said, her lips tilting down in a slight frown.

He laughed. "If you want to go back and work for your daddy, do that. I'm not going to call you. But maybe you'll appreciate my ways later. Other jobs will seem easy after this one."

She just looked at him, her jaw firmly set, her petite body rigid with determination. "What time do you want me here?"

"Seven o'clock. Don't be late. Or else…"

"You'll fire me. I've got the theme."

"Excellent. Hayley Thompson, you've got yourself a job."

Chapter 2

Hayley scrubbed her face as she walked into The Grind through the private entrance from her upstairs apartment. It was early. But she wanted to make sure she wasn't late to work.

On account of all the firing talk.

"Good morning," Cassie said from behind the counter, smiling cheerfully. Hayley wondered if Cassie was really thrilled to be at work this early in the morning. Hayley knew all about presenting a cheerful face to anyone who might walk in the door.

You couldn't have a bad day when you worked at the church.

"I need coffee," Hayley said, not bothering to force a grin. She wasn't at work yet. She paused. "Do you know Jonathan Bear?"

Cassie gave her a questioning look. "Yes, I'm friends

with his sister, Rebecca. She owns the store across the street."

"Right," Hayley said, frowning. "I don't think I've ever met her. But I've seen her around town."

Hayley was a few years younger than Cassie, and probably a bit younger than Rebecca, as well, which meant they had never been in classes together at school, and had never shared groups of friends. Not that Hayley had much in the way of friends. People tended to fear the pastor's daughter would put a damper on things.

No one had tested the theory.

"So yes, I know Jonathan in passing. He's… Well, he's not very friendly." Cassie laughed. "Why?"

"He just hired me."

Cassie's expression contorted into one of horror and Hayley saw her start to backpedal. "He's probably fine. It's just that he's very protective of Rebecca because he raised her, you know, and all that. And she had her accident, and had to have a lot of medical procedures done… So my perception of him is based entirely on that. I'm sure he's a great boss."

"No," Hayley said, "you were right the first time. He's a grumpy cuss. Do you have any idea what kind of coffee he drinks?"

Cassie frowned, a small notch appearing between her brows. "He doesn't come in that often. But when he does I think he gets a dark roast, large, black, no sugar, with a double shot of espresso."

"How do you remember that?"

"It's my job. And there are a lot of people I know by drink and not by name."

"Well, I will take one of those for him. And hope that it's still hot by the time I get up the mountain."

"Okay. And a coffee for you with room for cream?"

"Yes," Hayley said. "I don't consider my morning caffeination ritual a punishment like some people seem to."

"Hey," Cassie said, "some people just like their coffee unadulterated. But I am not one of them. I feel you."

Hayley paid for her order and made her way to the back of the store, looking around at the warm, quaint surroundings. Locals had filed in and were filling up the tables, reading their papers, opening laptops and dropping off bags and coats to secure the coveted positions in the tiny coffee shop.

Then a line began to form, and Hayley was grateful she had come as early as she had.

A moment later, her order was ready. Popping the lid off her cup at the cream and sugar station, she gave herself a generous helping of both. She walked back out the way she had come in, going to her car, which was parked behind the building in her reserved space.

She got inside, wishing she'd warmed up the vehicle before placing her order. It wasn't too cold this morning, but she could see her breath in the damp air. She positioned both cups of coffee in the cup holders of her old Civic, and then headed to the main road, which was void of traffic—and would remain that way for the entire day.

She liked the pace of Copper Ridge, she really did. Liked the fact that she knew so many people, that people waved and smiled when she walked by. Liked that there were no traffic lights, and that you rarely had to wait for more than one car at a four-way stop.

She loved the mountains, and she loved the ocean.

But she knew there were things beyond this place, too. And she wanted to see them.

Needed to see them.

She thought about all those places as she drove along the winding road to Jonathan Bear's house. She had the vague thought that if she went to London or Paris, if she looked at the Eiffel Tower or Big Ben, structures so old and lasting—structures that had been there for centuries—maybe she would learn something about herself.

Maybe she would find what she couldn't identify here. Maybe she would find the cure for the elusive ache in her chest when she saw Ace with Sierra and their kids.

Would find the freedom to be herself—whoever that might be. To flirt and date, and maybe drink a beer. To escape the confines that so rigidly held her.

Even driving out of town this morning, instead of to the church, was strange. Usually, she felt as though she were moving through the grooves of a well-worn track. There were certain places she went in town— her parents' home, the church, the grocery store, The Grind, her brother's brewery and restaurant, but never his bar—and she rarely deviated from that routine.

She supposed this drive would become routine soon enough.

She pulled up to the front of the house, experiencing a sharp sense of déjà vu as she walked up to the front porch to knock again. Except this time her stomach twisted with an even greater sense of trepidation.

Not because Jonathan Bear was an unknown, but because she knew a little bit about him now. And what she knew terrified her.

The door jerked open before she could pound against it. "Just come in next time," he said.

"Oh."

"During business hours. I was expecting you."

"Expecting me to be late?" she asked, holding out his cup of coffee.

He arched a dark brow. "Maybe." He tilted his head to the side. "What's that?"

"Probably coffee." She didn't know why she was being anything other than straightforward and sweet. He'd made it very clear that he had exacting standards. Likely, he wanted his assistant to fulfill his every whim before it even occurred to him, and to do so with a smile. Likely, he didn't want his assistant to sass him, even lightly.

Except, something niggled at her, telling her he wouldn't respect her at all if she acted like a doormat. She was good at reading people. It was a happy side effect of being quiet. Of having few friends, of being an observer. Of spending years behind the church desk, not sure who might walk through the door seeking help. That experience had taught Hayley not only kindness, but also discernment.

And that was why she chose to follow her instincts with Jonathan.

"It's probably coffee?" he asked, taking the cup from her, anyway.

"Yes," she returned. "Probably."

He turned away from her, heading toward the stairs,

but she noticed that he took the lid off the cup and examined the contents. She smiled as she followed him up the stairs to the office.

The doors were already open, the computer that faced the windows fired up. There were papers everywhere. And pens sat across nearly every surface.

"Why so many pens?" she asked.

"If I have to stop and look for one I waste an awful lot of time cussing."

"Fair enough."

"I have to go outside and take care of the horses, but I want you to go through that stack of invoices and enter all the information into the spreadsheet on the computer. Can you do that?"

"Spreadsheets are my specialty. You have horses?"

He nodded. "This is kind of a ranch."

"Oh," she said. "I didn't realize."

"No reason you should." Then he turned, grabbing a black cowboy hat off a hook and putting it firmly on his head. "I'll be back in a couple of hours. And I'm going to want more coffee. The machine is downstairs in the kitchen. Should be pretty easy. Probably."

Then he brushed his fingertips against the brim of his hat, nodding slightly before walking out, leaving her alone.

When he left, something in her chest loosened, eased. She hadn't realized just how tense she'd felt in his presence.

She took a deep breath, sitting down at the desk in front of the computer, eyeing the healthy stack of papers to her left. Then she looked over the monitor to the view below. This wouldn't be so bad. He wasn't here looking over her shoulder, barking orders. And really, in terms of work space, this office could hardly be beat.

Maybe this job wouldn't be so bad, after all.

By the time Jonathan made a run to town after finishing up with the horses, it was past lunchtime. So he brought food from the Crab Shanty and hoped his new assistant didn't have a horrible allergy to seafood.

He probably should have checked. He wasn't really used to considering other people. And he couldn't say he was looking forward to getting used to it. But he would rather she didn't die. At least, not while at work.

He held tightly to the white bag of food as he made his way to the office. Her back was to the door, her head bent low over a stack of papers, one hand poised on the mouse.

He set the bag down loudly on the table by the doorway, then deposited his keys there, too. He hung his hat on the hook. "Hungry?"

Her head popped up, her eyes wide. "Oh, I didn't hear you come in. You scared me. You should have announced yourself or something."

"I just did. I said, 'hungry?' I mean, I could have said I'm here, but how is that any different?"

She shook her head. "I don't have an answer to that."

"Great. I have fish."

"What kind?"

"Fried kind."

"I approve."

He sighed in mock relief. "Good. Because if you didn't, I don't know how I would live with myself. I would have had to eat both of these." He opened the bag, taking out two cartons and two cans of Coke.

He sat in the chair in front of the table he used for drawing plans, then held her portion toward her.

She made a funny face, then accepted the offered lunch. "Is one of the Cokes for me, too?"

"Sure," he said, sliding a can at her.

She blinked, then took the can.

"What?"

She shook her head. "Nothing."

"You expected me to hand everything to you, didn't you?"

She shook her head. "No. Well, maybe. But, I'm sorry. I don't work with my father anymore, as you have mentioned more than once."

"No," he said, "you don't. And this isn't a church. Though—" he took a french fry out of the box and bit it "—this is pretty close to a religious experience." He picked up one of the thoughtfully included napkins and wiped his fingers before popping the top on the Coke can.

"How did you know I worked at the church?" she asked.

"I pay attention. And I definitely looked at the address you included on your form. Also, I know your brother. Or rather, I know of him. My sister is engaged to his brother-in-law. I might not be chummy with him, but I know his dad is the pastor. And that he has a younger sister."

She looked crestfallen. "I didn't realize you knew my brother."

"Is that a problem?"

"I was trying to get a job based on my own merit. Not on family connections. And frankly, I can't find anyone who is not connected to my family in some way in this town. My father knows the saints, my brother knows the sinners."

"Are you calling me a sinner?"

She picked gingerly at a piece of fish. "All have sinned and so forth."

"That isn't what you meant."

She suddenly became very interested in her coleslaw, prodding it with her plastic fork.

"How is it you know I'm a sinner?" he asked, not intending to let her off the hook, because this was just so fun. Hell, he'd gone and hired himself a church secretary, so might as well play with her a little bit.

"I didn't mean that," she insisted, her cheeks turning pink. He couldn't remember the last time he'd seen a woman blush.

"Well, if it helps at all, I don't know your brother well. I just buy alcohol from him on the weekends. But you're right. I am a sinner, Hayley."

She looked up at him then. The shock reflected in those stormy eyes touched him down deep. Made his stomach feel tight, made his blood feel hot. All right, he needed to get a handle on himself. Because that was not the kind of fun he was going to have with the church secretary he had hired. No way.

Jonathan Bear was a ruthless bastard; that fact could not be disputed. He had learned to look out for himself at an early age, because no one else would. Not his father. Certainly not his mother, who had taken off when he was a teenager, leaving him with a younger sister to raise. And most definitely not anyone in town.

But, even he had a conscience.

In theory, anyway.

"Good to know. I mean, since we're getting to know each other, I guess."

They ate in relative silence after that. Jonathan took that opportunity to check messages on his phone. A damn smartphone. This was what he had come to. Used to be that if he wanted to spend time alone he could unplug and go out on his horse easily enough. Now, he could still do that, but his business partners—dammit all, he had business partners—knew that he should be accessible and was opting not to be.

"Why did you leave the church?" he asked after a long stretch of silence.

"I didn't. I mean, not as a member. But, I couldn't work there anymore. You know, I woke up one morning and looked in the mirror and imagined doing that exact same thing in forty years. Sitting behind that desk, in the same chair, talking to the same people, having the same conversations… I just didn't think I could do it. I thought…well, for a long time I thought if I sat in that chair life would come to me." She took a deep breath. "But it won't. I have to go get it."

What she was talking about… That kind of stability. It was completely foreign to him. Jonathan could scarcely remember a time in his life when things had stayed the same from year to year. He would say one thing for poverty, it was dynamic. It could be a grind, sure, but it kept you on your toes. He'd constantly looked for new ways to support himself and Rebecca.

To prove to child services that he was a fit guardian. To keep their dwelling up to par, to make sure they could always afford it. To keep them both fed and clothed— or at least her, if not him.

He had always craved what Hayley was talking about. A place secure enough to rest for a while. But not having it was why he was here now. In this house, with all this money. Which was the only real damned security in the world. Making sure you were in control of everything around you.

Even if it did mean owning a fucking smartphone.

"So, your big move was to be my assistant?"

She frowned. "No. This is my small move. You have to make small moves before you can make a big one."

That he agreed with, more or less. His whole life had been a series of small moves with no pausing in between. One step at a time as he climbed up to the top. "I'm not sure it's the best thing to let your employer know you think he's a small step," he said, just because he wanted to see her cheeks turn pink again. He was gratified when they did.

"Sorry. This is a giant step for me. I intend to stay here forever in my elevated position as your assistant."

He set his lunch down, leaning back and holding up his hands. "Slow down, baby. I'm not looking for a commitment."

At that, her cheeks turned bright red. She took another bite of coleslaw, leaving a smear of mayonnaise on the corner of her mouth. Without thinking, he leaned in and brushed his thumb across the smudge, and along the edge of her lower lip.

He didn't realize it was a mistake until the slug of heat hit him low and fast in the gut.

He hadn't realized it would be a mistake because she was such a mousy little thing, a church secretary. Because his taste didn't run to that kind of thing. At least, that's what he would have said.

But while his brain might have a conscience, he discovered in that moment that his body certainly did not.

Chapter 3

It was like striking a match, his thumb sweeping across her skin. It left a trail of fire where he touched, and made her feel hot in places he hadn't. She was... Well, she was immobilized.

Like a deer caught in the headlights, seeing exactly what was barreling down on her, and unable to move.

Except, of course, Jonathan wasn't barreling down on her. He wasn't moving at all.

He was just looking at her, his dark eyes glittering, his expression like granite. She followed his lead, unsure of what to do. Of how she should react.

And then, suddenly, everything clicked into place. Exactly what she was feeling, exactly what she was doing...and exactly how much of an idiot she was.

She took a deep breath, gasping as though she'd been submerged beneath water. She turned her chair sideways, facing the computer again. "Well," she said, "thank you for lunch."

Fiddlesticks. And darn it. And fudging graham crackers.

She had just openly stared at her boss, probably looking like a guppy gasping on dry land because he had wiped mayonnaise off her lip. Which was—as things went—probably one of the more platonic touches a man and a woman could share.

The problem was, she couldn't remember ever being touched—even platonically—by a man who wasn't family. So she had been completely unprepared for the reaction it created inside her. Which she had no doubt he'd noticed.

Attraction. She had felt *attracted* to him.

Backtracking, she realized the tight feeling in her stomach that had appeared the first moment she'd seen him was probably attraction.

That was bad. Very bad.

But what she was really curious about, was why this attraction felt different from what she'd felt around other men she had liked. She'd felt fluttery feelings before. Most notably for Grant Daniels, the junior high youth pastor, a couple years ago. She had really liked him, and she was pretty sure he'd liked her, too, but he hadn't seemed willing to make a move.

She had conversations with him over coffee in the Fellowship Hall, where he had brought up his feelings on dating—he didn't—and how he was waiting until he was ready to get married before getting into any kind of relationship with a woman.

For a while, she'd been convinced he'd told her that

because he was close to being ready, and he might want to marry her.

Another instance of sitting, waiting and believing what she wanted would come to her through the sheer force of her good behavior.

Looking back, she realized it was kind of stupid that she had hoped he'd marry her. She didn't know him, not really. She had only ever seen him around church, and of course her feelings for him were based on that. Everybody was on their best behavior there. Including her.

Not that she actually behaved badly, which was kind of the problem. There was what she did, what she showed the world, and then there were the dark, secret things that lived inside her. Things she wanted but was afraid to pursue.

The fluttery feelings she had for Grant were like public Hayley. Smiley, shiny and giddy. Wholesome and hopeful.

The tension she felt in her stomach when she looked at Jonathan…that was all secret Hayley.

And it scared her that there was another person who seemed to have access to those feelings she examined only late at night in the darkness of her room.

She had finally gotten up the courage to buy a romance novel when she'd been at the grocery store a month or so ago. She had always been curious about those books, but since she'd lived with her parents, she had never been brave enough to buy one.

So, at the age of twenty-four, she had gotten her very first one. And it had been educational. Very, *very* educational. She had been a little afraid of it, to be honest.

Because those illicit feelings brought about late at

night by hazy images and the slide of sheets against her bare skin had suddenly become focused and specific after reading that book.

And if that book had been the fantasy, Jonathan was the reality. It made her want to turn tail and run. But she couldn't. Because if she did, then he would know what no one else knew about her.

She couldn't risk him knowing.

They were practically strangers. They had nothing in common. These feelings were ridiculous. At least Grant had been the kind of person she was suited to.

Which begged the question—why didn't he make her feel this off-kilter?

Her face felt like it was on fire, and she was sure Jonathan could easily read her reaction. That was the problem. It had taken her longer to understand what she was feeling than it had likely taken him. Because he wasn't sheltered like she was.

Sheltered even from her own desire.

The word made her shiver. Because it was one she had avoided thinking until now.

Desire.

Did she desire him? And if she did, what did that mean?

Her mouth went dry as several possibilities floated through her mind. Each more firmly rooted in fantasy than the last, since she had no practical experience with any of this.

And it was going to stay that way. At least for now.

Small steps. This job was her first small step. And it was a job, not a chance for her to get ridiculous over a man.

"Did you have anything else you wanted me to do?" she asked, not turning to face him, keeping her gaze resolutely pinned to the computer screen.

He was silent for a moment, and for some reason, the silence felt thick. "Did you finish entering the invoices?"

"Yes."

"Good," he said. "Here." He handed her his phone. "If anyone calls, say I'm not available, but you're happy to take a message. And I want you to call the county office and ask about the permits listed in the other spreadsheet I have open. Just get a status update on that. Do you cook?"

She blinked. "What?"

"Do you cook? I hired you to be my assistant. Which includes things around the house. And I eat around the house."

"I cook," she said, reeling from the change of topic.

"Great. Have something ready for me, and if I'm not back before you knock off at five, just keep it warm."

Then he turned and walked out, leaving her feeling both relieved and utterly confused. All those positive thoughts from this morning seemed to be coming back to haunt her, mock her.

The work she could handle. It was the man that scared her.

The first week of working with Hayley had been pretty good, in spite of that hiccup on the first day.

The one where he had touched her skin and felt just how soft it was. Something he never should have done.

But she was a good assistant. And every evening

when he came in from dealing with ranch work his dinner was ready. That had been kind of a dick move, asking her to cook, but in truth, he hadn't put a very detailed job description in the ad. And she wasn't an employee of Gray Bear. She was his personal employee, and that meant he could expand her responsibilities.

At least, that was what he told himself as he approached the front porch Friday evening, his stomach already growling in anticipation. When he came in for the evening after the outside work was done, she was usually gone and the food was warming in the oven.

It was like having a wife. With none of the drawbacks *and* none of the perks.

But considering he could get those perks from a woman who wasn't in his house more than forty hours a week, he would take this happily.

He stomped up the front steps, kicking his boots off before he went inside. He'd been walking through sludge in one of the far pastures and he didn't want to track in mud. His housekeeper didn't come until later in the week.

The corner of his mouth lifted as he processed that thought. He had a housekeeper. He didn't have to get on his hands and knees and scrub floors anymore. Which he had done. More times than he would care to recount. Most of the time the house he and Rebecca had shared while growing up had been messy.

It was small, and their belongings—basic though they were—created a lot of clutter. Plus, teenage boys weren't the best at keeping things deep cleaned. Especially not when they also had full-time jobs and were trying to finish high school. But when he knew child services would be by, he did his best.

He didn't now. He paid somebody else to do it. For a long time, adding those kinds of expenses had made both pride and anxiety burn in his gut. Adjusting to living at a new income level was not seamless. And since things had grown exponentially and so quickly, the adjustments had come even harder. Often in a million ways he couldn't anticipate. But he was working on it. Hiring a housekeeper. Hiring Hayley.

Pretty soon, he would give in and buy himself a new pair of boots.

He drew nearer to the kitchen, smelling something good. And then he heard footsteps, the clattering of dishes.

He braced his arms on either side of the doorway. Clearly, she hadn't heard him approach. She was bending down to pull something out of the oven, her sweet ass outlined to perfection by that prim little skirt.

There was absolutely nothing provocative about it. It fell down past her knees, and when she stood straight it didn't display any curves whatsoever.

For a moment, he just admired his own commitment to being a dick. She could not be dressed more appropriately, and still his eyes were glued to her butt. And damn, his body liked what he saw.

"You're still here," he said, pushing away from the door and walking into the room. He had to break the tension stretching tight inside him. Step one was breaking the silence and making his presence known. Step two was going to be calling up one of the women he had associations with off and on.

Because he had to do something to take the edge off. Clearly, it had been too long since he'd gotten laid.

"Sorry," she said, wiping her hands on a dishcloth and making a few frantic movements. As though she wanted to look industrious, but didn't exactly have a specific task. "The roast took longer than I thought it would. But I did a little more paperwork while I waited. And I called the county to track down that permit."

"You don't have to justify all your time. Everything has gotten done this week. Plus, inefficient meat preparation was not on my list of reasons I might fire you."

She shrugged. "I thought you reserved the right to revise that list at any time."

"I do. But not today."

"I should be out of your hair soon." She walked around the counter and he saw she was barefoot. Earlier, he had been far too distracted by her backside to notice.

"Pretty sure that's a health code violation," he said.

She turned pink all the way up to her scalp. "Sorry. My feet hurt."

He thought of those low, sensible heels she always wore and he had to wonder what the point was to wearing shoes that ugly if they weren't even comfortable. The kind of women he usually went out with wore the kinds of shoes made for sitting. Or dancing on a pole.

But Hayley didn't look like she even knew what pole dancing was, let alone like she would jump up there and give it a try. She was… Well, she was damn near sweet.

Which was all wrong for him, in every way. He wasn't sweet.

He was successful. He was driven.

But he was temporary at best. And frankly, almost

everyone in his life seemed grateful for that fact. No one stayed. Not his mother, not his father. Even his sister was off living her own life now.

So why he should spend even one moment looking at Hayley the way he'd been looking at her, he didn't know. He didn't have time for subtlety. He never had. He had always liked obvious women. Women who asked for what they wanted without any game-playing or shame.

He didn't want a wife. He didn't even want a serious girlfriend. Hell, he didn't want a casual girlfriend. When he went out it was with the express intention of hooking up. When it came to women, he didn't like a challenge.

His whole damned life was a challenge, and always had been. When he'd been raising his sister he couldn't bring anyone back to his place, which meant he needed someone with a place of their own, or someone willing to get busy in the back of a pickup truck.

Someone who understood he had only a couple free hours, and he wouldn't be sharing their bed all night.

Basically, his taste ran toward women who were all the things Hayley wasn't.

Cute ass or not.

None of those thoughts did anything to ease the tension in his stomach. No matter how succinctly they broke down just why he shouldn't find Hayley hot.

He nearly scoffed. She *wasn't* hot. She was… She would not be out of place as the wholesome face on a baking mix. Much more Little Debbie than Debbie Does Dallas.

"It's fine. I don't want you going lame on me."

She grinned. "No. Then you'd have to put me down."

"True. And if I lose more than one personal assistant that way people will start asking questions."

He could tell she wasn't sure if he was kidding or not. For a second, she looked downright concerned.

"I have not sent, nor do I intend to send, any of my employees—present or former—to the glue factory. Don't look at me like that."

She bit her lower lip, and that forced him to spend a moment examining just how lush it was. He didn't like that. She needed to stop bending over, and to do nothing that would draw attention to her mouth. Maybe, when he revised the list of things he might fire her for, he would add drawing attention to attractive body parts to the list.

"I can never tell when you're joking."

"Me, either," he said.

That time she did laugh. "You know," she said, "you could smile."

"Takes too much energy."

The timer went off and she bustled back to the stove. "Okay," she said, "it should be ready now." She pulled a little pan out of the oven and took the lid off. It was full of roast and potatoes, carrots and onions. The kind of home-cooked meal he imagined a lot of kids grew up on.

For him, traditional fare had been more along the lines of flour tortillas with cheese or ramen noodles. Something cheap, easy and full of carbs. Just enough to keep you going.

His stomach growled in appreciation, and that was the kind of hunger associated with Hayley that he could accept.

"I should go," she said, starting to walk toward the kitchen door.

"Stay."

As soon as he made the offer Jonathan wanted to bite his tongue off. He did not need to encourage spending more time in closed off spaces with her. Although dinner might be a good chance to prove that he could easily master those weird bursts of attraction.

"No," she said, and he found himself strangely relieved. "I should go."

"Don't be an idiot," he said, surprising himself yet again. "Dinner is ready here. And it's late. Plus there's no way I can eat all this."

"Okay," she said, clearly hesitant.

"Come on now. Stop looking at me like you think I'm going to bite you. You've been reading too much *Twilight*. Indians don't really turn into wolves."

Her face turned really red then. "That's not what I was thinking. I don't... I'm not afraid of you."

She was afraid of something. And what concerned him most was that it might be the same thing he was fighting against.

"I really was teasing you," he said. "I have a little bit of a reputation in town, but I didn't earn half of it."

"Are you saying people in town are...prejudiced?"

"I wouldn't go that far. I mean, I wouldn't say it's on purpose. But whether it's because I grew up poor or it's because I'm brown, people have always given me a wide berth."

"I didn't... I mean, I've never seen people act that way."

"Well, they wouldn't. Not to you."

She blinked slightly. "I'll serve dinner now."

"Don't worry," he said, "the story has a happy ending. I have a lot of money now, and that trumps anything else. People have no issue hiring me to build these days. Though, I remember the first time my old boss put me on as the leader of the building crew, and the guy whose house we were building had a problem with it. He didn't think I should be doing anything that required too much skill. Was more comfortable with me just swinging the hammer, not telling other people where to swing it."

She took plates down from the cupboard, holding them close to her chest. "That's awful."

"People are awful."

A line creased her forehead. "They definitely can be."

"Stop hugging my dinner plate to your shirt. That really isn't sanitary. We can eat in here." He gestured to the countertop island. She set the plates down hurriedly, then started dishing food onto them.

He sighed heavily, moving to where she was and taking the big fork and knife out of her hands. "Have a seat. How much do you want?"

"Oh," she said, "I don't need much."

He ignored her, filling the plate completely, then filling his own. After that, he went to the fridge and pulled out a beer. "Want one?"

She shook her head. "I don't drink."

He frowned, then looked back into the fridge. "I don't have anything else."

"Water is fine."

He got her a glass and poured some water from the spigot in the fridge. He handed it to her, regarding her like she was some kind of alien life-form. The small conversation had really highlighted the gulf between them.

It should make him feel even more ashamed about looking at her butt.

Except shame was pretty hard for him to come by.

"Tell me what you think about people, Hayley." He took a bite of the roast and nearly gave her a raise then and there.

"No matter what things look like on the surface, you never know what someone is going through. It surprised me how often someone who had been smiling on Sunday would come into the office and break down in tears on Tuesday afternoon, saying they needed to talk to the pastor. Everyone has problems, and I do my best not to add to them."

"That's a hell of a lot nicer than most people deserve."

"Okay, what do you think about people?" she asked, clasping her hands in front of her and looking so damn interested and sincere he wasn't quite sure how to react.

"I think they're a bunch of self-interested bastards. And that's fair enough, because so am I. But whenever somebody asks for something, or offers me something, I ask myself what they will get out of it. If I can't figure out how they'll benefit, that's when I get worried."

"Not everyone is after money or power," she said. He could see she really believed what she said. He wasn't sure what to make of that.

"All right," he conceded, "maybe they aren't all after money. But they are looking to gain something. Everyone is. You can't get through life any other way. Trust me."

"I don't know. I never thought of it that way. In terms of who could get me what. At least, that's not how I've lived."

"Then you're an anomaly."

She shook her head. "My father is like that, too. He really does want to help people. He cares. Pastoring a small church in a little town doesn't net you much power or money."

"Of course it does. You hold the power of people's salvation in your hands. Pass around the plate every week. Of course you get power and money." Jonathan shook his head. "Being the leader of local spirituality is power, honey, trust me."

Her cheeks turned pink. "Okay. You might have a point. But my father doesn't claim to have the key to anyone's salvation. And the money in that basket goes right back into the community. Or into keeping the doors of the church open. My father believes in living the same way the community lives. Not higher up. So whatever baggage you might have about church, that's specific to your experience. It has nothing to do with my father or his faith."

She spoke with such raw certainty that Jonathan was tempted to believe her. But he knew too much about human nature.

Still, he liked all that conviction burning inside her. He liked that she believed what she said, even if he couldn't.

If he had been born with any ideals, he couldn't remember them now. He'd never had the luxury of having faith in humanity, as Hayley seemed to have. No, his earliest memory of his father was the old man's fist connecting with his face. Jonathan had never had the chance to believe the best of anybody.

He had been introduced to the worst far too early.

And he didn't know very many people who'd had different experiences.

The optimism she seemed to carry, the softness combined with strength, fascinated him. He wanted to draw closer to it, to her, to touch her skin, to see if she was strong enough to take the physical demands he put on a woman who shared his bed.

To see how shocked she might be when he told her what those demands were. In explicit detail.

He clenched his jaw tight, clamping his teeth down hard. He was not going to find out, for a couple reasons. The first being that she was his employee, and off-limits. The second being that all those things that fascinated him would be destroyed if he got close, if he laid even one finger on her.

Cynicism bled from his pores, and he damn well knew it. He had earned it. He wasn't one of those bored rich people overcome by ennui just because life had gone so well he wanted to create problems so he had something to battle against.

No. He had fought every step of the way, and he had been disappointed by people in every way imaginable. He had earned his feelings about people, that was for damn sure.

But he wasn't certain he wanted to pass that cynicism on to Hayley. No, she was like a pristine wilderness area. Unspoiled by humans. And his first inclination was to explore every last inch, to experience all that beauty, all that majesty. But he had to leave it alone. He had to leave it looked at, not touched.

Hayley Thompson was the same. Untouched. He had to leave her unspoiled. Exploring that beauty would only leave it ruined, and he couldn't do that. He wouldn't.

"I think it's sad," she said, her voice muted. "That you can't see the good in other people."

"I've been bitten in the ass too many times," he said, his tone harder than he'd intended it to be. "I'm glad you haven't been."

"I haven't had the chance to be. But that's kind of the point of what I'm doing. Going out, maybe getting bitten in the ass." Her cheeks turned bright red. "I can't believe I said that."

"What?"

"That word."

That made his stomach feel like it had been hollowed out. *"Ass?"*

Her cheeks turned even redder. "Yes. I don't say things like that."

"I guess not… Being the church secretary and all."

Now he just felt… Well, she made him feel rough and uncultured, dirty and hard and unbending as steel. Everything she was not. She was small, delicate and probably far too easy to break. Just like he'd imagined earlier, she was…set apart. Unspoiled. And here he had already spoiled her a little bit. She'd said ass, right there in his kitchen.

And she'd looked shocked as hell by her own behavior.

"You don't have to say things like that if you don't want to," he said. "Not every experience is a good experience. You shouldn't try things just to try them. Hell, if I'd had the choice of staying innocent of human nature, maybe I would have taken that route instead. Don't ruin that nice vision of the world you have."

She frowned. "You know, everybody talks about going out and experiencing things…"

"Sure. But when people say that, they want control over those experiences. Believe me, having the blinders ripped off is not necessarily the best thing."

She nodded slowly. "I guess I understand that. What kinds of experiences do you think are bad?"

Immediately, he thought of about a hundred bad things he wanted to do to her. Most of them in bed, all of them naked. He sucked in a sharp breath through his teeth. "I don't think we need to get into that."

"I'm curious."

"You know what they say about curiosity and the cat, right?"

"But I'm not a cat."

"No," he said, "you are Hayley, and you should be grateful for the things you've been spared. Maybe you should even go back to the church office."

"No," she said, frowning. "I don't want to. Maybe I don't want to *experience everything*—I can see how you're probably right about that. But I can't just stay in one place, sheltered for the rest of my life. I have to figure out…who I am and what I want."

That made him laugh, because it was such a naive sentiment. He had never stood back and asked himself who the hell Jonathan Bear was, and what he wanted out of life. He hadn't given a damn how he made his money as long as he made it.

As far as he was concerned, dreams were for people with a lot of time on their hands. He had to *do*. Even as a kid, he couldn't think, couldn't wonder; he had to act.

She might as well be speaking a foreign language. "You'll have to tell me what that's like."

"What?"

"That quest to find yourself. Let me know if it's any more effective than just living your life and seeing what happens."

"Okay, now you've made me feel silly."

He took another bite of dinner. Maybe he should back down, because he didn't want her to quit. He would like to continue eating her food. And, frankly, he would like to keep looking at her.

Just because he should back down didn't mean he was going to.

"There was no safety net in my life," he said, not bothering to reassure her. "There never has been. I had to work my ass off from the moment I was old enough to get paid to do something. Hell, even before then. I would get what I could from the store, expired products, whatever, so we would have something to eat. That teaches you a lot about yourself. You don't have to go looking. In those situations, you find out whether you're a survivor or not. Turns out I am. And I've never really seen what more I needed to know."

"I don't… I don't have anything to say to that."

"Yeah," he returned. "My life story is kind of a bummer."

"Not now," she said softly. "You have all this. You have the business, you have this house."

"Yeah, I expect a man could find himself here. Well,

unless he got lost because it was so big." He smiled at her, but she didn't look at all disarmed by the gesture. Instead, she looked thoughtful, and that made his stomach feel tight.

He didn't really do meaningful conversation. He especially didn't do it with women.

Yet here he was, telling this woman more about himself than he could remember telling anyone. Rebecca knew everything, of course. Well, as much as she'd observed while being a kid in that situation. They didn't need to talk about it. It was just life. But other people... Well, he didn't see the point in talking about the deficit he'd started with. He preferred people assume he'd sprung out of the ground powerful and successful. They took him more seriously.

He'd had enough disadvantages, and he wouldn't set himself up for any more.

But there was something about Hayley—her openness, her honesty—that made him want to talk. That made him feel bad for being insincere. Because she was just so...so damn real.

How would he have been if he'd had a softer existence? Maybe he wouldn't be as hard. Maybe a different life would have meant not breaking a woman like this the moment he put his hands on her.

It was moot. Because he hadn't had a different life. And if he had, he probably wouldn't have made half as much of himself.

"You don't have to feel bad for wanting more," he said finally. "Just because other people don't have it easy, doesn't mean you don't have your own kind of hard."

"It's just difficult to decide what to do when other people's expectations feel so much bigger than your own dreams."

"I know a little something about that. Only in my case, the expectations other people had for me were that I would end up dead of a drug overdose or in prison. So, all things considered, I figured I would blow past those expectations and give people something to talk about."

"I just want to travel."

"Is that it?"

A smile played in the corner of her lips, and he found himself wondering what it might be like to taste that smile. "Okay. And see a famous landmark. Like the Eiffel Tower or Big Ben. And I want to dance."

"Have you never danced?"

"No!" She looked almost comically horrified. "Where would I have danced?"

"Well, your brother does own a bar. And there is line dancing."

"I can't even go into Ace's bar. My parents don't go. We can go to the brewery. Because they serve more food there. And it's not called a bar."

"That seems like some arbitrary shit."

Her cheeks colored, and he didn't know if it was because he'd pointed out a flaw in her parents' logic or because he had cursed. "Maybe. But I follow their lead. It's important for us to keep away from the appearance of evil."

"Now, that I don't know anything about. Because nobody cares much about my appearance."

She cleared her throat. "So," she said. "Dancing."

Suddenly, an impulse stole over him, one he couldn't

quite understand or control. Before he knew it, he was pushing his chair back and standing up, extending his hand. "All right, Hayley Thompson, Paris has to wait awhile. But we can take care of the dancing right now."

"What?" Her pretty eyes flew wide, her soft lips rounded into a perfect O.

"Dance with me, Hayley."

Chapter 4

Hayley was pretty sure she was hallucinating.

Because there was no way her stern boss was standing there, his large, work-worn hand stretched toward her, his dark eyes glittering with an intensity she could only guess at the meaning of, having just asked her to dance. Except, no matter how many times she blinked, he was still standing there. And the words were still echoing in her head.

"There's no music."

He took his cell phone out of his pocket, opened an app and set the phone on the table, a slow country song filling the air. "There," he said. "Music accomplished. Now, dance with me."

"I thought men *asked* for a dance, I didn't think they demanded one."

"Some men, maybe. But not me. But remember, I don't give a damn about appearances."

"I think I might admire that about you."

"You should," he said, his tone grave.

She felt… Well, she felt breathless and fluttery, and she didn't know what to do. But if she said no, then he would know just how inexperienced she was. He would know she was making a giant internal deal about his hand touching hers, about the possibility of being held against his body. That she felt strange, unnerving sensations skittering over her skin when she looked at him. She was afraid he could see her too clearly.

Isn't this what you wanted? To reach out? To take a chance?

It was. So she did.

She took his hand. She was still acclimating to his heat, to being touched by him, skin to skin, when she found herself pressed flush against his chest, his hand enveloping hers. He wrapped his arm around her waist, his palm hot on her lower back.

She shivered. She didn't know why. Because she wasn't cold. No. She was hot. And so was he. Hot and hard, so much harder than she had imagined another person could be.

She had never, ever been this close to a man before. Had never felt a man's skin against hers. His hand was rough, from all that hard work. What might it feel like if he touched her skin elsewhere? If he pushed his other hand beneath her shirt and slid his fingertips against her lower back?

That thought sent a sharp pang straight to her stomach, unfurling something inside her, making her blood run faster.

She stared straight at his shoulder, at an innocuous

spot on his flannel shirt. Because she couldn't bring herself to raise her eyes and look at that hard, lean face, at the raw beauty she had never fully appreciated before.

He would probably be offended to be characterized as beautiful. But he was. In the same way that a mountain was beautiful. Tall, strong and unmoving.

She gingerly curled her fingers around his shoulder, while he took the lead, his hold on her firm and sure as he established a rhythm she could follow.

The grace in his steps surprised her. Caused her to meet his gaze. She both regretted it and relished it at the same time. Because it was a shame to stare at flannel when she could be looking into those dark eyes, but they also made her feel…absolutely and completely undone.

"Where did you learn to dance?" she asked, her voice sounding as breathless as she had feared it might.

But she was curious about this man who had grown up in such harsh circumstances, who had clearly devoted most of his life to hard work with no frills, who had learned to do this.

"A woman," he said, a small smile tugging at the edges of his lips.

She was shocked by the sudden, sour turn in her stomach. It was deeply unpleasant, and she didn't know what to do to make it stop. Imagining what other woman he might have learned this from, how he might have held her…

It hurt. In the strangest way.

"Was she…somebody special to you? Did you love her?"

His smile widened. "No. I've never loved anybody. Not anybody besides my sister. But I sure as hell *wanted* something from that woman, and she wanted to dance."

It took Hayley a while to figure out the meaning behind those words. "Oh," she said, "she wanted to dance and you wanted..." That feeling in her stomach intensified, but along with it came a strange sort of heat. Because he was holding *her* now, dancing with her. *She* wanted to dance. Did that mean that he...?

"Don't look at me like that, Hayley. This," he said, tightening his hold on her and dipping her slightly, his face moving closer to hers, "is just a dance."

She was a tangle of unidentified feelings—knots in her stomach, an ache between her thighs—and she didn't want to figure out what any of it meant.

"Good," she said, wishing she could have infused some conviction into that word.

The music slowed, the bass got heavier. And he matched the song effortlessly, his hips moving firmly against hers with every deep pulse of the beat.

This time, she couldn't ignore the lyrics. About two people and the fire they created together. She wouldn't have fully understood what that meant even a few minutes ago, but in Jonathan's arms, with the heat that burned from his body, fire was what she felt.

Like her nerve endings had been set ablaze, like a spark had been stoked low inside her. If he moved in just the wrong way—or just the right way—the flames in him would catch hold of that spark in her and they would combust.

She let her eyes flutter closed, gave herself over to the moment, to the song, to the feel of him, the scent of him. She was dancing. And she liked it a lot more than she had anticipated and in a way she hadn't imagined she could.

She had pictured laughing, lightness, with people all around, like at the bar she had never been to before. But this was something else. A deep intimacy that grew from somewhere inside her chest and intensified as the music seemed to draw them more tightly together.

She drew in a breath, letting her eyes open and look up at him. And then she froze.

He was staring at her, the glitter in his dark eyes almost predatory. She didn't know why that word came to mind. Didn't even know what it might mean in this context. When a man looked at you like he was a wildcat and you were a potential meal.

Then her eyes dipped down to his mouth. Her own lips tingled in response and she was suddenly aware of how dry they were. She slid her tongue over them, completely self-conscious about the action even as she did it, yet unable to stop.

She was satisfied when that predatory light in his eyes turned sharper. More intense.

She didn't know what she was doing. But she found herself moving closer to him. She didn't know why. She just knew she had to. With the same bone-deep impulse that came with the need to draw breath, she had to lean in closer to Jonathan Bear. She couldn't fight it; she didn't want to. And until her lips touched his, she didn't even know what she was moving toward.

But when their mouths met, it all became blindingly clear.

She had thought about these feelings in terms of fire,

but this sensation was something bigger, something infinitely more destructive. This was an explosion. One she felt all the way down to her toes; one that hit every place in between.

She was shaking. Trembling like a leaf in the wind. Or maybe even like a tree in a storm.

He was the storm.

His hold changed. He let go of her hand, withdrew his arm from around her waist, pressed both palms against her cheeks as he took the kiss deeper, harder.

It was like drowning. Like dying. Only she didn't want to fight it. Didn't want to turn away. She couldn't have, even if she'd tried. Because his grip was like iron, his body like a rock wall. They weren't moving in time with the music anymore. No. This was a different rhythm entirely. He propelled her backward, until her shoulder blades met with the dining room wall, his hard body pressed against hers.

He was hard. Everywhere. Hard chest, hard stomach, hard thighs. And that insistent hardness pressing against her hip.

She gasped when she realized what that was. And he consumed her shocked sound, taking advantage of her parted lips to slide his tongue between them.

She released her hold on him, her hands floating up without a place to land, and she curled her fingers into fists. She surrendered herself to the kiss, to him. His hold was tight enough to keep her anchored to the earth, to keep her anchored to him.

She let him have control. Let him take the lead. She didn't know how to dance, and she didn't know how to do this. But he did.

So she let him show her. This was on her list, too, though she hadn't been brave enough to say it, even to herself. To know passion. To experience her first kiss.

She wanted it to go on and on. She never wanted it to end. If she could just be like this, those hot hands cupping her face, that insistent mouth devouring hers, she was pretty sure she could skip the Eiffel Tower.

She felt him everywhere, not just his kiss, not just his touch. Her breasts felt heavy. They ached. In any other circumstances, she might be horrified by that. But she didn't possess the capacity to be horrified, not right now. Not when everything else felt so good. She wasn't ashamed; she wasn't embarrassed—not of the heavy feeling in her breasts, not of the honeyed, slick feeling between her thighs.

This just made sense.

Right now, what she felt was the only thing that made sense. It was the only thing she wanted.

Kissing Jonathan Bear was a necessity.

He growled, flexing his hips toward hers, making it so she couldn't ignore his arousal. And the evidence of his desire carved out a hollow feeling inside her. Made her shake, made her feel like her knees had dissolved into nothing and that without his powerful hold she would crumple onto the floor.

She still wasn't touching him. Her hands were still away from his body, trembling. But she didn't want to do anything to break the moment. Didn't want to make a sound, didn't want to make the wrong move. She didn't want to turn him off or scare him away. Didn't want to do anything to telegraph her innocence. Because it would probably freak him out.

Right, Hayley, like he totally believes you're a sex kitten who's kissed a hundred men.

She didn't know what to do with her hands, let alone her lips, her tongue. She was receiving, not giving. But she had a feeling if she did anything else she would look like an idiot.

Suddenly, he released his hold on her, moving away from her so quickly she might have thought she'd hurt him.

She was dazed, still leaning against the wall. If she hadn't been, she would have collapsed. Her hands were still in the air, clenched into fists, and her breath came in short, harsh bursts. So did his, if the sharp rise and fall of his chest was anything to go by.

"That was a mistake," he said, his voice hard. His words were everything she had feared they might be.

"No, it wasn't," she said, her lips feeling numb, and a little bit full, making it difficult for her to talk. Or maybe the real difficulty came from feeling like her head was filled with bees, buzzing all around and scrambling her thoughts.

"Yes," he said, his voice harder, "it was."

"No," she insisted. "It was a great kiss. A really, really good kiss. I didn't want it to end."

Immediately, she regretted saying that. Because it had been way too revealing. She supposed it was incredibly gauche to tell the guy you'd just kissed that you could have kissed him forever. She tried to imagine how Grant, the youth pastor, might have reacted to that. He would have told her she needed to go to an extra Bible study. Or that she needed to marry him first.

He certainly wouldn't have looked at her the way

Jonathan was. Like he wanted to eat her whole, but was barely restraining himself from doing just that. "That's exactly the problem," he returned, the words like iron, "because I *did* want it to end. But in a much different way than it did."

"I don't understand." Her face was hot, and she was humiliated now. So she didn't see why she shouldn't go whole hog. Let him know she was fully outside her comfort zone and she wasn't keeping up with all his implications. She needed stated facts, not innuendo.

"I didn't want to keep kissing you forever. I wanted to pull your top off, shove your skirt up and bury myself inside of you. Is that descriptive enough for you?"

It was. And he had succeeded in shocking her. She wasn't stupid. She knew he was hard, and she knew what that meant. But even given that fact, she hadn't really imagined he wanted... Not with her.

And this was just her first kiss. She wasn't ready for more. Wasn't ready for another step away from the person she had been taught to be.

What about the person you want to be?

She looked at her boss, who was also the most beautiful man she had ever seen. That hadn't been her immediate thought when she'd met him, but she had settled into it as the truth. As certain as the fact the sky was blue and the pine trees that dotted the mountains were deep forest green.

So maybe... Even though it was shocking. Even though it would be a big step, and undoubtedly a big mistake... Maybe she did want it.

"You better go," he said, his voice rough.

"Maybe I don't—"

"You do," he said. "Trust me. And I want you to."

She was confused. Because he had just said he wanted her, and now he was saying he wanted her to go. She didn't understand men. She didn't understand this. She wanted to cry. But a lick of pride slid its way up her spine, keeping her straight, keeping her tears from falling.

Pride she hadn't known she possessed. But then, she hadn't realized she possessed the level of passion that had just exploded between them, either. So it was a day for new discoveries.

"That's fine. I just wanted to have some fun. I can go have it with someone else."

She turned on her heel and walked out of the dining room, out the front door and down the porch steps as quickly as possible. It was dark now, trees like inky bottle brushes rising around her, framing the midnight-blue sky dotted with stars. It was beautiful, but she didn't care. Not right now. She felt…hurt. Emotionally. Physically. The unsatisfied ache between her thighs intensified with the pain growing in her heart.

It was awful. All of it.

It made her want to run. Run back to her parents' house. Run back to the church office.

Being *good* had always been safe.

She had been so certain she wanted to escape safety. Only a few moments earlier she'd needed that escape, felt it might be her salvation. Except she could see now that it was ruin. Utter and complete ruin.

With shaking hands, she pushed the button that undid the locks on her car door and got inside, jamming the key into the ignition and starting it up, a tear sliding down her cheek as she started to back out of the driveway.

She refused to let this ruin her, or this job, or this step she was taking on her own.

She was finding independence, learning new things.

As she turned onto the two-lane highway that would take her back home, she clung to that truth. To the fact that, even though her first kiss had ended somewhat disastrously, it had still shown her something about herself.

It had shown her exactly why it was a good thing she hadn't gotten married to that youthful crush of hers. It would have been dishonest, and not fair to him or to her.

She drove on autopilot, eventually pulling into her driveway and stumbling inside her apartment, lying down on her bed without changing out of her work clothes.

Was she a fallen woman? To want Jonathan like she had. A man she wasn't in love with, a man she wasn't planning to marry.

Had that passion always been there? Or was it created by Jonathan? This feeling. This *need*.

She bit back a sob and forced a smile. She'd had her first kiss. And she wouldn't dwell on what it might mean. Or on the fact that he had sent her away. Or on the fact that—for a moment at least—she had been consumed with the desire for more.

She'd had her first kiss. At twenty-four. And that felt like a change deep inside her body.

Hayley Thompson had a new apartment, a new job, and she had been kissed.

So maybe it wasn't safe. But she had decided she wanted something more than safety, hadn't she?

She would focus on the victories and simply ignore the rest.

No matter that this victory made her body burn in a way that kept her up for the rest of the night.

Chapter 5

He hadn't expected her to show up Monday morning. But there she was, in the entryway of the house, hands clasped in front of her, dark hair pulled back in a neat bun. Like she was compensating for what had happened between them Friday night.

"Good morning," he said, taking a sip of his coffee. "I half expected you to take the day off."

"No," she said, her voice shot through with steel, "I can't just take days off. My boss is a tyrant. He'll fire me."

He laughed, mostly to disguise the physical response those words created in him. There was something about her. About all that softness, that innocence, combined with the determination he hadn't realized existed inside her until this moment.

She wasn't just soft, or innocent. She was a force to

be reckoned with, and she was bent on showing him that now.

"If he's so bad why do you want to keep the job?"

"My job history is pathetic," she said, walking ahead of him to the stairs. "And, as he has pointed out to me many times, he is not my daddy. My previous boss was. I need something a bit more impressive on my résumé."

"Right. For when you do your traveling."

"Maybe I'll get a job in London," she shot back.

"What's the biggest city you've been to, Hayley?" he asked, following her up the stairs and down the hall toward the office.

"Portland," she said.

He laughed. "London is a little bit bigger."

"I don't care. That's what I want. I want a city where I can walk down the street and not run into anybody that I've ever seen before. All new people. All new faces. I can't imagine that. I can't imagine living a life where I do what I want and not hear a retelling of the night before coming out of my mother's mouth at breakfast the next morning."

"Have you ever done anything worthy of being recounted by your mother?"

Color infused her cheeks. "Okay, specifically, the incident I'm referring to is somebody telling my mother they were proud of me because they saw me giving a homeless woman a dollar."

He laughed. He couldn't help himself, and her cheeks turned an even more intense shade of pink that he knew meant she was furious.

She stamped. Honest to God stamped, like an old-time movie heroine. "What's so funny?"

"Even the gossip about you is good, Hayley Thompson. For the life of me, I can't figure out why you hate that so much."

"Because I can't *do* anything. Jonathan, if you had kissed me in my brother's bar... Can you even imagine? My parents' phone would have been ringing off the hook."

His body hardened at the mention of the kiss. He had been convinced she would avoid the topic.

But he should've known by now that when it came to Hayley he couldn't anticipate her next move. She was more direct, more up-front than he had thought she might be. Was it because of her innocence that she faced things so squarely? Because she hadn't experienced a whole range of consequences for much of anything yet?

"I wouldn't do that to you," he said. "Because you're right. If anybody suspected something unprofessional had happened between us, it would cause trouble for you."

"I didn't mean it that way." She looked horrified. "I mean, the way people would react if they thought I was... It has nothing to do with you."

"It does. More than you realize. You've been sheltered. But just because you don't know my reputation, that doesn't mean other people in town don't know it. Most people who know you're a good girl know I am a bad man, Hayley. And if anyone suspected I had put my hands on you, I'm pretty sure there would be torches and pitchforks at my front door by sunset."

"Well," she said, "that isn't fair. Because *I* kissed *you*."

"I'm going out on a limb here—of the two of us, I have more experience."

She clasped her hands in front of her and shuffled her feet. "Maybe."

"Maybe nothing, honey. I'm not the kind of man you need to be seen with. So, you're right. You do need to get away. Maybe you should go to London. Hell, I don't know."

"Now you want to get rid of me?"

"Now you're just making it so I can't win."

"I don't mean to," she said, with that trademark sincerity that was no less alarming for being typical of her. "But I don't know what to do with…with this."

She bit her lip, and the motion drew his eye to that lush mouth of hers. Forced him back to the memory of kissing it. Of tasting her.

He wanted her. No question about it.

He couldn't pretend otherwise. But he could at least be honest with himself about why. He wanted her for all the wrong reasons. He wanted her because some sick, caveman part of him wanted to get all that *pretty* dirty. Part of him wanted to corrupt her. To show her everything she was missing. To make her fall from grace a lasting one.

And that was some fucked up shit.

Didn't mean he didn't feel it.

"Well, after I earn enough money, that's probably what I'll do," she said. "And since this isn't going anywhere… I should probably just get to work. And we shouldn't talk about it anymore."

"No," he said, "we shouldn't."

"It was just a kiss."

His stomach twisted. Not because it disappointed him to hear her say that, but because she had to say it for her own peace of mind. She was innocent enough that a kiss worked her up. It meant something to her. Hell, sex barely meant anything to him. Much less a kiss.

Except for hers. You remember hers far too well.

"Just a kiss," he confirmed.

"Good. So give me some spreadsheets."

The rest of the week went well. If well meant dodging moments alone with Jonathan, catching herself staring at him at odd times during the day and having difficulty dreaming of anything except him at night.

"Thank God it's Friday," she said into the emptiness of her living room.

She didn't feel like cooking. She had already made a meal for Jonathan at his house, and then hightailed it out of there as quickly as possible. She knew that if she'd made enough for herself and took food with her he wouldn't have minded, but she was doing her best to keep the lines between them firm.

She couldn't have any more blurred lines. They couldn't have any more…kissing and other weirdness. Just thinking about kissing Jonathan made her feel restless, edgy. She didn't like it. Or maybe she liked it too much.

She huffed out a growl and wandered into the kitchen, opening the cupboard and pulling out a box of chocolate cereal.

It was the kind of cereal her parents never would have bought. Because it wasn't good for you, and it was expensive. So she had bought it for herself, because she had her own job, she was an adult and she made her own decisions.

Do you?

She shut out that snotty little voice. Yes, she *did* make her own decisions. Here she was, living in her own place, working at the job she had chosen. Yes, she very much made her own decisions. She had even kissed Jonathan. Yes, that had been her idea.

Which made the fallout her fault. But she wasn't going to dwell on that.

"I'm dwelling," she muttered. "I'm a liar, and I'm dwelling." She took down a bowl and poured herself a large portion of the chocolaty cereal. Then she stared at it. She didn't want to eat cereal by herself for dinner.

She was feeling restless, reckless.

She was feeling something a whole lot like desperation.

Because of that kiss.

The kiss she had just proposed she wasn't going to think about, the kiss she couldn't let go of. The kiss that made her burn, made her ache and made her wonder about all the mysteries in life she had yet to uncover.

Yeah, *that* kiss.

She had opened a floodgate. She'd uncovered all this potential for passion inside herself, and then she had to stuff it back down deep.

Jonathan Bear was not the only man in the world. Jonathan Bear wasn't even the only man in Copper Ridge.

She could find another guy if she wanted to.

Of course, if she went out, there would be all those gossip issues she and Jonathan had discussed earlier in the week.

That was why she had to get out of this town.

It struck her then, like a horse kicking her square in the chest, that she was running away. So she could be who she wanted to be without anybody knowing about it. So she could make mistakes and minimize the consequences.

So she could be brave and a coward all at the same time.

That's what it was. It was cowardice. And she was not very impressed with herself.

"Look at you," she scolded, "eating cold cereal on a Friday night by yourself when you would rather be out getting kissed."

Her heart started to beat faster. Where would she go?

And then it hit her. There was one place she could go on a Friday night where nobody from church would recognize her, and even if they did recognize her, they probably wouldn't tell on her because by doing so they would be telling on themselves.

Of course, going there would introduce the problem of her older brother. But Ace had struck out on his own when he was only seventeen years old. He was her inspiration in all this. So he should understand Hayley's need for independence.

And that was when she made her decision. It was Friday night, and she was going out.

She was going to one of the few places in town where she had never set foot before.

Ace's bar.

Chapter 6

"I'd like a hamburger," Hayley said, adjusting her dress and trying not to look like she was about to commit a crime.

"Hayley?" Her brother looked at her as if she had grown another head. "What are you doing in my bar?"

"I'm here to have a hamburger. And…a beer."

Ace shook his head. "You don't want beer."

Darn him for being right. She couldn't stand the smell of the stuff, and she'd honestly never even been tempted to taste it.

"No," she agreed. "I want a Coke."

"I will get you a Coke. Are Mom and Dad here?"

She sighed heavily. "No, they're not. I do go places without them. I moved out."

"I know. We talked about it last time Sierra and I went over for dinner."

Hayley's brother had never much cared about his reputation, or about what anyone thought of him. She had been jealous of that for a long time. For years, Ace had been a total hellion and a womanizer, until he'd settled down and married the town rodeo princess, Sierra West. Now the two of them had one child and another on the way, and Ace's position in the community had improved vastly.

"Right. Well, I'm just saying." She traced an imaginary pattern over the bar top with the tip of her finger. "Did I tell you I quit working at the church?"

Ace look surprised by that. "No."

"Well," she said, "I did. I'm working for Jonathan Bear. Helping out with things around the house and in the office."

Ace frowned. "Well, that probably isn't very much fun. He's kind of a grumpy sumbitch."

"I didn't know you knew him all that well."

"He's my future sister-in-law's brother," Ace said, "but no, I don't know him *well*. He's not very sociable. It's not like he comes to the West family gatherings."

"He said he knows you because he buys beer from you."

"That's how everybody knows me," Ace said.

"Except for me."

"You were *trying* to buy beer from me. I'm just not going to sell one to you."

"That's not fair."

"Sure it is," he said, smiling. "Because you don't actually want to buy beer from me. You're just trying to prove a point."

She scowled. She hated that Ace seemed to understand her so well. "Okay, maybe so. I'm kind of proving a point by being here, I guess."

"Well," he said, "it's all right by me."

"Good."

"I kind of wish you would have come on another night, though," he said, "because I have to go. I promised Sierra I would be home early, so I'm about to take off. But I'll tell Jasmine to keep an eye on you."

"I don't need anybody to keep an eye on me."

"Yes," Ace said, laughing, "you do."

Hayley frowned, and plotted how to order a beer when her brother was gone. Ultimately, she decided to stick with Coke, but when the dancing started, she knew that while she might stay away from alcohol, she didn't want to stay seated. She had danced once. And she had liked it.

She was going to do it again.

Jonathan didn't know what in blazes he was doing at Ace's. Sure, he knew what he'd told himself while getting ready, his whole body restless thanks to memories of kissing Hayley.

He had continued to push those thoughts down while pacing around the house, and then, after a while, he'd decided to go out and find someone to hook up with. He didn't do that kind of thing, not anymore. He had a couple of women he called; he didn't go trawling bars. He was too old for that.

But right now, he was too much of a hazard to his innocent assistant, and he needed to take the edge off.

And it occurred to him that if he went to Ace's bar and found somebody, the news might filter back to Hayley.

Even though she might find it upsetting, it would be beneficial in the long run. She didn't want to mess with a man like him, not really. It was only that she was too innocent realize the dangers. But she would, eventually, and she would thank him.

That decision made, he'd hauled his ass down to the bar as quickly as possible.

By the time he walked in, his mood had not improved. He had thought it might. The decision to find a willing woman should have cheered him up. But he felt far from cheered. Maybe because an anonymous body was the last thing he wanted.

He wanted *Hayley*.

Whether he should or not. But he wasn't going to have Hayley. So he would have to get the hell over it.

He moved to the bar and then looked over at the dance floor. His chest tightened up. His body hardened. There was a petite brunette in a formfitting dress dancing with no one in particular. Two men hovered nearby, clearly not minding as she turned to and away from each of them, giving them both just a little bit of attention.

She reminded him of Hayley. Out there on the dance floor acting like nothing close to Hayley.

Then she turned, her dark hair shimmering behind her in a stream, a bright smile on her face, and he could barely process his thoughts. Because it was Hayley. *His* Hayley, out there in the middle of the dance floor, wearing a dress that showed off the figure her clothes had only hinted at before. Sure, in comparison to a lot of women, there was nothing flashy about it, but for Hayley Thompson, it was damned flashy.

And he was… Well, he would be damned if he was going to let those guys put their hands on her.

Yeah, he was bad news. Yeah, he was the kind of guy she should stay well away from. But those guys weren't any better. College douche bags. Probably in their twenties, closer to her age, sure, but not the kind of men who knew how to handle a woman. Especially not one as inexperienced as Hayley.

She would need a man who could guide the experience, show her what she liked. A man who could unlock the mysteries of sex, of her body.

Dickwads that age were better off with an empty dorm room and a half bottle of lotion.

And there was no way in hell they were getting their hands on her.

Without ordering, he moved away from the bar and went out on the dance floor. "You're done here," he said to one of the guys, who looked at him as though Jonathan had just threatened his life. His tone had been soft and even, but it was nice to know the younger man had heard the implied threat loud and clear.

Hayley hadn't noticed his approach, or that the other guy had scurried off to the other end of the dance floor. She was too involved with the guy she was currently dancing with to notice. She was shaking her head, her eyes closed, her body swaying to the music. A completely different kind of dancing than the two of them had done last week.

Then her current dance partner caught Jonathan's eye and paled. He slunk off into the shadows, too.

If Jonathan hadn't already found them wanting when it came to Hayley, he would have now. If they were any kind of men, they would have stood up and declared their interest. They would have proclaimed their desire for her, marked their territory.

He still would have thrown punches, but at least he would've respected them a bit.

Not now.

"Mind if I dance with you?"

Her eyes flew open and she looked around, her head whipping from side to side, her hair following suit. "Where are…"

"Tweedledee and Tweedledum had somewhere to be."

"Where?"

"Someplace where I wouldn't beat their asses."

"Why are you going to beat their…butts?"

"What are you doing here, Hayley?"

She looked around, a guilty expression on her face. "I was just dancing. I have to say, when I imagined getting in trouble in a bar, I figured it would be my dad dragging me outside, not my boss."

"I haven't dragged you outside. *Yet*." He added that last bit because at this point he wasn't sure how this night was going to end. "What are you doing?"

She lifted a shoulder. "Dancing."

"Getting ready to have your first threesome?"

Her mouth dropped open. "I don't even know how that would work."

He huffed out a laugh. "Look it up. On second thought, don't."

She rolled her eyes like a snotty teenager. "We were just dancing. It wasn't a big deal."

"Little girl, what you don't know about men could

fill a library. Men don't *just want to dance*. And men don't *just want to kiss*. You can't play these kinds of games. You don't know the rules. You're going to get yourself into trouble."

"I'm not going to get myself into trouble. Did it ever occur to you that maybe some men are nicer than you?"

He chuckled, a low, bitter sound. "Oh, I know that most men are a lot nicer than me. Even then, they want in your pants."

"I don't know what your problem is. You don't want me, so what do you care if they do?"

"Hayley, honey, I don't *want* to want you, but that is not the same thing as not wanting you. It is not even close. What I want is something you can't handle."

"I know," she said, looking to the right and then to the left, as though making sure no one was within earshot. Then she took a step toward him. "You said you wanted to…be inside of me."

That simple statement, that repetition of his words, had him hard as an iron bar. "You better back off."

"See, I thought you didn't want me. I thought you were trying to scare me away when you said that. Because why would you want me?"

"I'd list the reasons, but I would shock you."

She tilted her head to the side, her hair falling over her shoulder like a glossy curtain. "Maybe I want to be shocked. Maybe I want something I'm not quite ready for."

"No," he said, his tone emphatic now. "You're on this big kick to have experiences. And there are much nicer men you can have experiences with."

She bared her teeth. "I was trying! You just scared them off."

"You're not having experiences with those clowns. They wouldn't know how to handle a woman if she came with an instruction manual. And let me tell you, women do not come with an instruction manual. You just have to know what to do."

"And you know what to do?"

"Damn straight," he returned.

"So," she said, tilting her chin up, looking stubborn. "Show me."

"Not likely, babe."

He wanted to. He wanted to pick her up, throw her over his shoulder and drag her back to his cave. He wanted to bury himself inside her and screw them both senseless, breathless. He wanted to chase every man in the vicinity away from her. He wanted to make it known, loud and clear that—for a little while at least— she was his.

But it was wrong. On about a thousand levels. And the fact that she didn't seem to know it was just another bit of evidence that he needed to stay away.

"You're playing with fire," he said.

"I know. When you kissed me, that was the closest to being burned I've ever experienced in my life. I want more of that."

"We're not having this conversation in the middle of a bar." He grabbed her arm and hauled her off the dance floor, steering them both to the door.

"Hayley!"

He turned and saw one of the waitresses standing by the bar with her hands on her hips.

"Is everything all right?" she asked.

"Yes," Hayley responded. "Jasmine, it's fine. This is my boss."

Jasmine arched her brow. "Really?"

Hayley nodded. "Really. Just work stuff."

Then she broke free of him and marched out ahead of him. When they were both outside, she rounded on him, her words coming out on a frosty cloud in the night air.

"You're so concerned about my reputation, but then you wander in and make a spectacle."

"You were dancing with two men when I got there," he said. "And what's happening with that dress?"

"Oh please," she said, "I wear this dress to church. It's fine."

"You wear that to *church*?" He supposed, now that he evaluated it with more neutrality, it was pretty tame. The black stretch cotton fell past her knees and had a fairly high neckline. But he could see the curves of her breasts, the subtle slope of her waist to her hips, and her ass looked incredible.

He didn't know if hers was the sort of church that did confession, but he would sure as hell need to confess if he were seated in a row behind her during service.

"Yes," she said. "And it's fine. You're being crazy. Because…because you…*like* me. You *like me* like me."

There she went again, saying things that revealed how innocent she was. Things that made him want her even more, when they should send him running.

"I don't have relationships," he said. He would tell her the truth. He would be honest. It would be the fastest way to chase her off. "And I'm betting a nice girl like you wants a relationship. Wants romance, and flowers, and at least the possibility of commitment. You don't get any of those things with me, Hayley."

She looked up at him, her blue eyes glittering in the security light. He could hear the waves crashing on the shore just beyond the parking lot, feel the salt breeze blowing in off the water, sharp and cold.

"What would I get?" she asked.

"A good, hard fuck. A few orgasms." He knew he'd shocked her, and he was glad. She needed to be shocked. She needed to be scared away.

He couldn't see her face, not clearly, but he could tell she wasn't looking at him when she said, "That's… that's a good thing, right?"

"If you don't know the answer, then the answer is no. Not for you."

The sounds of the surf swelled around them, wind whipping through the pines across the road. She didn't speak for a long time. Didn't move.

"Kiss me again," she said, finally.

The words hit him like a sucker punch. "What? What did I just tell you about men and kissing?"

"It's not for you," she said, "it's for me. Before I give you an answer, you need to kiss me again."

She raised her head, and the light caught her face. She stared at him, all defiance and soft lips, all innocence and intensity, and he didn't have it in him to deny her.

Didn't have it in him to deny himself.

Before he could stop, he wrapped his arm around her waist, crushed her against his chest and brought his lips crashing down on hers.

Chapter 7

She was doing this. She wasn't going to turn back. Not now. And she kept telling herself that as she followed Jonathan's pickup truck down the long, empty highway that took them out of town, toward his house.

His house. Where she was going to spend the night.

Where she was going to lose her virginity.

She swallowed hard, her throat suddenly dry and prickly like a cactus.

This wasn't what she had planned when she'd started on her grand independence journey. Yes, she had wanted a kiss, but she hadn't really thought as far ahead as having a sexual partner. For most of her life she had imagined she would be married first, and then, when she'd started wavering on that decision, she had at least imagined she would be in a serious relationship.

This was... Well, it wasn't marriage. It wasn't the beginning of a relationship, either. Of that, she was certain. Jonathan hadn't been vague. Her cheeks heated at the memory of what he'd said, and she was grateful they were driving in separate cars so she had a moment alone for a private freak-out.

She was so out of her league here.

She could turn around. She could head back to town, back to Main Street, back to her little apartment where she could curl up in bed with the bowl of cereal she'd left dry and discarded on the counter earlier.

And in the morning, she wouldn't be changed. Not for the better, not for the worse.

She seriously considered that, though she kept on driving, her eyes on the road and on Jonathan's taillights.

This decision was a big deal. She wouldn't pretend it wasn't. Wouldn't pretend she didn't put some importance on her first sexual experience, on sex in general. And she wouldn't pretend it probably wasn't a mistake.

It was just that maybe she needed to make the mistake. Maybe she needed to find out for herself if Jonathan was right, if every experience wasn't necessary.

She bit her lip and allowed herself a moment of undiluted honesty. When this was over, there would be fallout. She was certain of it.

But while it was happening, it would feel really, really good.

If the kissing was anything to go by, it would be amazing.

She would feel…wild. And new. And maybe sex with Jonathan would be just the kind of thing she needed. He was hot; touching him burned.

Maybe he could be her own personal trial by fire.

She had always imagined that meant walking through hard times. And maybe, conventionally, it did. But she was walking into the heat willingly, knowing the real pain would come after.

She might be a virgin, but she wasn't an idiot. Jonathan Bear wasn't going to fall in love with her. And anyway, she didn't want him to.

She wanted freedom. She wanted something bigger than Copper Ridge.

That meant love wasn't on her agenda, either.

They pulled up to the house and he got out of his truck, closing the door solidly behind him. And she... froze. Sitting there in the driver's seat, both hands on the steering wheel, the engine still running.

The car door opened and cool air rushed in. She looked up and saw Jonathan's large frame filling the space. "Second thoughts?"

She shook her head. "No," she said, and yet she couldn't make herself move.

"I want you," he said, his voice rough, husky, the words not at all what she had expected. "I would like to tell you that if you are having second thoughts, you should turn the car around and go back home. But I'm not going to tell you that. Because if I do, then I might miss out on my chance. And I want this. Even though I shouldn't."

She tightened her hold on the steering wheel. "Why shouldn't you?" she asked, her throat constricted now.

"Do you want the full list?"

"I've got all night."

"All right. You're a nice girl. You seem to believe

the best of people, or at least, you want to, until they absolutely make it so you can't. I'm not a nice man. I don't believe the best of anyone, even when they prove I should. People like me, we tend to drag people like you down to our level. Unfortunately. And that's likely what's going to happen here. I'm going to drag you right down to my level. Because let me tell you, I like dirty. And I'm going to get you filthy. I can promise you that."

"Okay," she said, feeling breathless, not quite certain how to respond. Part of her wanted to fling herself out of the car and into his arms, while another, not insignificant part wanted to throw the car in Reverse and drive away.

"I can only promise you two things. This—you and me—won't last forever. And tonight, I will make you come. If you're okay with those promises, then get out of the car and up to my room. If you're not, it's time for you to go."

For some reason, that softly issued command was what it took to get her moving. She released her hold on the steering wheel and turned sideways in her seat. Then she looked up at him, pushing herself into a standing position. He had one hand on the car door, the other on the side mirror, blocking her in.

Her breasts nearly touched his chest, and she was tempted to lean in and press against him completely.

"Come on then," he said, releasing his hold on the car and turning away.

The movement was abrupt. It made her wonder if he was struggling with indecision, too. Which didn't really make sense, since Jonathan was the most decisive man she had ever met. He seemed certain about everything, all the time, even if he was sure it was a bad decision.

That certainty was what she wanted. Yeah, she was certain this was a bad decision, too, but she was going for it, anyway.

She had walked into this house five days a week for the past couple weeks, yet this time was different. Because this time she wasn't headed to the office. This time she was going to his bedroom. And she wasn't his employee; he wasn't her boss. Not now.

Her stomach tightened, her blood heated at the idea of following orders. His orders. Lord knew she would need instruction. Direction. She had no idea what she was doing; she was just following her gut instinct.

When they reached the long hallway, they stopped at a different door than usual. His bedroom. She had never been inside Jonathan's bedroom. It was strange to be standing there now. So very deliberate.

It might have been easier if they had started kissing here in the house, and let things come to their natural conclusion… On the floor or something. She was reasonably sure people did it on the floor sometimes.

Yeah, that would have been easier. This was so *intentional*.

She was about to say something about the strangeness of it when he reached out, cupped her chin and tilted her face upward. Then he closed the distance between them, claiming her mouth.

She felt his possession, all the way down to her toes.

He didn't wait for her to part her lips this time. Instead, he invaded her, sliding his tongue forcibly against hers, his arms wrapped tight around her like steel bands.

There was nothing gentle about this kiss. It was consuming, all-encompassing. And all her thoughts about the situation feeling premeditated dissolved.

This time, she didn't stand there as a passive participant. This time, she wrapped her arms around his neck—pressing her breasts flush against his chest, forking her fingers through his hair—and devoured him right back.

She couldn't believe this was her. Couldn't believe this was her life, that this man wanted her. That he was hard for her. That he thought she might be a mistake, and he was willing to make her, anyway. God knew, she was willing to make him.

Need grew inside her, prowling around like a restless thing. She rocked her hips forward, trying to tame the nameless ache between her thighs. Trying to calm the erratic, reckless feeling rioting through her.

He growled, sliding his hands down her back, over her bottom, down to her thighs. She squeaked as he gripped her tightly, pulling both her feet off the ground and picking her up, pressing that soft, tender place between her legs against his arousal.

"Wrap your legs around me," he said against her mouth, the command harsh, and sexier because of that.

She obeyed him, locking her ankles behind his back. He reversed their positions, pressing her against the wall and deepening his kiss. She gasped as he made even firmer contact with the place that was wet and aching for him.

He ground his hips against her, and her internal muscles pulsed. An arc of electricity lanced through her. She gripped his shoulders hard, vaguely aware that she might be digging her fingernails into his skin, not really sure that she cared. Maybe it would hurt him, but she wasn't exactly sure if he was hurting her or not. She was suspended between pleasure and pain, feelings so intense she could scarcely breathe.

And through all that, he continued to devour her mouth, the rhythm of his tongue against hers combining with the press of his firm length between her thighs, ensuring that her entire world narrowed down to him. Jonathan Bear was everything right now. He was her breath; he was sensation. He was heaven and he was hell.

She needed it to end. Needed to reach some kind of conclusion, where all this tension could be defused.

And yet she wanted it to go on forever.

Her face was hot, her limbs shaking. A strange, hollow feeling in the pit of her stomach made her want to cry. It was too much. And it was not enough. That sharp, insistent ache between her legs burrowed deeper with each passing second, letting her know this kiss simply wasn't enough at all.

She moved her hands up from his broad shoulders, sliding them as far as she could into his long, dark hair. Her fingers snagged on the band that kept his hair tied back and she internally cursed her clumsiness, hoping he wouldn't notice. She had enthusiasm guiding her through this, but that was about it. Enthusiasm and a healthy dose of adrenaline that bordered on terror. But she didn't want to stop. She couldn't stop.

Those big, rough hands gripped her hips and braced her as he rocked more firmly against her, and suddenly, stars exploded behind her eyes. She gasped, wrenching her lips away from his as something that felt like thunder rolled through her body, muscles she'd never been aware of before pulsing like waves against the shore.

She pressed her forehead against his shoulder, did her best to grit her teeth and keep herself from crying out, but a low, shaky sound escaped when the deepest wave washed over her.

Then it ended, and she felt even more connected to reality, to this moment, than she had a second ago. And she felt…so very aware that she was pressed against the wall and him, that something had just happened, that she hadn't been fully cognizant of her actions. She didn't know what she might have said.

That was when she realized she was digging her nails into his back, and she had probably punctured his skin. She started to move against him, trying to get away, and he gripped her chin again, steadying her. "Hey," he said, "you're not going anywhere."

"I need to… I have to…"

"You don't have to do anything, baby. Nothing at all. Just relax." She could tell he was placating her. She couldn't bring herself to care particularly, because she needed placating. Her heart was racing, her hands shaking, and that restlessness that had been so all-consuming earlier was growing again. She had thought the earthquake inside her had handled that.

That was when she realized exactly what that earthquake had been.

Her cheeks flamed, horror stealing through her. She'd had… Well, she'd had an orgasm. And he hadn't even touched her. Not with his hands. Not under her clothes.

"I'm sorry," she said, putting her hands up, patting

his chest, then curling her hands into fists because she had patted him and that was really stupid. "I'm just sorry."

He frowned. "What are you sorry about?"

"I'm sorry because I—I… I did that. And we didn't…"

He raised one eyebrow. "Are you apologizing for your orgasm?"

She squeezed her eyes tightly shut. "Yes."

"Why?"

She tightened her fists even more, pressing them against her own chest, keeping her eyes closed. "Because we didn't even… You didn't… We're still dressed."

"Honey," he said, taking hold of her fists and drawing them toward him, pressing them against his chest. "You don't need to apologize to me for coming."

She opened one eye. "I… I don't?"

"No."

"But that…" She looked fully at him, too curious to be embarrassed now. "That ruins it, doesn't it? We didn't…"

"You can have as many orgasms as I can give you. That's the magical thing about women. There's no ceiling on that."

"There isn't?"

"You didn't know?"

"No."

"Hayley," he said, his tone grave, "I need to ask you a question."

Oh great. Now he was actually going to ask if she was a virgin. Granted, she thought he'd probably guessed, but apparently he needed to hear it. "Go ahead," she said, bracing herself for utter humiliation.

"Have you never had an orgasm before?"

"Yes," she said, answering the wrong question before he even got his out. "I mean… No. I mean, just a minute ago. I wasn't even sure what it was right when it was happening."

"That doesn't… Not even with yourself?"

Her face felt so hot she thought it might be on fire. She was pretty sure her heart was beating in her forehead. "No." She shook her head. "I can't talk to you about things like that."

"I just gave you your first orgasm, so you better be able to talk to me about things like that. Plus I'm aiming to give you another one before too long here."

"I bet you can't."

He chuckled, and then he bent down, sweeping her up into his arms. She squeaked, curling her fingers around his shirt. "You should know better than to issue challenges like that." He turned toward the bedroom door, kicking it open with his boot before walking inside and kicking it closed again. Then he carried her to the bed and threw her down in the center.

"Wait," she said, starting to feel panicky, her heart fluttering in her chest like a swarm of butterflies. "Just wait a second."

"I'm not going to fall on you like a ravenous beast," he said, his hands going to the top button of his shirt. "Yet." He started to undo the button slowly, revealing his tan, muscular chest.

She almost told him to stop, except he stripped the shirt off, and she got completely distracted by the play of all those muscles. The sharp hitch of his abs as he cast the flannel onto the floor, the shift and bunch of his pectoral muscles as he pushed his hand over his hair.

She had never seen a shirtless man that looked like him. Not in person, anyway. And most definitely not this close, looking at her like he had plans. Very, very dirty plans.

"I'm a virgin," she blurted out. "Just so you know."

His eyes glowed with black fire. For one heart-stopping moment she was afraid he might pick up his shirt and walk out of the room. His eyes looked pure black; his mouth pressed into a firm line. He stood frozen, hands on his belt buckle, every line in his cut torso still.

Then something in his expression shifted. Nearly imperceptible, and mostly unreadable, but she had seen it. Then his deft fingers went to work, moving his belt through the buckle. "I know," he said.

"Oh." She felt a little crestfallen. Like she must have made some novice mistake and given herself away.

"You're a church secretary who confessed to having never had an orgasm. I assumed." He lowered his voice. "If you hadn't told me outright, I could have had plausible deniability. Which I was sort of counting on."

She blinked. "Did you…need it?"

"My conscience is screwed, anyway. So not really."

She didn't know quite what to say, so she didn't say anything.

"Have you ever seen a naked man before?"

She shook her head. "No."

"Pictures?"

"Does medieval art count?"

"No, it does not."

"Then no," she said, shaking her head even more vigorously.

He rubbed his hand over his forehead, and she was sure she heard him swear beneath his breath. "Okay," he said, leaving his belt hanging open, but not going any further. He pressed his knee down on the mattress, kneeling beside her. Then he took her hand and placed it against his chest. "How's that?"

She drew shaking fingers across his chest slowly, relishing his heat, the satiny feel of his skin. "Good," she said. "You're very…hot. I mean, temperaturewise. Kind of smooth."

"You don't have to narrate," he said.

"Sorry," she said, drawing her hand back sharply.

"No," he said, pressing her palm back against his skin. "Don't apologize. Don't apologize for anything that happens between us tonight, got that?"

"Okay," she said, more than happy to agree, but not entirely sure if she could keep to the agreement. Because every time she moved her hand and his breath hissed through his teeth, she wanted to say she was sorry. Every time she took her exploration further, she wanted to apologize for the impulse to do it.

She bit her lip, letting her hands glide lower, over his stomach, which was as hard and rippled as corrugated steel. Then she found her hands at the waistband of his jeans, and she pulled back.

"Do you want me to take these off?" he asked.

"In a minute," she said, losing her nerve slightly. "Just a minute." She rose up on her knees, pressed her mouth to his and lost herself in kissing him. She really liked kissing. Loved the sounds he made, loved being enveloped in his arms, and she really loved it when he laid them both down, pressing her deep into the mattress and settling between her thighs.

Her dress rode up high, and she didn't care. She felt rough denim scraping her bare skin, felt the hard press of his zipper, and his arousal behind it through the thin fabric of her panties.

She lost herself in those sensations. In the easy, sensual contact that pushed her back to the brink again. She could see already that Jonathan was going to win the orgasm challenge. And she was okay with that.

Very, very okay with that.

Then he took her hem and pulled the cotton dress over her head, casting it onto the floor. Her skin heated all over, and she was sure she was pink from head to toe.

"Don't be embarrassed," he said, touching her collarbone, featherlight, then tracing a trail down to the curve of her breast, to the edge of her bra. "You're beautiful."

She didn't know quite how to feel about that. Didn't know what to do with that husky, earnest compliment. She wasn't embarrassed because she lacked beauty, but because she had always been taught to treasure modesty. To respect her body, to save it.

He *was* respecting it, though. And right now, she felt like she had been saving it for him.

He reached behind her, undoing her bra with one hand and flicking the fabric to the side.

"You're better at that than I am," she said, laughing nervously as he bared her breasts, her nipples tightening as the cold air hit her skin.

He smiled. "You'll appreciate that in a few minutes."

"What will I appreciate?" she asked, shivering. She crossed her arms over her chest.

"My skill level." Instead of moving her hands, he bent his head and nuzzled the tender spot right next to her hand, the full part of her breast that was still exposed. She gasped, tightening her hold on herself.

He was not deterred.

He nosed her gently and shifted her hand to the side, pressing a kiss to her skin, sending electric sensations firing through her. "Don't be shy," he said, "not with me."

She waited for a reason why. He didn't give one, but she found that the more persistent he was—the more hot, open-mouthed kisses he pressed to her skin—the less able she was to deny him anything. Anything at all. She found herself shifting her hands and then letting them fall away.

As soon as she did, he closed his lips over her nipple, sucking deep. She gasped, her hips rocking up off the bed. He wrapped his arm around her, holding her against his hardness as he teased her with his lips and tongue.

Every time she wiggled, either closer to him, or in a moment of self-consciousness, away, it only brought him more in contact with that aching place between her thighs, and then she would forget why she was moving at all. Why she wasn't just letting him take the lead.

So she relaxed into him, and let herself get lost. She was in a daze when he took her hand and pushed it down his stomach, to the front of his jeans. She gasped when his hard, denim-covered length filled her palm.

"Feel that? That's how much I want you. That's what you do to me."

A strange surge of power rocketed through her. That she could cause such a raw, sexual response… Well, it was intoxicating in a way she hadn't appreciated it could be.

Especially because he was such a man. A hot man. A sexy man, and she had never thought of anyone that way in her life. But he was. He most definitely was.

"Are you ready?" he asked.

She nodded, sliding her hand experimentally over him. He moved, undoing his pants and shoving them quickly down, hardly giving her a chance to prepare. Her mouth dried when she saw him, all of him. She hadn't really… Well, she had been content to allow her fantasies to be somewhat hazy. Though reading that romance novel had made those fantasies a little sharper.

Still, she hadn't really imagined specifically how large a man might be. But suffice it to say, he was a bit larger than she had allowed for.

Her breath left her lungs in a rush. But along with the wave of nerves that washed over her came a sense of relief. "You are… I like the way you look," she said finally.

A crooked smile tipped his mouth upward. "Thank you."

"I told you, I've never seen a naked man before. I was a little afraid I wouldn't like it."

"Well, I'm glad you do. Because let me tell you, that's a lot of pressure. Being the first naked man you've ever seen." His eyes darkened and his voice got lower, huskier. "Being the first naked man you've ever touched."

He took her hand again and placed it around his bare shaft, the skin there hotter and much softer than she had imagined. She slid her thumb up and down, marveling at the feel of him.

"You're the first man I've ever kissed," she said, the words slurred, because she had lost the full connection between her brain and her mouth. All her blood had flowed to her extremities.

He swore, and then crushed her to him, kissing her deeply and driving her back down to the mattress. His erection pressed into her stomach, his tongue slick against hers, his lips insistent. She barely noticed when he divested her of her underwear, until he placed his hand between her legs. The rough pads of his fingers sliding through her slick flesh, the white-hot pleasure his touch left behind, made her gasp.

"I'm going to make sure you're ready," he said.

She had no idea what that meant. But he started doing wicked, magical things with his fingers, so she didn't much care. Then he slid one finger deep inside her and she arched away, not sure whether she wanted more of that completely unfamiliar sensation, or if she needed to escape it.

"It's okay," he said, moving his thumb in a circle over a sensitive bundle of nerves as he continued to slide his finger in and out of her body.

After a few passes of his thumb, she agreed.

He shifted his position, adding a second finger, making her gasp. It burned slightly, made her feel like she was being stretched, but after a moment, she adjusted to that, too.

That lovely, spiraling tension built inside her again,

and she knew she was close to the edge. But every time he took her to the brink, he would drop back again.

"Please," she whispered.

"Please what?" he asked, being dastardly, asking her to clarify, when he knew saying the words would embarrass her.

"You know," she said, placing her hand over his, like she might take control, increase the pressure, increase the pace, since he refused.

But, of course, he was too strong for her to guide him at all. "I need to hear it."

"I need… I need to have an orgasm," she said quickly.

For a moment, he stopped. He looked at her like she mystified him. Like he had never seen anything like her before. Then he withdrew his hand and slid down her body, gripping her hips roughly before drawing her quickly against his mouth.

She squeaked when his lips and tongue touched her right in her most intimate place. She reached down, grabbing hold of his hair, because she was going to pull him away, but then his tongue touched her in the most amazing spot and she found herself lacing her fingers through his hair instead.

She found herself holding him against her instead of pushing him away.

She moved her hips in time with him, gasping for air as pleasure, arousal, built to impossible heights. She had been on the edge for so long now it felt like she was poised on the brink of something else entirely. But right when she was about to break, he moved away from her, drawing himself up her body. He grabbed a small, round packet from the bedspread that she hadn't noticed until now, and tore it open, quickly sheathing himself before moving to position the blunt head of his arousal at her entrance.

He flexed his hips, thrusting deep inside her, and her arousal broke like a mirror hit with a hammer. She gritted her teeth as pain—sharp and jagged—cut through all the hidden places within her. But along with the pain came the intense sensation of being full. Of being connected to another person like she never had been before.

She reached up, taking his heavily muscled arms and holding him, just holding him, as he moved slowly inside her.

He was *inside* her.

She marveled at that truth even as the pain eased, even as pleasure began to push its way into the foreground again.

"Move with me," he said, nuzzling her neck, kissing the tender skin there.

So she did, meeting his every thrust, clinging to him. She could see the effort it took for him to maintain control, and she could see when his control began to fray. When his thrusts became erratic, his golden skin slick with sweat, his breathing rough and ragged, matching her own.

When he thrust deep, she arched her hips, an electric shower of sparks shimmering through her each time.

His hands were braced on either side of her shoulders, his strong fingers gripping the sheets. His movements became hard, rough, but none of the earlier pain remained, and she welcomed him. Opened her thighs wider and then wrapped her legs around his lean hips so she could take him even deeper.

There was no pain. There was no shame. There was no doubt at all.

As far as she was concerned, there was only the two of them.

He leaned down, pressing his forehead against hers, his dark gaze intense as his rhythm increased. He went shallow, then deep, the change pushing her even closer to the edge.

Then he pulled out almost completely, his hips pulsing slightly. The denial of that deep, intimate contact made her feel frantic. Made her feel needy. Made her feel desperate.

"Jonathan," she said. "Jonathan, please."

"Tell me you want to come," he told her, the words a growl.

"I want to come," she said, not wasting a moment on self-consciousness.

He slammed back home, and she saw stars. This orgasm grabbed her deep, reached places she hadn't known were there. The pleasure seemed to go on and on, and when it was done, she felt like she was floating on a sea, gazing up at a sky full of infinite stars.

She felt adrift, but only for a moment. Because when she came back to herself, she was still clutching his strong arms, Jonathan Bear rooting her to the earth.

And then she waited.

Waited for regret. Waited for guilt.

But she didn't feel any of it. Right now, she just felt a bone-deep satisfaction she hoped never went away.

"I..." He started to say something, moving away from her. Then he frowned. "You don't have a toothbrush or anything, do you?"

It was such a strange question that it threw her for a loop. "What?"

"It doesn't matter," he said. He bent down, pressing a kiss to her forehead. "We'll work something out in the morning."

She was glad he'd said there was nothing to worry about, because her head was starting to get fuzzy and her eyelids were heavy. Which sucked, because she didn't want to sleep. She wanted to bask in her new-found warm and fuzzy feelings.

But she was far too sleepy, far too sated to do anything but allow herself to be enveloped by that warmth. By him.

He drew her into his arms, and she snuggled into his chest, pressing her palm against him. She could feel his heartbeat, hard and steady, beneath her hand.

And then, for the first time in her life, Hayley Thompson fell asleep in a man's arms.

Chapter 8

Jonathan didn't sleep. As soon as Hayley drifted off, he went into his office, busying himself with work that didn't need to be done.

Women didn't spend the night at his house. He had never even brought a woman back to this house. But when Hayley had looked up at him like that… He hadn't been able to tell her to leave. He realized that she expected to stay. Because as far as she was concerned, sex included sleeping with somebody.

He had no idea where she had formed her ideas about relationships, but they were innocent. And he was a bastard. He had already known that, but tonight just confirmed it.

Except he had let her stay.

He couldn't decide if that was a good thing or not. Couldn't decide if letting her stay had been a kindness or a cruelty. Because the one thing it hadn't been was the reality of the situation.

The reality was this wasn't a relationship. The reality was, it had been… Well, a very bad idea.

He stood up from his desk, rubbing the back of his neck. It was getting light outside, pale edges beginning to bleed from the mountaintops, encroaching on the velvet middle of the sky.

He might as well go outside and get busy on morning chores. And if some of those chores were in the name of avoiding Hayley, then so be it.

He made his way downstairs, shoved his feet into his boots and grabbed his hat, walking outside with heavy footsteps.

He paused, inhaling deeply, taking a moment to let the scent of the pines wash through him. This was his. All of it was his. He didn't think that revelation would ever get old.

He remembered well the way it had smelled on his front porch in the trailer park. Cigarette smoke and exhaust from cars as people got ready to leave for work. The noise of talking, families shouting at each other. It didn't matter if you were inside the house or outside. You lived way too close to your neighbors to avoid them.

He had fantasized about a place like this back then. Isolated. His. Where he wouldn't have to see another person unless he went out of his way to do so. He shook his head. And he had gone and invited Hayley to stay the night. He was a dumb ass.

He needed a ride to clear his head. The fact that he got to take weekends off now was one of his favorite

things about his new position in life. He was a worka-
holic, and he had never minded that. But ranching was
the kind of work he really enjoyed, and that was what
he preferred to do with his free time.

He saddled his horse and mounted up, urging the bay
gelding toward the biggest pasture. They started out
at a slow walk, then Jonathan increased the pace until
he and his horse were flying over the grass, patches of
flowers blurring on either side of them, blending with
the rich green.

It didn't matter what mess he had left behind at the
house. Didn't matter what mistakes he had made last
night. It never did, not when he was on a horse. Not
when he was in his sanctuary. The house… Well, he
would be lying if he said that big custom house hadn't
been a goal for him. Of course it had been. It was evidence that he had made it.

But this… The trees, the mountains, the wind in his
face, being able to ride his horse until his lungs burned,
and not reach the end of his property… That was the
real achievement. It belonged to him and no one else.
In this place he didn't have to answer to anyone.

Out here it didn't matter if he was bad. You couldn't
let the sky down. You couldn't disappoint the mountains.

He leaned forward to go uphill, tightening his hold
on the reins as the animal changed its gait. He pulled
back, easing to a stop. He looked down the mountain,
at the valley of trees spread out before him, an ever-
green patchwork stitched together by rock and river.
And beyond that, the ocean, brighter blue than usual

on this exceptionally clear morning, the waves capped with a rosy pink handed down from the still-rising sun.

Hayley would love this.

That thought brought him up short, because he wasn't exactly sure why he thought she would. Or why he cared. Why he suddenly wanted to show her. He had never shown this view to anybody. Not even to his sister, Rebecca.

He had wanted to keep it for himself, because growing up, he'd had very little that belonged to him and him alone. In fact, up here, gazing at everything that belonged to him now, he couldn't think of a single damn thing that had truly belonged to him when he'd been younger.

It had all been for a landlord, for his sister, for the future.

This was what he had worked for his entire life.

He didn't need to show it to some woman he'd slept with last night.

He shook his head, turning the horse around and trotting down the hill, moving to a gallop back down to the barn.

When he exited the gate that would take him out of the pasture and back to the paddock, Jonathan saw Hayley standing in the path. Wearing last night's dress, her hair disheveled, she was holding two mugs of coffee.

He was tempted to imagine he had conjured her up just by thinking of her up on the ridge. But if it were a fantasy, she would have been wearing nothing, rather than being back in that black cotton contraption.

She was here, and it disturbed him just how happy that made him.

"I thought I might find you out here," she said. "And I figured you would probably want your coffee."

He dismounted, taking the reins and walking the horse toward Hayley. "It's your day off. You don't have to make me coffee."

Her cheeks turned pink, and he marveled at the blush. And on the heels of that marveling came the sharp bite of guilt. She was a woman who blushed routinely. And he had... Well, he had started down the path of corrupting her last night.

He had taken her virginity. Before her he'd never slept with a virgin in his damn life. In high school, that hadn't been so much out of a sense of honor as it had been out of a desire not to face down an angry dad with a shotgun. Better to associate with girls who had reputations worse than his own.

All that restraint had culminated in him screwing the pastor's daughter.

At least when people came with torches and pitchforks, he would have a decent-sized fortress to hole up in.

"I just thought maybe it would be nice," she said finally, taking a step toward him and extending the coffee mug in his direction.

"It is," he said, taking the cup, knowing he didn't sound quite as grateful as he might have. "Sorry," he conceded, sipping the strong brew, which was exactly the way he liked it. "I'm not used to people being nice. I'm never quite sure what to make of it when you are."

"Just take it at face value," she said, lifting her shoulder.

"Yeah, I don't do that."

"Why not?" she asked.

"I have to take care of the horse," he said. "If you want story time, you're going to have to follow me."

He thought his gruff demeanor might scare her off, but instead, she followed him along the fence line. He tethered his horse and set his mug on the fence post, then grabbed the pick and started on the gelding's hooves.

Hayley stepped up carefully on the bottom rung of the fence, settling herself on the top rung, clutching her mug and looking at him with an intensity he could feel even with his focus on the task at hand.

"I'm ready," she said.

He looked up at her, perched there like an inquisitive owl, her lips at the edge of her cup, her blue eyes round. She was…a study in contradictions. Innocent as hell. Soft in some ways, but determined in others.

It was her innocence that allowed her to be so open— that was his conclusion. The fact that she'd never really been hurt before made it easy for her to come at people from the front.

"It's not a happy story," he warned.

It wasn't a secret one, either. Pretty much everybody knew his tragic backstory. He didn't go around talking about it, but there was no reason not to give her what she was asking for.

Except for the fact that he never talked to the women he hooked up with. There was just no point to it.

But then, the women he usually hooked up with never stumbled out of his house early in the morning with cups of coffee. So he supposed it was an unusual situation all around.

"I'm a big girl," she said, her tone comically serious. It was followed by a small slurp as she took another sip of coffee. The sound should not have been cute, but it was.

"Right." He looked up at her, started to speak and then stopped.

Would hearing about his past, about his childhood, change something in her? Just by talking to her he might ruin some of her optimism.

It was too late for worrying about that, he supposed. Since sleeping with her when she'd never even kissed anyone before had undoubtedly changed her.

There had been a lot of points in his life when he had not been his own favorite person. The feeling was intense right now. He was a damned bastard.

"I'm waiting," she said, kicking her foot slightly to signify her impatience.

"My father left when I was five," he said.

"Oh," she said, blinking, clearly shocked. "I'm sorry."

"It was the best thing that had happened to me in all five years of my life, Hayley. The very best thing. He was a violent bastard. He hit my mother. He hit me. The day he left… I was a kid, but I knew even then that life was going to be better. I was right. When I was seven, my mom had another kid. And she was the best thing. So cute. Tiny and loud as hell, but my mother wasn't all that interested in me, and my new sister was. Plus she gave me, I don't know…a feeling of importance. I had someone to look after, and that mattered. Made me feel like maybe I mattered."

"Rebecca," Hayley said.

"Yeah," he replied. "Then, when Rebecca was a teenager, she was badly injured in a car accident. Needed a lot of surgeries, skin grafts. All of it was paid for by the family responsible for the accident, in exchange for keeping everything quiet. Of course, it's kind of an open secret now that Gage West was the one who caused the accident."

Hayley blinked. "Gage. Isn't she… Aren't they… Engaged?"

Familiar irritation surged through him. "For now. We'll see how long that lasts. I don't have a very high opinion of that family."

"Well, you know my brother is married into that family."

He shrugged. "All right, maybe I'll rephrase that. I don't have anything against Colton, or Sierra, or Maddy. But I don't trust Gage or his father one bit. I certainly don't trust him with my sister, any more now than I did then. But if things fall apart, if he ends up breaking off the engagement, or leaves her ten years into the marriage… I'll have a place for her. I've always got a place for her."

Hayley frowned. "That's a very cynical take. If Rebecca can love the man who caused her accident, there must be something pretty exceptional about him."

"More likely, my sister doesn't really know what love looks like," he said, his voice hard, the words giving voice to the thing he feared most. "I have to backtrack a little. A few months after the accident, my mom took the cash payout Nathan West gave her and took off. Left me with Rebecca. Left Rebecca without a mother, when she needed her mother the most. My mom just couldn't handle it. So I had to. And I was a piss-poor replacement for parents. An older brother with a crappy construction job and not a lot of patience." He shook his head. "Every damn person in my life who was supposed to be there for me bailed. Everyone who was supposed to be there for Rebecca."

"And now you're mad at her, too. For not doing what you thought she should."

Guilt stabbed him right in the chest. Yeah, he was angry at his sister. And he felt like he had no damn right to be angry. Shouldn't she be allowed to be happy? Hadn't that been the entire point of taking care of her for all those years? So she could get out from under the cloud of their family?

So she'd done it. In a huge, spectacular way. She'd ended up with the man she'd been bitter about for years. She had let go of the past. She had embraced it, and in a pretty damned literal way.

But Jonathan couldn't. He didn't trust in sudden changes of heart or professions of love. He didn't trust much of anything.

"I'll be mad if she gets hurt," he said finally. "But that's my default. I assume it's going to end badly because I've only ever seen these things end badly. I worked my ass off to keep the two of us off the streets. To make sure we had a roof over our heads, as much food in our stomachs as I could manage. I protected her." He shook his head. "And there's no protecting somebody if you aren't always looking out for what might go wrong. For what might hurt them."

"I guess I can't blame you for not trusting the good in people. You haven't seen it very many times."

He snorted. "Understatement of the century." He

straightened, undoing the girth and taking the saddle off the bay in a fluid movement, then draping it over the fence. "But my cynicism has served me just fine. Look at where I am now. I started out in a single-wide trailer, and I spent years working just to keep that much. I didn't advance to this place by letting down my guard, by stopping for even one minute." He shook his head again. "I probably owe my father a thank-you note. My mother, too, come to that. They taught me that I couldn't trust anyone but myself. And so far that lesson's served me pretty well."

Hayley was looking at him like she was sad for him, and he wanted to tell her to stop it. Contempt, disgust and distrust were what he was used to getting from people. And he had come to revel in that reaction, to draw strength from it.

Pity had been in short supply. And if it was ever tossed in his general direction, it was mostly directed at Rebecca. He wasn't comfortable receiving it himself.

"Don't look at me like I'm a sad puppy," he said.

"I'm not," she returned.

He untied the horse and began to walk back into the barn. "You are. I didn't ask for your pity." He unhooked the lead rope and urged the gelding into his stall. "Don't go feeling things for me, Hayley. I don't deserve it. In fact, what you should have done this morning was walked out and slapped me in the face, not given me a cup of coffee."

"Why?"

"Because I took advantage of you last night. And you should be upset about that."

She frowned. "I should be?" She blinked. "I'm not. I thought about it. And I'm not."

"I don't know what you're imagining this is. I don't know what you think might happen next..."

She jumped down from the fence and set her coffee cup on the ground. Then she took one quick step forward. She hooked an arm around his neck and pushed herself onto her tiptoes, pressing her lips to his.

He was too stunned to react. But only for a moment. He wrapped an arm around her waist, pressing his forefinger beneath her chin and urging the kiss deeper.

She didn't have a lot of skill. That had been apparent the first and second times they'd kissed. And when they had come together last night. But he didn't need skill, he just needed her.

Even though it was wrong, he consumed her, sated his hunger on her mouth.

She whimpered, a sweet little sound that only fueled the driving hunger roaring in his gut. He grabbed her hair, tilting her head back farther, abandoning her mouth to scrape his teeth over her chin and down her neck, where he kissed her again, deep and hard.

He couldn't remember ever feeling like this before. Couldn't remember ever wanting a woman so much it was beyond the need for air. Sure, he liked sex. He was a man, after all. But the need had never been this specific. Had never been for one woman in particular.

But what he was feeling wasn't about sex, or about lust or desire. It was about her. About Hayley. The sweet little sounds she made when he kissed the tender skin on her neck, when he licked his way back up to her lips. The way she trembled with her need for him. The way she had felt last night, soft and slick and made only for him.

This was beyond anything he had ever experienced before. And he was a man who had experienced a hell of a lot.

That's what it was, he thought dimly as he scraped his teeth along her lower lip. And that said awful things about him, but then so did a lot of choices in his life.

He had conducted business with hard, ruthless precision, and he had kept his personal life free of any kind of connection beyond Rebecca—who he was loyal to above anyone else.

So maybe that was the problem. Now that he'd arrived at this place in life, he was collecting those things he had always denied himself. The comfortable home, the expansive mountains and a sweet woman.

Maybe this was some kind of latent urge. He had the homestead, now he wanted to put a woman in it.

He shook off that thought and all the rest. He didn't want to think right now. He just wanted to feel. Wanted to embrace the heat firing through his veins, the need stoking the flame low in his gut, which burned even more with each pass of her tongue against his.

She pulled away from him, breathing hard, her pupils dilated, her lips swollen and rounded into a perfect O. "That," she said, breathlessly, "was what I was thinking might happen next. And that we might… Take me back to bed, please."

"I can't think of a single reason to refuse," he said—a lie, as a litany of reasons cycled through his mind.

But he wasn't going to listen to them. He was going to take her, for as long as she was on offer. And when it ended, he could only hope he hadn't damaged her too much. Could only hope he hadn't broken her beyond repair.

Because there were a couple things he knew for sure. It would end; everything always did. And he would be the one who destroyed it.

He just hoped he didn't destroy her, too.

Chapter 9

It was late in the afternoon when Hayley and Jonathan finally got back out of bed. Hayley felt... Well, she didn't know quite what she felt. Good. Satisfied. Jonathan was... Well, if she'd ever had insecurities about whether or not she might be desirable to a man, he had done away with those completely. He had also taught her things about herself—about pleasure, about her own body—that she'd never in her wildest dreams conceived of.

She didn't know what would happen next, though. She had fallen asleep after their last time together, and when she'd awoken he was gone again. This morning, she had looked for him. She wasn't sure if she should do that twice.

Still, before she could even allow herself to ponder making the decision, she got out of bed, grabbed his T-shirt from the floor and pulled it over her head. Then she padded down the hallway, hoping he didn't have any surprise visitors. That would be a nightmare. Getting caught wearing only a T-shirt in her boss's hallway. There would be a lot of questions about what they had just spent the last few hours doing, that was for sure.

She wondered if Jonathan might be outside again, but she decided to check his office first. And was rewarded when she saw him sitting at the computer, his head lowered over the keyboard, some of his dark hair falling over his face after coming loose from the braid he normally kept it in.

Her heart clenched painfully, and it disturbed her that her heart was the first part of her body to tighten. The rest of her followed shortly thereafter, but she really wished her reaction was more about her body than her feelings. She couldn't afford to have feelings for him. She wasn't staying in Copper Ridge. And even if she were, he wouldn't want her long-term, anyway.

She took a deep breath, trying to dispel the strange, constricted feeling that had overtaken her lungs. "I thought I might find you here," she said.

He looked up, his expression betraying absolutely no surprise. He sneaked up on her all the time, but of course, as always, Jonathan was unflappable. "I just had a few schematics to check over." He pushed the chair away from the desk and stood, reaching over his head to stretch.

She was held captive by the sight of him. Even fully dressed, he was a beautiful thing.

His shoulders and chest were broad and muscular, his waist trim. His face like sculpted rock, or hardened bronze, uncompromising. But she knew the secret way to make those lips soften. Only for her.

No, not only for you. He does this all the time. They are just softening for you right now.

It was good for her to remember that.

"I'm finished now," he said, treating her to a smile that made her feel like melting ice cream on a hot day.

"Good," she said, not quite sure why she said it, because it wasn't like they had made plans. She wondered when he would ask her to leave. Or maybe he wanted her to leave, but didn't want to tell her. "It's late," she said. "I could go."

"Do you need to go?"

"No," she said, a little too quickly.

"Then don't."

Relief washed over her, and she did her best not to show him just how pleased she was by that statement. "Okay," she said, "then I won't go."

"I was thinking. About your list."

She blinked. "My list?"

"Yeah, your list. You had dancing on there. Pretty sure you had a kiss. And whether or not it was on the list…you did lose your virginity. Since I helped you with those items, I figured I might help you with some of the others."

A deep sense of pleasure and something that felt a lot like delight washed through her. "Really?"

"Yes," he said, "really. I figure we started all of this, so we might as well keep going."

"I don't have an official list."

"Well, that's ridiculous. If you're going to do this thing, you have to do it right." He grabbed a sheet of paper out of the printer and settled back down in the office chair. "Let's make a list."

He picked up a pen and started writing.

"What are you doing? I didn't tell you what I wanted yet."

"I'm writing down what we already did so you have the satisfaction of checking those off."

Her stomach turned over. "Don't write down all of it."

"Oh," he said, "I am. All of it. In detail."

"No!" She crossed the space between them and stood behind him, wrapping her arms around his broad shoulders as if she might restrain him. He kept on writing. She peered around his head, then slapped the pen out of his hand when she saw him writing a very dirty word. "Stop it. If anybody finds that list I could be... incriminated."

He laughed and swiveled the chair to the side. He wrapped his arm around her waist and pulled her onto his lap. "Oh no. We would hate for you to be incriminated. But on the other hand, the world would know you spent the afternoon with a very firm grip on my—"

"No!"

He looked at her and defiantly put a checkmark by what he had just written. She huffed, but settled into his hold. She liked this too much. Him smiling, him holding her when they had clothes on as if he just wanted to hold her.

It was nice to have him want her in bed. Very nice. But this was something else, and it was nice, too.

"Okay, so we have dancing, kissing, sex, and all of

the many achievements beneath the sex," he said, ignoring her small noises of protest. "So what else?"

"I want to go to a place where I need a passport," she said.

"We could drive to Canada."

She laughed. "I was thinking more like Europe. But... Could we really drive to Canada?"

"Well," he said, "maybe not today, since I have to be back here by Monday."

"That's fine. I was thinking more Paris than Vancouver."

"Hey, they speak French in Canada."

"Just write it down," she said, poking his shoulder.

"Fine. What next?"

"I feel like I should try alcohol," she said slowly. "Just so I know."

"Fair enough." He wrote *get hammered*.

"That is not what I said."

"Sorry. I got so excited about the idea of getting you drunk. Lowering your inhibitions."

She rolled her eyes. "I'm already more uninhibited with you than I've ever been with anyone else." It was true, she realized, as soon as she said it. She was more herself with Jonathan than she had ever been with anyone, including her family, who had known her for her entire life.

Maybe it was the fact that, in a town full of people who were familiar with her, at least by reputation, he was someone she hadn't known at all until a couple weeks ago.

Maybe it was the fact that he had no expectations of her beyond what they'd shared. Whatever the case, around him she felt none of the pressure that she felt around other people in the community.

No need to censor herself, or hide; no need to be respectable or serene when she felt like being disreputable and wild.

"I want to kiss in the rain," she said.

"Given weather patterns," he said slowly, "we should be able to accomplish that, too."

She was ridiculously pleased he wanted to be a part of that, pleased that he hadn't said anything about her finding a guy to kiss in the rain in Paris. She shouldn't be happy he was assuming he would be the person to help her fulfill these things. She should be annoyed. She should feel like he was inserting himself into her independence, but she didn't. Mostly because he made her independence seem…well, like *more*.

"You're very useful, aren't you?"

He looked at her, putting his hand on her cheek, his dark gaze serious as it met hers. "I'm glad I can be useful to you."

She felt him getting hard beneath her backside, and that pleased her, too. "Parts of you are very useful," she said, reaching behind her and slowly stroking his length.

The light in his eyes changed, turning much more intense. "Hayley Thompson," he said, "I would say that's shocking behavior."

"I would say you're responsible, Jonathan Bear."

He shook his head. "No, princess, you're responsible for this. For all of this. This is you. It's what you want, right? The things on your list that you don't even want to write down. It's part of you. You don't get to blame it all on me."

She felt strangely empowered by his words. By the idea that this was her, and not just him leading her somewhere.

"That's very… Well, that's very… I like it." She furthered her exploration of him, increasing the pressure of her touch. "At least, I like it with you."

"I'm not complaining."

"That's good," she said softly, continuing to stroke him through the fabric of his pants.

She looked down, watched herself touching him. It was…well, now that she had started, she didn't want to stop.

"I would be careful if I were you," he said, his tone laced with warning, "because you're about to start something, and it's very likely you need to take a break from all that."

"Do I? Why would I need a break?"

"Because you're going to get sore," he said, maddeningly pragmatic.

And, just as maddeningly, it made her blush to hear him say it. "I don't really mind," she said finally.

"You don't?" His tone was calm, but heat flared in the depths of his dark eyes.

"No," she replied, still trailing her fingertips over his hardening body. "I like feeling the difference. In me. I like being so…aware of everything we've done." For her, that was a pretty brazen proclamation, though she had a feeling it paled in comparison to the kinds of things other women had said to him in the past.

But she wasn't one of those other women. And right now he was responding to her, so she wasn't going to waste a single thought on anyone who had come before her. She held his interest now. That was enough.

"There's something else on my list," she said, fighting to keep her voice steady, fighting against the nerves firing through her.

"Is that so?"

She sucked in a sharp breath. "Yes. I want to… That is… What you did for me… A couple of times now… I want to… I want to…" She gave up trying to get the words out. She wasn't sure she had the right words for what she wanted to do, anyway, and she didn't want to humiliate herself by saying something wrong.

So, with unsteady hands, she undid the closure on his jeans and lowered the zipper. She looked up at him. If she expected to get any guidance, she was out of luck. He just stared at her, his dark eyes unfathomable, his jaw tight, a muscle in his cheek ticking.

She shifted on his lap, sliding gracefully to the floor in front of the chair. Then she went to her knees and turned to face him, flicking her hair out of her face.

He still said nothing, watching her closely, unnervingly so. But she wasn't going to turn back now. She lifted the waistband of his underwear, pulling it out in order to clear his impressive erection, then she pulled the fabric partway down his hips, as far as she could go with him sitting.

He was beautiful.

That feeling of intimidation she'd felt the first time she'd seen him had faded completely. Now she knew what he could do, and she appreciated it greatly. He had shown her so many things; he'd made her pleasure the number one priority. And she wanted to give to him in return.

Well, she also knew this would be for her, too.

She slid her hands up his thighs, then curled her fingers around his hardened length, squeezing him firmly. She was learning that he wasn't breakable there. That he liked a little bit of pressure.

"Hayley," he said, his voice rough, "I don't think you know what you're doing."

"No," she said, "I probably don't. But I know what I want. And it's been so much fun having what I want." She rose up slightly, then leaned in, pressing her lips to the head of his shaft. He jerked beneath her touch, and she took that as approval.

A couple hours ago she would have been afraid that she'd hurt him. But male pleasure, she was discovering, sometimes looked a little like pain. Heck, female pleasure was a little like pain. Sex was somewhere between. The aching need to have it all and the intense rush of satisfaction that followed.

She shivered just thinking about it.

And then she flicked her tongue out, slowly testing this new territory. She hummed, a low sound in the back of her throat, as she explored the taste of him, the texture. Jonathan Bear was her favorite indulgence, she was coming to realize. There was nothing about him she didn't like. Nothing he had done to her she didn't love. She liked the way he felt, and apparently she liked the way he tasted, too.

She parted her lips slowly, worked them over the head, then swallowed down as much of him as she could. The accompanying sound he made hollowed out her stomach, made her feel weak and powerful at the same time.

His body was such an amazing thing. So strong, like it had been carved straight from the mountain. Yet it wasn't in any way cold or unmovable; it was hot. His body had changed hers. Yes, he'd taken her virginity, but he had also taught her to feel pleasure she hadn't realized she had the capacity to feel.

Such power in his body, and yet, right now, it trembled beneath her touch. The whisper-soft touch of her lips possessed the power to rock him, to make him shake. To make him shatter.

Right now, desire was enough. She didn't need skill. She didn't need experience. And she felt completely confident in that.

She slipped her tongue over his length as she took him in deep, and he bucked his hips lightly, touching the back of her throat. Her throat contracted and he jerked back.

"Sorry," he said, his voice strained.

"No," she said, gripping him with one hand and bringing her lips back against him. "Don't apologize. I like it."

"You're inexperienced."

She nodded slowly, then traced him with the tip of her tongue. "Yes," she agreed, "I am. I've never done this for any other man. I've never even thought about it before." His hips jerked again, and she realized he liked this. That he—however much he tried to pretend he didn't—liked that her desire was all for him.

"I think you might be corrupting me," she said, keeping her eyes wide as she took him back into her mouth.

He grunted, fisting his hands in her hair, but he didn't pull her away again.

The muscles in his thighs twitched beneath her fingertips, and he seemed to grow larger, harder in her mouth. She increased the suction, increased the friction, used her hands as well as her mouth to drive him as crazy as she possibly could.

There was no plan. There was no skill. There was just the need to make him even half as mindless as he'd made her over the past couple days.

He had changed her. He had taken her from innocence...to this. She would be marked by him forever. He would always be her first. But society didn't have a term for a person's experience after virginity. So she didn't have a label for the impact she wanted to make on him.

Jonathan hadn't been a virgin for a very long time, she suspected. And she probably wasn't particularly special as a sexual partner.

So she had to try to make herself special.

She had no tricks to make this the best experience he'd ever had. She had only herself. And so she gave it to him. All of her. Everything.

"Hayley," he said, his voice rough, ragged. "You better stop."

She didn't. She ignored him. She had a feeling he was close; she recognized the signs now. She had watched him reach the point of pleasure enough times that she had a fair idea of what it looked like. Of what it felt like. His whole body tensing, his movements becoming less controlled.

She squeezed the base of him tightly, pulling him in

deeper, and then he shattered. And she swallowed down every last shudder of need that racked his big body.

In the aftermath, she was dazed, her heart pounding hard, her entire body buzzing. She looked up at him from her position on the floor, and he looked down at her, his dark eyes blazing with…anger, maybe? Passion? A kind of sharp, raw need she hadn't ever seen before.

"You're going to pay for that," he said.

"Oh," she returned, "I hope so."

He swept her up, crushed her against his chest. "You have to put it on my list first," she said.

Then he brought his mouth down to hers, and whatever she'd intended to write down was forgotten until morning.

Chapter 10

Sometime on Sunday afternoon Hayley had gone home. Because, she had insisted, she wasn't able to work in either his T-shirt or the dress she had worn to the bar on Friday.

He hadn't agreed, but he had been relieved to have the reprieve. He didn't feel comfortable sharing the bed with her while he slept. Which had meant sleeping on the couch in the office after she drifted off.

He just… He didn't sleep with women. He didn't see the point in inviting that kind of intimacy. Having her spend the night in his bed was bad enough. But he hadn't wanted to send her home, either. He didn't want to think about why. Maybe it was because she expected to stay, because of her general inexperience.

Which made him think of the moment she had taken him into her mouth, letting him know he was the first man she had ever considered doing that for. Just the thought of it made his eyes roll back in his head.

Now, it was late Monday afternoon and she had been slowly driving him crazy with the prim little outfit she had come back to work in, as though he didn't know what she looked like underneath it.

Who knew he'd like a good girl who gave head like a dream.

She had also insisted that they stay professional during work hours, and it was making it hard for him to concentrate. Of course, it was always hard for him to concentrate on office work. In general, he hated it.

Though bringing Hayley into the office certainly made it easier to bear.

Except for the part where it was torture.

He stood up from his chair and stretched slowly, trying to work the tension out of his body. But he had a feeling that until he was buried inside Hayley's body again, tension was just going to be the state of things.

"Oh," Hayley said, "Joshua Grayson just emailed and said he needs you to go by the county office and sign a form. And no, it can't be faxed."

For the first time in his life, Johathan was relieved to encounter bureaucracy. He needed to get out of this space. He needed to get his head on straight.

"Great," he said.

"Maybe I should go with you," she said. "I've never been down to the building and planning office, and you might need me to run errands in the future."

He gritted his teeth. "Yeah, probably."

"I'll drive my own car." She stood, grabbing her

purse off the desk. "Because by the time we're done it will be time for me to get off."

He ground his teeth together even harder, because he couldn't ignore her double entendre even though he knew it had been accidental. And because, in addition to the double meaning, it was clear she intended to stay in town tonight and not at his place.

He should probably be grateful she wasn't being clingy. He didn't like to encourage women to get too attached to him, not at all.

"Great idea," he said.

But he didn't think it was a great idea, and he grumbled the entire way to town in the solitude of his pickup truck, not missing the irony that he had been wanting alone time, and was now getting it, and was upset about it.

The errand really did take only a few minutes, and afterward it still wasn't quite time for Hayley to clock out.

"Do you want to grab something to eat?" he asked, though he had no earthly idea why. He should get something for himself and go home, deal with that tension he had been pondering earlier.

She looked back and forth, clearly edgy. "In town?"

"Yes," he returned, "in town."

"Oh. I don't… I guess so."

"Calm down," he said. "I'm not asking you to Beaches. Let's just stop by the Crab Shanty."

She looked visibly relieved, and again he couldn't quantify why that annoyed him.

He knew they shouldn't be seen together in town. He had a feeling she also liked the casual nature of the restaurant. It was much more likely to look like a boss and employee grabbing something to eat than it was to look like a date.

They walked from where they had parked a few streets over, and paused at the crosswalk. They waited for one car to crawl by, clearly not interested in heeding the law that said pedestrians had the right-of-way. Then Jonathan charged ahead of her across the street and up to the faded yellow building. A small line was already forming outside the order window, and he noticed that Hayley took pains to stand slightly behind him.

When it was their turn to order, he decided he wasn't having any of her missish circumspection. They shouldn't be seen together as anything more than a boss and an assistant.

But right now, hell if he cared. "Two orders of fish and chips, the halibut. Two beers and a Diet Coke."

He pulled his wallet out and paid before Hayley could protest, then he grabbed the plastic number from the window, and the two of them walked over to a picnic table positioned outside the ramshackle building. There was no indoor seating, which could be a little bracing on windy days, and there weren't very many days that didn't have wind on the Oregon coast.

Jonathan set the number on the wooden table, then sat down heavily, looking up at the blue-and-white-striped umbrella wiggling in the breeze.

"Two beers?"

"One of them is for you," he said, his words verging on a growl.

"I'm not going to drink a beer." She looked sideways. "At least not here."

"Yeah, right out here on Main Street in front of God and everybody? You're a lot braver in my bedroom."

He was goading her, but he didn't much care. He was… Well dammit, it pissed him off. To see how ashamed she was to be with him. How desperate she was to hide it. Even if he understood it, it was like a branding iron straight to the gut.

"You can't say that so loud," she hissed, leaning forward, grabbing the plastic number and pulling it to her chest. "What if people heard you?"

"I thought you were reinventing yourself, Hayley Thompson."

"Not for the benefit of…the town. It's about me."

"It's going to be about you not getting dinner if you keep hiding our number." He snatched the plastic triangle from her hands.

She let out a heavy sigh and leaned back, crossing her arms. "Well, the extra beer is for you. Put it in your pocket."

"You can put it in your own pocket. Drink it back at your place."

"No, thanks."

"Don't you want to tick that box on your list? We ticked off some pretty interesting ones last night."

Her face turned scarlet. "You're being obnoxious, Jonathan."

"I've been obnoxious from day one. You just found it easy to ignore when I had my hand in your pants."

Her mouth dropped open, then she snapped it shut again. Their conversation was cut off when their food was placed in front of them.

She dragged the white cardboard box toward her

and opened it, removing the container of coleslaw and setting it to the side before grabbing a french fry and biting into it fiercely. Her annoyance was clearly telegraphed by the ferocity with which she ate each bite of food. And the determination that went into her looking at anything and everything around them except for him.

"Enjoying the view?" he asked after a moment.

"The ocean is very pretty," she snapped.

"And you don't see it every day?"

"I never tire of the majesty of nature."

His lips twitched, in spite of his irritation. "Of course not."

The wind whipped up, blowing a strand of dark hair into Hayley's face. Reflexively, he reached across the table and pushed it out of her eyes. She jerked back, her lips going slack, her expression shocked.

"You're my boss," she said, her voice low. "As far as everyone is concerned."

"Well," he said, "I'm your lover. As far as I'm concerned."

"Stop."

"I thought you wanted new experiences? I thought you were tired of hiding? And here you are, hiding."

"I don't want to…perform," she said. "My new experiences are for me. Not for everyone else's consumption. That's why I'm leaving. So I can…do things without an audience."

"You want your dirty secrets, is that it? You want me to be your dirty secret."

"It's five o'clock," she said, her tone stiff. "I'm going to go home now."

She collected her food, and left the beer, standing up

in a huff and taking off down the street in the opposite direction from where they had parked.

"Where are you going?"

"Home," she said sharply.

He gathered up the rest of the food and stomped after her. "You parked the other way."

"I'll get it in the morning."

"Then you better leave your house early. Unless this is you tendering your resignation."

"I'm not quitting," she said, the color heightening in her face. "I'm just… I'm irritated with you."

She turned away from him, continuing to walk quickly down the street. He took two strides and caught up with her. "I see that." He kept pace with her, but she seemed bound and determined not to look at him. "Would you care to share why?"

"Not even a little bit."

"So you're insisting that you're my employee, and that you want to be treated like my employee in public. But that clearly excludes when you decide to run off having a temper tantrum."

She whirled around then, stopping in her tracks. "Why are you acting like this? You've been…much more careful than this up till now." She sniffed. "Out of deference to my innocence?"

"What innocence, baby? Because I took that." He smiled, knowing he was getting to her. That he was making her feel as bad as he did. "Pretty damn thoroughly."

"I can't do this with you. Not here." She paused at the street corner and looked both ways before hurrying across the two-lane road. He followed suit. She walked down the sidewalk, passed the coffeehouse, which was closing up for the day, then rounded the side of the brick building and headed toward the back.

"Is this where you live?" he asked.

"Maybe," she returned, sounding almost comically stubborn. Except he didn't feel like much was funny about this situation.

"Here in the alley?" he asked, waving his hand around the mostly vacant space.

"Yes. In the Dumpster with the mice. It's not so bad. I shredded up a bunch of newspaper and made a little bed."

"I suspect this is the real reason you've been spending the night at my place, then."

She scowled. "If you want to fight with me, come upstairs."

He didn't want to fight with her. He wanted to grab her, pull her into his arms and kiss her. He wanted to stop talking. Wanted to act logical instead of being wounded by something he knew he should want to avoid.

It didn't benefit him to have anyone in town know what he was doing with Hayley. He should want to hide it as badly as she did.

But the idea that she was enjoying his body, enjoying slumming it with him in the sheets, and was damned ashamed of him in the streets burned like hell.

But he followed her through the back door to a little hallway that contained two other doors. She unlocked one of them and held it open for him. Then she gestured to the narrow staircase. "Come on."

"Who's the boss around here?"

"I'm off the clock," she said.

He shrugged, then walked up the stairs and into an open-plan living room with exposed beams and brick. It was a much bigger space than he had expected it to be, though it was also mostly empty. As if she had only half committed to living there.

But then, he supposed, her plan *was* to travel the world.

"Nice place," he said.

"Yeah," she said. "Cassie gave me a deal."

"Nice of her."

"Some people are nice, Jonathan."

"Meaning I'm not?" he asked.

She nodded in response, her mouth firmly sealed, her chin jutting out stubbornly.

"Right. Because I bought you fish and french fries and beer. And I give you really great orgasms. I'm a monster."

"I don't know what game you're playing," she said, suddenly looking much less stubborn and a little more wobbly. And that made him feel something close to guilty. "What's the point in blurring the lines while we walk through town? We both know this isn't a relationship. It's…it's boxes being ticked on a list."

"Sure. But why does it matter if people in town know you're doing that?"

"You know why it matters. Don't play like you don't understand. You do. I know you do. You know who I am, and you know that I feel like I'm under a microscope. I shared all of that with you. Don't act surprised by it now."

"Well," he said, opting for honesty even though he

knew it was a damned bad idea. "Maybe I don't like being your dirty secret."

"It's not about you. Any guy that I was… Anyone that I was…doing this with. It would be a secret. It has to be."

"Why?"

"Because!" she exploded. "Because everyone will be…disappointed."

"Honey," he said, "I don't think people spend half as much time thinking about you as you think they do."

"No," she said. "They do. You know Ace. He's the pastor's son. He ran away from home, he got married, he got divorced. Then he came back and opened a bar. My parents…they're great. They really are. But they had a lot of backlash over that. People saying that the Bible itself says if you train up a child the way he should go, he's not going to depart from it. Well, he departed from it, at least as far as a lot of the congregants were concerned. People actually left the church." She sucked in a sharp breath, then let it out slowly. "I wanted to do better than that for them. It was important. For me to be…the good one."

Caring about what people thought was a strange concept. Appearances had never mattered to Jonathan. For him, it had always been about actions. What the hell did Rebecca care if he had been good? All she cared about was being taken care of. He couldn't imagine being bound by rules like that.

For the first time, he wondered if there wasn't some kind of freedom in no one having a single good expectation of you.

"But you don't like being the good one. At least, not by these standards."

Her eyes glittered with tears now. She shook her head. "I don't know. I just… I don't know. I'm afraid. Afraid of what people will think. Afraid of what my parents will think. Afraid of them being disappointed. And hurt. They've always put a lot of stock in me being what Ace wasn't. They love Ace, don't get me wrong. It's just…"

"He made things hard for them."

Hayley nodded, looking miserable. "Yes. He did. And I don't want to do that. Only…only, I was the good one and he still ended up with the kind of life I want."

"Is that all?" Jonathan asked. "Or are you afraid of who you might be if you don't have all those rules to follow?"

A flash of fear showed in her eyes, and he felt a little guilty about putting it there. Not guilty enough to take it back. Not guilty enough to stay away from her. Not guilty enough to keep his hands to himself. He reached out, cupping her cheek, then wrapped his arm around her waist and drew her toward him. "Does it scare you? Who you might be if no one told you what to do? I don't care about the rules, Hayley. You can be whoever you want with me. Say whatever you want. Drink whatever you want. Do whatever you want."

"I don't know," she said, wiggling against him, trying to pull away. "I don't know what I want."

"I think you do. I just think you wish you wanted something else." He brushed his thumb over her cheekbone. "I think you like having rules because it keeps you from going after what scares you."

He ignored the strange reverberation those words set off inside him. The chain reaction that seemed to burst all the way down his spine.

Recognition.

Truth.

Yeah, he ignored all that, and he dipped his head, claiming her mouth with his own.

Suddenly, it seemed imperative that he have her here. In her apartment. That he wreck this place with his desire for her. That he have her on every surface, against every wall, so that whenever she walked in, whenever she looked around, he was what she thought of. So that she couldn't escape this. So that she couldn't escape him.

"You think you know me now?" she asked, her eyes squinting with challenge. Clearly, she wasn't going to back down without a fight. And that was one of the things he liked about her. For all that she was an innocent church secretary, she had spirit. She had the kind of steel backbone that he admired, that he respected. The kind of strength that could get you through anything. But there was a softness to her as well, and that was something more foreign to him. Something he had never been exposed to, had never really been allowed to have.

"Yeah," he said, tightening his hold and drawing her against his body. "I know you. I know what you look like naked. I know every inch of your skin. How it feels, how it tastes. I know you better than anybody does, baby. You can tell yourself that's not true. You can say that this, what we have, is the crazy thing. That it's a break from your real life. That it's some detour you don't want anyone in town to know you're taking. But I know the truth. And I think somewhere deep down you know it, too. This isn't the break. All that other stuff... prim, proper church girl. That's what isn't real." He cupped her face, smoothing his thumbs over her cheeks. "You're fire, honey, and together we are an explosion."

He kissed her then, proving his point. She tasted like anger, like need, and he was of a mind to consume both. Whatever was on offer. Whatever she would give him.

He was beyond himself. He had never wanted a woman like this before. He had never wanted anything quite like this before. Not money, not security, not his damned house on the hill.

All that want, all that need, paled in comparison to what he felt for Hayley Thompson. The innocent little miss who should have bored him to tears by now, had him aching, panting and begging for more.

He was so hard he was in physical pain.

And when she finally capitulated, when she gave herself over to the kiss, soft fingertips skimming his shoulders, down his back, all the way to his ass, he groaned in appreciation.

There was something extra dirty about Hayley exploring his body. About her wanting him the way she did, because she had never wanted another man like she wanted him. By her own admission. And she had never had a man the way she'd had him, which was an admission she didn't have to make.

He gripped her hips, then slipped his hands down her thighs, grabbing them and pulling her up, urging her legs around his waist. Then he propelled them both across the living room, down onto the couch. He covered her, pressing his hardness against the soft, sweet apex of her thighs. She gasped as he rolled his hips forward.

"Not so ashamed of this now, are you?" He growled, pressing a kiss to her neck, then to her collarbone, then to the edge of her T-shirt.

"I'm not ashamed," she said, gasping for air.

"You could've fooled me, princess."

"It's not about you." She sifted her fingers through his hair. "I'm not ashamed of you."

"Not ashamed of your dirty, wrong-side-of-the-tracks boyfriend?"

Her eyes flashed with hurt and then fascination. "I've never thought of you that way. I never... *Boyfriend?*"

Something burned hot in his chest. "Lover. Whatever."

"I'm not ashamed of you," she reiterated. "Nothing about you. You're so beautiful. If anything, you ought to be ashamed of me. I'm not pretty. Not like you. And I don't even know what I'm doing. I just know what I want. I want you. And I'm afraid for anybody to know the truth. I'm so scared. The only time I'm not scared is when you're holding me."

He didn't want to talk anymore. He consumed her mouth, tasting her deeply, ramping up the arousal between them with each sweet stroke of his tongue across hers. With each deep taste of the sweet flavor that could only ever be Hayley.

He gripped the hem of her top, yanking it over her head, making quick work of her bra. Exposing small, perfect breasts to his inspection. She was pale. All over. Ivory skin, coral-pink nipples. He loved the look of her.

Loved the feel of her. Loved so many things about her that it was tempting to just go ahead and say he loved *her*.

That thought swam thick and dizzy in his head. He could barely grab hold of it, didn't want to. So he shoved it to the side. He wasn't going to claim that. Hell no.

He didn't love people. He loved *things*.

He could love her tits, and he could love her skin, could love the way it felt to slide inside her, slick and tight. But he sure as hell couldn't love *her*.

He bent his head, taking one hardened nipple into his mouth, sucking hard, relishing the horse sound of pleasure on her lips as he did so. Then he kissed his way down her stomach, to the edge of her pants, pulling them down her thighs, leaving her bare and open.

He pressed his hand between her legs, slicked his thumb over her, teased her entrance with one finger. She began to whimper, rolling her hips under him, arching them to meet him, and he watched. Watched as she took one finger inside, then another.

He damn well watched himself corrupt her, and he let himself enjoy it. Because he was sick, because he was broken, but at least it wasn't a surprise.

Everyone in his life was familiar with it.

His father had tried to beat it out of him. His mother had run from it.

Only Rebecca had ever stayed, and it was partly because she didn't know any better.

Hayley didn't know any better, either, come to that. Not really. Not when it came to men. Not when it came to sex. She was blinded by what he could make her body feel, so she had an easy enough time ignoring the rest. But that wouldn't last forever.

Fair enough, since they wouldn't last forever, anyway. They both knew it. So there was no point in worrying about it. Not really.

Instead, he would embrace this, embrace the rush. Embrace the hollowed out feeling in his gut that bordered on sickness. The tension in his body that verged on pain. The need that rendered him hard as iron and hot as fire.

"Come for me," he commanded, his voice hoarse. All other words, all other thoughts were lost to him. All he could do was watch her writhing beneath his touch, so hot, so wet for him, arching her hips and taking his fingers in deeper.

"Not yet," she gasped, emitting little broken sounds.

"Yes," he said. "You will. You're going to come for me now, Hayley, because I told you to. Your body is mine. You're mine." He slid his thumb over the delicate bundle of nerves there.

And then he felt her shatter beneath his touch. Felt her internal muscles pulse around his knuckles.

He reached into his back pocket, took out his wallet and found a condom quickly. He tore it open, then wrenched free his belt buckle and took down the zipper. He pushed his jeans partway down his hips, rolled the condom on his hard length and thrust inside her, all the way to the hilt. She was wet and ready for him, and he had to grit his teeth to keep from embarrassing himself, to keep it from being over before it had begun.

She gasped as he filled her, and then grabbed his ass when he retreated. Her fingernails dug into his skin, and he relished the pain this petite little thing could inflict on him. Of course, it was nothing compared to the pain he felt from his arousal. From the great, burning need inside him.

No, nothing compared to that. Nothing at all.

He adjusted their positions, dragging her sideways on the couch, bringing her hips to the edge of the cushion, going down on his knees to the hardwood floor.

He knelt there, gripping her hips and pulling her tightly against him, urging her to wrap her legs around him. The floor bit into his knees, but he didn't care. All he cared about was having her, taking her, claiming her. He gripped her tightly, his blunt fingertips digging into her flesh.

He wondered if he would leave a mark. He hoped he might.

Hoped that she would see for days to come where he had held her. Even if she wouldn't hold his hand in public, she would remember when he'd held her hips in private, when he'd driven himself deep inside her, clinging to her like she might be the source of all life.

Yeah, she would remember that. She would remember this.

He watched as a deep red flush spread over her skin, covering her breasts, creeping up her neck. She was on the verge of another orgasm. He loved that. Another thing he was allowed to love.

Loved watching her lose control. Loved watching her so close to giving it up for him again, completely. Utterly. He was going to ruin her for any other man. That was his vow, there and then, on the floor of her apartment, with a ragged splinter digging into his knee through the fabric of his jeans. She was never going to fuck anyone else without thinking of him. Without wanting him. Without wishing it were him.

She would go to Paris, and some guy would do her with a view of the Eiffel tower in the background. And she would wish she were here, counting the familiar beams on her ceiling.

And when she came home for a visit and she passed him on the street, she would shiver with a longing that she would never quite get rid of.

So many people in his life had left him. As far as he'd known, they had done it without a backward glance. But Hayley would never forget him. He would make sure of it. Damn sure.

His own arousal ratcheted up to impossible proportions. He was made entirely of his need for her. Of his need for release. And he forgot what he was trying to do. Forgot that this was about her. That this was about making her tremble, making her shake. Because he was trembling. He was shaking.

He was afraid he might be the one who was indelibly marked by all this.

He was the one who wouldn't be able to forget. The one who would never be with anyone else without thinking of her. No matter how skilled the woman was who might come after her, it would never be the same as the sweet, genuine urging of Hayley's hips against his. It would never be quite like the tight, wet clasp of her body.

He had been entirely reshaped, remade, to fit inside her, and no one else would do.

That thought ignited in his stomach, overtook him completely, lit him on fire.

When he came, it was with her name on his lips, with a strange satisfaction washing through him that left him only hungrier in the end, emptier. Because this was ending, and he knew it.

She wasn't going to work for him forever. She wasn't going to stay in Copper Ridge. She might hold on to him in secret, but in public, she would never touch him.

And as time passed, she would let go of him by inches, walking off to the life of freedom she was so desperate for.

Walking off like everyone else.

Right now, she was looking up at him, a mixture of wonder and deep emotion visible in her blue eyes. She reached up, stroking his face. Some of his hair had been tugged from the leather strap, and she brushed the strands out of his eyes.

It was weird how that hit him. How it touched him. After all the overtly sexual ways she'd put her hands on him, why that sweet gesture impacted him low and deep.

"Stay with me," she said, her voice soft. "The night. In my bed."

That hit even harder.

He had never slept with her. He didn't sleep with women. But that was all about to change. He was going to sleep with her because he wanted to. Because he didn't want to release his hold on her for one moment, not while he still had her.

"Okay," he said.

Then, still buried deep inside her, he picked her up from the couch, brought them both to a standing position and started walking toward the door at the back of the room. "Bedroom is this way?"

"How did you know?"

"Important things, I know. Where the bedroom is." He kissed her lips. "How to make you scream my name. That I know."

"Care to make me scream it a few more times?"

"The neighbors might hear."

It was a joke, but he could still see her hesitation. "That's okay," she said slowly.

And even though he was reasonably confident that was a lie, he carried her into her bedroom and lay down on the bed with her.

It didn't matter if it was a lie. Because they had all night to live in it. And that was good enough for him.

Chapter 11

When he woke up the next morning he was disoriented. He was lying in a bed that was too small for his large frame, and he had a woman wrapped around him. Of course, he knew immediately which woman it was. It couldn't be anyone else. Even in the fog of sleep, he wasn't confused about Hayley's identity.

She smelled like sunshine and wildflowers. Or maybe she just smelled like soap and skin and only reminded him of sunshine and wildflowers, because they were innocent things. New things. The kinds of things that could never be corrupted by the world around them.

The kinds of things not even he could wreck.

She was that kind of beautiful.

But the other reason he was certain it was Hayley was that there was no other woman he would have fallen asleep with. It was far too intimate a thing, sharing a bed with someone when you weren't angling for an orgasm. He had never seen the point of it. It was basically the same as sharing a toothbrush, and he wasn't interested in that, either.

He looked at Hayley, curled up at his side, her brown hair falling across her face, her soft lips parted, her breathing easy and deep. The feeling carved out in his chest was a strange one.

Hell, lying there in the early morning, sharing a toothbrush with Hayley didn't even seem so insane.

He sat up, shaking off the last cobwebs of sleep and extricating himself from Hayley's hold. He groaned when her fingertips brushed the lower part of his stomach, grazing his insistent morning erection. He had half a mind to wake her up the best way he knew how.

But the longer the realization of what had happened last night sat with him, the more eager he was to put some distance between them.

He could get some coffee, get his head on straight and come back fully clothed. Then maybe the two of them could prepare for the workday.

He needed to compartmentalize. He had forgotten that yesterday. He had let himself get annoyed about something that never should have bothered him. Had allowed old hurts to sink in when he shouldn't give a damn whether or not Hayley wanted to hold his hand when they walked down the street. She wasn't his girlfriend. And all the words that had passed between them in the apartment, all the anger that had been rattling around inside him, seemed strange now. Like it had all happened to somebody else. The morning had brought clarity, and it was much needed.

He hunted around the room, collecting his clothes and tugging them on quickly, then he walked over to the window, drew back the curtains and tried to get a sense of what time it was. She didn't have a clock in her room. He wondered if she just looked at her phone.

The sky was pink, so it had to be nearing six. He really needed to get home and take care of the horses. He didn't want to mess up their routine. But he would come back. Or maybe Hayley would just come to his place on time.

Then he cursed, realizing he had left his car at the other end of Main Street. He walked back to the living room, pulled on his boots and headed out the door, down the stairs. His vision was blurry, and he was in desperate need of caffeine. There were two doors in the hallway, and he reached for the one closest to him.

And nearly ran right into Cassie Caldwell as he walked into The Grind.

The morning sounds of the coffee shop filled his ears, the intense smell of the roast assaulting him in the best way.

But Cassie was staring at him, wide-eyed, as were the ten people sitting inside the dining room. One of whom happened to be Pastor John Thompson.

Jonathan froze, mumbled something about coming in through the back door, and then walked up to the counter. He was going to act like there was nothing remarkable about where he had just come from. Was going to do his very best to look like there was nothing at all strange about him coming through what he now realized was a private entrance used only by the tenant upstairs. It didn't escape his notice that the pastor was eyeballing him closely. And so was Cassie. Really, so was everybody. Damn small town.

Now, he could see why Hayley had been so vigilant yesterday.

If only he could go back and be vigilant in his door choice.

"Black coffee," he said, "two shots of espresso."

Cassie's gaze turned hard. "I know."

"I came through the wrong door," he said.

She walked over to the espresso machine, wrapped a damp cloth around the wand that steamed the milk and twisted it, a puff of steam coming out as she jerked the cloth up and down roughly, her eyes never leaving his. "Uh-huh."

"I did."

"And it's just a coincidence that my tenant happens to live upstairs. My tenant who works for you." She said that part softly, and he was sure nobody else in the room heard it.

"That's right," he said. "Just a coincidence."

Suddenly, the door to the coffee shop opened again, and Hayley appeared, wearing a T-shirt and jeans, her hair wild, like she had just rolled out of bed.

Her eyes widened when she saw her father. Then she looked over at the counter and her eyes widened even further when she saw Jonathan.

"Good morning," he said, his voice hard. "Fancy meeting you here before work."

"Yes," she said. "I'm just gonna go get ready."

She turned around and walked back out of the coffee shop, as quickly as she had come in. So much for being casual. If he hadn't already given it away, he was pretty sure Hayley's scampering had.

"You were saying?" Cassie said, her tone brittle.

"I'm sorry," he said, leaning in. "Is she your sister?"

"No."

"Best friend?"

"No."

"Is she your daughter? Because I have a feeling I'm about to catch hell from the reverend here in a few minutes, but I'm not really sure why I'm catching it from you."

"Because I know her. I know all about you. I am friends with your sister, and I know enough through her."

"Undoubtedly all about my great personal sacrifice and sparkling personality," he said.

Cassie's expression softened. "Rebecca loves you. But she's also realistic about the fact that you aren't a love-and-commitment kind of guy. Also, I do believe Ms. Hayley Thompson is younger than your sister."

"And last I checked, I wasn't committing any crimes. I will just take the coffee. You can keep the lecture."

He was not going to get chased out of the coffee shop, no matter how many people looked at him. No matter how much Cassie lectured him.

He was not the poor kid he'd once been. He was more than just a boy who had been abandoned by both parents. He was a damned boon to the town. His business brought in good money. *He* brought in good money. He wasn't going to be treated like dirt beneath anybody's shoe.

Maybe Hayley was too good for him, but she was sleeping with him. She wanted him. So it wasn't really up to anybody to say that she shouldn't.

When he turned around after Cassie gave him his coffee, the pastor stood up at his table and began to make his way over to Jonathan.

"Hello. Jonathan, right?" the older man said, his voice shot through with the same kind of steel that Jonathan often heard in Hayley's voice. Clearly, she got her strength from her father. It was also clear to Jonathan that he was not being spoken to by a pastor at the moment. But by a fairly angry dad.

"Pastor John," Jonathan said by way of greeting.

"Why don't you join me for a cup of coffee?"

Not exactly the words Jonathan had expected, all things considered. He could sense the tension in the room, sense the tension coming off Hayley's father.

People were doing their very best to watch, without appearing to do so. Any hope Jonathan had retained that they were oblivious to what it meant that he had come down from the upstairs apartment was dashed by just how fascinated they all were. And by the steady intent on Pastor John's face.

If the old man wanted to sit him down and humiliate him in front of the town, wanted to talk about how Jonathan wasn't fit to lick the dust off Hayley's boots, Jonathan wouldn't be surprised. Hell, he welcomed it. It was true, after all.

"I think I will," Jonathan said, following the other man back to his table.

He took a seat, his hand curled tightly around his coffee cup.

"I don't think we've ever formally met," John said, leaning back in his chair.

"No," Jonathan said, "we wouldn't have. I don't recall

darkening the door of the church in my lifetime. Unless it was to repair something."

Let him know just what kind of man Jonathan was. That's where this was headed, anyway. Jonathan had never met a woman's parents before. He had never been in a relationship that was serious enough to do so. And this wasn't serious, either. But because of this damn small town and Hayley's role in it, he was being forced into a position he had never wanted to be in.

"I see," the pastor said. "Hayley has been working for you for the past couple of weeks, I believe."

He was cutting right to the chase now. To Jonathan's connection to Hayley, which was undeniable. "Yes."

"I've been very protective of Hayley. Possibly overprotective. But when my son, Ace, went out on his own, he didn't find much but heartbreak. I transferred some of my fear of that happening again onto Hayley, to an unfair degree. So I kept her close. I encouraged her to keep working at the church. To live at home for as long as possible. You have a sister, don't you?"

Damn this man and his ironclad memory for detail. "I didn't think it was Christian to gossip. But I can see that you've certainly heard your share about me."

"I do know a little something about you, yes. My son is married to one of Nathan West's children, as I'm sure you know. And your sister has a connection to that family, as well."

Jonathan gritted his teeth. "Yes. My sister is with Gage. Though only God knows why. Maybe you could ask Him."

"Matters of the heart are rarely straightforward. Whether it's in the case of romantic love, or the love you feel for your children, or your sister. It's a big emotion. And it is scary at times. Not always the most rational. What you feel about Rebecca being with Gage I suppose is similar to the concerns I have about Hayley."

"That she's with a bastard who doesn't deserve her?"

The pastor didn't even flinch. "That she's involved deeply enough that she could be hurt. And if we're going to speak plainly, I suppose the question I could ask you is whether or not you would think any man was good enough for Rebecca, or if you would be concerned—no matter who it was—that he wouldn't handle her with the care you would want."

Jonathan didn't have much to say about that. Only because he was trying to be angry. Trying to take offense at the fact that the older man was questioning him. Trying to connect this conversation to what he knew to be true—everybody looked at him and saw someone who wasn't worthy. He certainly didn't deserve kindness from this man, not at all. Didn't deserve for him to sit here and try to forge some kind of connection.

Jonathan had taken advantage of Hayley. Regardless of her level of experience, she was his employee. Even if she had been with a hundred men, what he had done would be problematic. But, as far as he was concerned, the problem was compounded by the fact that Hayley had been innocent.

So he waited. He waited for that hammer to fall. For the accusations to fly.

But they didn't come. So he figured he might try to create a few.

"I'm sure there's a certain type of man you would prefer your daughter be with. But it's definitely not the guy with the bad reputation you'd want stumbling out of her apartment early in the morning."

John nodded slowly, and Jonathan thought—with a certain amount of triumph—that he saw anger flicker briefly in the older man's eyes.

"I told you already that I feel very protective of her," Pastor John said. "But I wonder if, by protecting her as much as I did, I shielded her too effectively from the reality of life. I don't want her to get hurt." He let out a long, slow breath. "But that is not within my control."

"Is this the part where you ask me about my intentions toward your daughter? Because I highly doubt we're ever going to sit around a dinner table and try to make small talk. This isn't that sort of thing." With those words, Jonathan effectively told Hayley's father that all he was doing was fooling around with her. And that wasn't strictly true. Also, he hated himself a little bit for pretending it was.

For saying that sort of thing to her father when he knew it would embarrass her.

But in a way, it would be a mercy. She cared what people in town thought about her. She cared about her father's opinion. And this conversation would make it so much easier for her to let Jonathan go when the time came.

She was always going to let you go. She has traveling to do, places to see. You were her dirty detour along the way. You're the one who needs distance. You're the one who needs to find a way to make it easier.

He ignored that voice, ignored the tightening in his chest.

"Why isn't it that sort of thing?" The question, issued

from Hayley's father, his tone firm but steady, reached something deep inside Jonathan, twisted it, cracked it.

It couldn't be anything more than temporary. Because of him. Because of what he was. Who he was. That should be obvious. It would have been even more obvious if Pastor John had simply sat down and started hurling recriminations. About how Jonathan was beneath the man's pure, innocent daughter. About why a formerly impoverished man from the wrong side of the tracks could never be good enough for a woman like her.

It didn't matter that he had money now. He was the same person he had been born to be. The same boy who had been beaten by his father, abandoned by his mother. All that was still in him. And no custom home, no amount of money in his bank account, was ever going to fix it.

If John Thompson wouldn't look at him and see that, if he wouldn't shout it from across a crowded coffee shop so the whole town would hear, then Jonathan was going to have to make it clear.

"Because it's not something I do," he returned, his voice hard. "I'm in for temporary. That's all I've got."

"Well," John said, "that's a pretty neat lie you've been telling yourself, son. But the fact of the matter is, it's only the most you're willing to give, not the most you have the ability to give."

"And you're saying you want me to dig down deep and find it inside myself to be with your daughter forever? Something tells me that probably wouldn't be an ideal situation as far as you're concerned."

"That's between you and Hayley. I have my own personal feelings about it, to be sure. No father wants to believe that his daughter is being used. But if I believe that, then it means I don't see anything good in you, and that isn't true. Everybody knows how you took care of your sister. Whatever you think the people in this town believe about you, they do know that. I can't say you haven't been mistreated by the people here, and it grieves me to think about it."

He shook his head, and Jonathan was forced to believe the older man was being genuine. He didn't quite know what to do with that fact, but he saw the same honesty shining from John that he often saw in Hayley's eyes. An emotional honesty Jonathan had limited experience with.

The older man continued. "You think you don't have the capacity for love? When you've already mentioned your concern for Rebecca a couple of times in this conversation? When the past decade and a half of your life was devoted to caring for her? It's no secret how hard you've worked. I may never have formally met you until this moment, but I know about you, Jonathan Bear, and what I know isn't the reputation you seem to think you have."

"Well, regardless of my reputation, you should be concerned about Hayley's. When I came through that door this morning, it was unintentional. But it's important to Hayley that nobody realizes what's happening between us. So the longer I sit here talking to you, the more risk there is of exposing her to unnecessary chatter. And that's not what I want. So," he said, "out of respect for keeping it a secret, like Hayley wants—"

"That's not what I want."

Chapter 12

Hayley was shaking. She had been shaking from the moment she had walked into The Grind and seen Jonathan there, with her father in the background.

Somehow, she had known—just known—that everyone in the room was putting two and two together and coming up with sex.

And she also knew she had definitely made it worse by running away. If she had sauntered in and acted surprised to see Jonathan there, she might have made people think it really was coincidental that the two of them were both in the coffeehouse early in the morning, coming through the same private door. For reasons that had nothing to do with him spending the night upstairs with her.

But she had spent the past five minutes pacing around upstairs, waiting for her breath to normalize, waiting for her heart to stop beating so hard. Neither thing had happened.

Then she had cautiously crept back downstairs and come in to see her father sitting at the table with Jonathan. Fortunately, Jonathan hadn't looked like he'd been punched in the face. But the conversation had definitely seemed tense.

And standing there, looking at what had been her worst nightmare not so long ago, she realized that it just...wasn't. She'd never been ashamed of Jonathan. He was...the most determined, hardworking, wonderful man she had ever known. He had spent his life raising his sister. He had experienced a childhood where he had known nothing but abandonment and abuse, and he had turned around and given love to his sister, unconditionally and tirelessly.

And, yeah, maybe it wasn't ideal to announce her physical affair with him at the coffee shop, all things considered, but...whatever she had expected to feel... She didn't.

So, it had been the easiest thing in the world to walk over to their table and say that she really didn't need to keep their relationship a secret. Of course, now both Jonathan and her father were looking at her like she had grown a second head.

When she didn't get a response from either of them, she repeated, "That's not what I want."

"Hayley," Jonathan said, his tone firm. "You don't know what you're saying."

"Oh, please," she returned. "Jonathan, that tone wouldn't work on me in private, and it's not going to work on me here, either."

She took a deep breath, shifting her weight from foot to foot, gazing at her father, waiting for him to say something. He looked… Well, it was very difficult to say if John Thompson could ever really be surprised. In his line of work, he had seen it all, heard it all. While Protestants weren't much for confession, people often used him as a confessional, she knew.

Still, he looked a little surprised to be in this situation.

She searched his face for signs of disappointment. That was her deepest fear. That he would be disappointed in her. Because she had tried, she really had, to be the child Ace wasn't.

Except, as she stood there, she realized that was a steaming pile of bull-pucky. Her behavior wasn't about being what Ace hadn't been. It was all about desperately wanting to please people while at the same time wishing there was a way to please herself. And the fact of the matter was, she couldn't have both those things. Not always.

That contradiction was why she had been hell-bent on running away, less because she wanted to experience the wonders of the world and more because she wanted to go off and do what she wanted without disappointing anyone.

"Jonathan isn't just my boss," she said to her dad. "He's my… Well, I don't really know. But…you know." Her throat tightened, tears burning behind her eyes.

Yes, she wanted to admit to the relationship, and she wanted to live out in the open, but that didn't make the transition from good girl to her own woman any easier.

She wanted to beg her dad for his approval. He wasn't

a judgmental man, her father, but he had certainly raised her in a specific fashion, and this was not it. So while he might not condemn her, she knew she wasn't going to get his wholesale approval.

And she would have to live with that.

Living without his approval was hard. Much harder than she had thought it might be. Especially given the fact that she thought she'd accepted it just a few moments ago. But being willing to experience disapproval and truly accepting it were apparently two different things.

"Why don't you have a seat, Hayley," her father said slowly.

"No, thank you," she replied. "I'm going to stand, because if I sit down… Well, I don't know. I have too much energy to sit down. But I—I care about him." She turned to Jonathan. "I care about you. I really do. I'm so sorry I made you feel like you were a dirty secret. Like I was ashamed of you. Because any woman would be proud to be involved with you." She took a deep breath and looked around the coffee shop. "I'm dating him," she said, pointing at Jonathan. "Just so you all know."

"Hayley," her father said, standing up, "come to dinner this week."

"With him?"

"If you want to. But please know that we want to know about your life. Even if it isn't what we would choose for you, we want to know." He didn't mean Jonathan specifically. He meant being in a physical relationship without the benefit of any kind of commitment, much less marriage.

But the way he looked at her, with nothing but love,

made her ache all over. Made her throat feel so tight she could scarcely breathe.

She felt miserable. And she felt strong. She wasn't sure which emotion was more prominent. She had seen her father look at Ace like this countless times, had seen him talk about her brother with a similar expression on his face. Her father was loving, and he was as supportive as he could be, but he also had hard lines.

"I guess we'll see," she said.

"I suppose. I also imagine you need to have a talk with him," he said, tilting his head toward Jonathan, who was looking uncertain. She'd never seen Jonathan look uncertain before.

"Oh," she said, "I imagine I do."

"Come home if you need anything."

For some reason, she suddenly became aware of the tension in her father's expression. He was the pastor of Copper Ridge. And the entire town was watching him. So whether he wanted to or not, he couldn't haul off and punch Jonathan. He couldn't yell at her—though he never had yelled in all her life. And he was leaving her to sort out her own circumstances, when she could feel that he very much wanted to stay and sort them out for her.

Maybe Jonathan was right. Maybe she had never put a foot out of line because the rules were easier. There were no rules to what she was doing now, and no one was going to step in and tell her what to do. No one was going to pull her back if she went too far. Not even her father. Maybe that had been her real issue with taking this relationship public. Not so much the disappointment as the loss of a safety net.

Right now, Hayley felt like she was standing on the edge of an abyss. She had no idea how far she might fall, how bad it might hurt when she landed. If she would even survive it.

She was out here, living her potential mistakes, standing on the edge of a lot of potential pain.

Because with the barrier of following the rules removed, with no need to leave to experience things... Well, it was just her. Her heart and what she felt for Jonathan.

There was nothing in the way. No excuses. No false idea that this could never be anything, because she was leaving in the end.

As her father walked out of the coffeehouse, taking with him an entire truckload of her excuses, she realized exactly what she had been protecting herself from.

Falling in love. With Jonathan. With a man who might never love her back. Wanting more, wanting everything, with the man least likely to give it to her.

She had been hiding behind the secretary desk at the church, listening to everybody else's problems, without ever incurring any of her own. She had witnessed a whole lot of heartbreak, a whole lot of struggle, but she had always been removed from it.

She didn't want to protect herself from this. She didn't want to hide.

"Why did you do that?" Jonathan asked.

"Because you were mad at me yesterday. I hurt your feelings."

He laughed, a dark, humorless sound. "Hayley," he said, "I don't exactly have feelings to hurt."

"That's not true," she said. "I know you do."

"Honey, that stuff was beaten out of me by my father before I was five years old. And whatever was left… It pretty much dissolved when my mother walked away and left me with a wounded sister to care for. That stuff just kind of leaves you numb. All you can do is survive. Work on through life as hard as you can, worry about putting food on the table. Worry about trying to do right by a kid who's had every unfair thing come down on her. You think you being embarrassed to hold my hand in public is going to hurt my feelings after that?"

She hated when he did this. When he drew lines between their levels of experience and made her feel silly.

She closed the distance between them and put her fingertips on his shoulder. Then she leaned in and kissed him, in full view of everybody in the coffeehouse. He put his hand on her hip, and even though he didn't enthusiastically kiss her back, he made no move to end it, either.

"Why do I get the feeling you are a little embarrassed to be with *me*?" she asked, when she pulled away from him.

He arched his brow. "I'm not embarrassed to be with you."

Maybe he wasn't. But there was something bothering him. "You're upset because everyone knows. And now there will be consequences if you do something to hurt me."

"When," he said, his tone uncompromising. "*When* I do something. That's what everyone is thinking. Trust me, Hayley, they don't think for one second that this might end in some fairy-tale wedding bullshit."

Hayley jerked back, trying to fight the feeling that

she had just been slapped in the face. For whatever reason, he was trying to elicit exactly that response, and she really didn't want to give it to him. "Fine. Maybe that is what they think. But why does it matter? That's the question, isn't it? Why does what other people think matter more than what you or I might want?

"You were right about me. My choices were less about what other people might think, and more about what might happen to me if I found out I had never actually been reined in." She shook her head. "If I discovered that all along I could have done exactly what I wanted to, with no limit on it. Before now, I never took the chance to find out who I was. I was happy to be told. And I think I've been a little afraid of who I might be beneath all of these expectations."

"Why? Because you might harbor secret fantasies of shoplifting doilies out of the Trading Post?"

"No," Hayley said, "because I might go and get myself hurt. If I had continued working at the church, if I'd kept on gazing at the kind of men I met there from across the room, never making a move because waiting for them to do it was right, pushing down all of my desires because it was lust I shouldn't feel… I would have been safe. I wouldn't be sitting here in this coffee shop with you, shaking because I'm scared, because I'm a little bit turned on thinking about what we did last night."

"I understand the turned on part," he said, his voice rough like gravel. He lifted his hand, dragging his thumb over her lower lip. "Why are you afraid?"

"I'm afraid because just like you said… There's a very low chance of this ending in some fairy-tale wedding…nonsense. And I want all of that." Her chest seized tight, her throat closing up to a painful degree. "With you. If you were wondering. And that is… That's so scary. Because I knew you would look at me like that if I told you."

His face was flat, his dark eyes blazing. He was… well, he was angry, rather than indifferent. Somehow, she had known he would be.

"You shouldn't be afraid of not getting your fairy tale with me. If anything, you should be relieved. Nobody wants to stay with me for the rest of their life, Hayley, trust me. You're supposed to go to Paris. And you're going to Paris."

"I don't want to go," she said, because she wanted to stay here, with him. Or take him with her. But she didn't want to be without him.

"Dammit," he said, his voice like ground-up glass. "Hayley, you're not going to change your plans because of me. That would last how long? Maybe a year? Maybe two if you're really dedicated. But I know exactly how that ends—with you deciding you would rather be anywhere but stuck in my house, stuck in this town."

"But I don't feel stuck. I never did. It was all…me being afraid. But the thing is, Jonathan, I never wanted anything more than I wanted my safety. Thinking I needed to escape was just a response to this missing piece inside of me that I couldn't put a name to. But I know what it is now."

"Don't," he bit out.

"It was you," she said. "All of this time it was you. Don't you see? I never wanted anyone or anything badly enough to take the chance. To take the risk. To expose myself, to step out of line. But you… I do want you that badly."

"Because you were forced to take the risk. You had to own it. Yesterday, you didn't have to, and so you didn't. You pulled away from me when we walked down the street, didn't want anyone to see."

"That wasn't about you. It was about me. It was about the fact that…basically, everybody in town knows I've never dated anybody. So in my case it's a little bit like announcing that I lost my virginity, and it's embarrassing."

Except now she was having this conversation with him in a coffeehouse, where people she knew were sitting only a few feet away, undoubtedly straining to hear her over the sound of the espresso machine. But whatever. She didn't care. For the first time in her life, she really, really didn't care. She cared about him. She cared about this relationship. About doing whatever she needed to do to make him see that everything she was saying was true.

"I'm over it," she added. "I just had to decide that I was. Well, now I have. Because it doesn't get any more horrifying than having to admit that you were having your first affair to your father."

"You see," he said. "I wouldn't know. Nobody was all that invested in me when I lost my virginity, or why. I was fifteen, if you were curious. So forgive me if your concerns seem foreign to me. It's just that I know how this all plays out. People say they love you, then they punch you in the face. You take care of somebody all of their damn life, and then they take off with the one person you spent all that time protecting them from. Yeah, they say they love you, and then they leave. That's life."

Hayley's chest tightened, her heart squeezing painfully. "I didn't say I loved you."

He looked stricken by that. "Well, good. At least you didn't lie to me."

She did love him, though. But he had introduced the word. Love and its effects were clearly the things that scared him most about what was happening between them.

Love loomed large between them. Love was clearly on the table here. Even if he didn't want it to be, there it was. Even if he was going to deny it, there it was.

Already in his mind, in his heart, whether she said it or not.

She opened her mouth to say it, but it stuck in her throat.

Because he had already decided it would be a lie if she spoke the words. He was so dedicated to that idea. To his story about who Jonathan Bear was, and who he had to be, and how people treated him. His behavior was so very close to what she had been doing for so long.

"Jonathan—"

He cut her off. "I don't love people," he said. "You know what I love? I love things. I love my house. I love my money. I love that company that I've spent so many hours investing in. I love the fact that I own a mountain, and can ride a horse from one end of my land to the other, and get a sense of everything that can never be taken from me. But I'll never love another person, not again." He stood up, gripping her chin with his thumb and forefinger. "Not even you. Because I will never love anything I can't buy right back, do you understand?"

She nodded, swallowing hard. "Yes," she said.

His pain was hemorrhaging from him, bleeding out of every pore, and there was nothing she could do to stop it. He was made of fury, of rage, and he was made of hurt, whether he would admit it or not.

"I think we're done then, Hayley."

He moved away from her, crossing the coffeehouse and walking out the door. Every eye in the room was on her, everybody watching to see what she would do next. So she did the only thing she could.

She stood up and she ran after Jonathan Bear for the entire town to see.

Jonathan strode down the street. The heavy gray sky was starting to crack, raindrops falling onto his head. His shoulders. Good. That was just about perfect.

It took him a few more strides to realize he was headed away from his car, but he couldn't think clearly enough to really grasp where he was going. His head was pounding like horse hooves over the grass, and he couldn't grab hold of a thought to save his life.

"Jonathan!"

He turned, looking down the mostly empty street, to see Hayley running after him, her dark hair flying behind her, rain flying into her face. She was making a spectacle of herself, right here on Main, and she didn't seem to care at all. Something about that made him feel like he'd been turned to stone, rooted to the spot, his heart thundering heavily in his chest.

"Don't run from me," she said, coming to a stop in front of him, breathing hard. "Don't run from us."

"You're the one who's running, honey," he said, keeping his voice deliberately flat.

"We're not done," she said. "We're not going to be done just because you say so. You might be the boss at your house, but you're not the boss here." Her words were jumbled up, fierce and ferocious. "What about what I want?"

He gritted his teeth. "Well, the problem is you made the mistake of assuming I might care what you want."

She sprang forward, pounding a closed fist on his shoulder. The gesture was so aggressive, so very unlike Hayley that it immobilized him. "You do care. You're not a mountain, you're just a man, and you do care. But you're awfully desperate to prove that you don't. You're awfully desperate to prove you have no worth. And I have to wonder why that is."

"I don't have to prove it. Everyone who's ever wandered through my life has proved it, Hayley. You're a little bit late to this party. You're hardly going to take thirty-five years of neglect and make me feel differently about it. Make me come to different conclusions than I've spent the past three decades drawing."

"Why not?" she asked. "That's kind of the point of knowing someone. Of being with them. They change you. You've certainly changed me. You made me...well, more me than I've ever been."

"I never said I needed to change."

"That's ridiculous. Of course you need to change. You live in that big house all by yourself, you're angry at your sister because she figured out how to let something go when you can't. And you're about ready to blow this up—to blow us up—to keep yourself safe." She shivered, the rain making dark spots on her top, drops rolling down her face.

"There's no reason any of this has to end, Hayley." He gritted his teeth, fighting against the slow, expanding feeling growing in his chest, fighting against the pain starting to push against the back of his eyes. "But you have to accept what I'm willing to give. And it may not be what you want, what you're looking for. If it's not, if that makes you leave, then you're no different from anyone else who's ever come through my life, and you won't be any surprise to me."

Hayley looked stricken by that, pale. And he could see her carefully considering her words. "Wow. That's a very smart way to build yourself an impenetrable fort there, Jonathan. How can anyone demand something of you, if you're determined to equate high expectations with the people who abandoned you? If you're determined to believe that someone asking anything of you is the same as not loving you at all?"

"You haven't said you loved me." His voice was deliberately hard. He didn't know why he was bringing that up again. Didn't know why he was suspended between the desire for her to tell him she didn't, and the need—the intense, soul-shattering need—to hear her say it, even if he could never accept it. Even if he could never return it.

"My mistake," she said, her voice thin. "What will you do if I tell you, Jonathan? Will you say it doesn't matter, that it isn't real? Because you know everything, don't you? Even my heart."

"I know more about the world than you do, little girl," he said, his throat feeling tight for some reason. "Whatever your intentions, I have a better idea of what the actual outcome might be."

She shocked him by taking two steps forward, eliminating the air between them, pressing her hand against his chest. His heart raged beneath her touch, and he had a feeling she could tell.

"I love you." She stared at him for a moment, then she stretched up on her toes and pressed a kiss to his lips. Her lips were slick and cold from the rain, and he wanted to consume her. Wanted to pretend that words didn't matter. That there was nothing but this kiss.

For a moment, a heartbeat, he pretended that was true.

"I love you," she said again, when they parted. "But that doesn't mean I won't expect something from you. In fact, that would be pretty sorry love if I expected to come into your life and change nothing, mean nothing. I want you to love me back, Jonathan. I want you to open yourself up. I want you to let me in. I want you to be brave."

He grabbed hold of her arms, held her against his chest. He didn't give a damn who might see them. "You're telling me to be brave? What have you ever faced down that scared you? Tell me, Hayley."

"You," she said breathlessly.

He released his hold on her and took a step back, swearing violently. "All the more reason you should walk away, I expect."

"Do you know why you scare me, Jonathan? You make me want something I can't control. You make me want something I can't predict. There are no rules for this. There is no safety. Loving you... I have no guarantees. There is no neat map for how this might work out. It's not a math equation, where I can add doing the right things with saying the right things and make you change. You have to decide. You have to choose this. You have to choose us. The rewards for being afraid, or being good, aren't worth as much as the reward for being brave. So I'm going to be brave.

"I love you. And I want you to love me back. I want you to take a chance—on me."

She was gazing at him, her eyes blazing with light and intensity. How long would it take for that light to dim? How long would it take for him to kill it? How long would it take for her to decide—like everyone else in his life—that he wasn't worth the effort?

It was inevitable. That was how it always ended.

"No," he said, the word scraping his throat raw as it escaped.

"No?" The devastation in her voice cut him like a knife.

"No. But hey, one more for your list," he said, hating himself with every syllable.

"What?"

"You got your kiss in the rain. I did a lot for you, checked off a lot of your boxes. Go find some other man to fill in the rest."

Then he turned and left her standing in the street.

And in front of God and everybody, Jonathan Bear walked away from Hayley Thompson, and left whatever remained of his heart behind with her.

Chapter 13

This was hell. Perhaps even literally. Hayley had wondered about hell a few times, growing up the daughter of a pastor. Now, she thought that if hell were simply living with a broken heart, with the rejection of the person you loved more than anything else echoing in your ears, it would be pretty effective eternal damnation.

She was lying on her couch, tears streaming down her face. She was miserable, and she didn't even want to do anything about it. She just wanted to sit in it.

Oh, she had been so cavalier about the pain that would come when Jonathan ended things. Back in the beginning, when she had been justifying losing her virginity to him, she had been free and easy about the possibility of heartbreak.

But she hadn't loved him then. So she really hadn't known.

Hadn't known that it would be like shards of glass digging into her chest every time she took a breath. Hadn't known that it was actual, physical pain. That her head would throb and her eyes would feel like sandpaper from all the crying.

That her body, and her soul, would feel like they had been twisted, wrung out and draped over a wire to dry in the brutal, unfeeling coastal air.

This was the experience he had talked about. The one that wasn't worth having.

She rolled onto her back, thinking over the past weeks with Jonathan. Going to his house, getting her first job away from the church. How nervous she had been. How fluttery she had felt around him.

Strangely, she felt her lips curve into a smile.

It was hard to reconcile the woman she was now with the girl who had first knocked on his door for that job interview.

She hadn't even realized what all that fluttering meant. What the tightening in her nipples, the pressure between her thighs had meant. She knew now. Desire. Need. Things she would associate with Jonathan for the rest of her life, no matter where she went, no matter who else she might be with.

He'd told her to find someone else.

Right now, the idea of being with another man made her cringe.

She wasn't ready to think about that. She was too raw. And she still wanted him. Only him.

Jonathan was more than an experience.

He had wrenched her open. Pulled her out of the

safe space she'd spent so many years hiding in. He had shown her a love that was bigger than fear.

Unfortunately, because that love was so big, the desolation of it was crippling.

She sat up, scrubbing her arm over her eyes. She needed to figure out what she was going to do next.

Something had crystallized for her earlier today, during the encounter with Jonathan and her father. She didn't need to run away. She didn't need to leave town, or gain anonymity, in order to have what she wanted. To be who she wanted.

She didn't need to be the church secretary, didn't need to be perfect or hide what she was doing. She could still go to her father's church on Sunday, and go to dinner at her parents' house on Sunday evening.

She didn't have to abandon her home, her family, her faith. Sure, it might be uncomfortable to unite her family and her need to find herself, but if there was one thing loving Jonathan had taught her, it was that sometimes uncomfortable was worth it.

She wasn't going to let heartbreak stop her.

She thought back to how he had looked at her earlier today, those black eyes impassive as he told her he wouldn't love her back.

Part of her wanted to believe she was right about him. That he was afraid. That he was protecting himself.

Another part of her felt that was a little too hopeful. Maybe that gorgeous, experienced man simply couldn't love his recently-a-virgin assistant.

Except…she had been so certain, during a few small moments, that she had given something to him, too. Just like he had given so much to her.

For some reason, he was dedicated to the idea that nobody stayed. That people looked at him and saw the worst. She couldn't understand why he would find that comforting, and yet a part of him must.

It made her ache. Her heart wasn't broken only for her, but for him, too. For all the love he wouldn't allow himself to accept.

She shook her head. Later. Later she would feel sorry for him. Right now, she was going to wallow in her own pain.

Because at the end of the day, Jonathan had made the choice to turn away from her, to turn away from love.

Right now, she would feel sorry for herself. Then maybe she would plan a trip to Paris.

"Do you want to invite me in?"

Jonathan looked at his sister, standing on the porch, looking deceptively calm.

"Do I have a choice?"

Rebecca shook her head, her long dark hair swinging behind her like a curtain. "Not really. I didn't drive all the way out here to have this conversation with moths buzzing around me."

It was dark out, and just as Rebecca had said, there were bugs fluttering around the porch light near her face.

"Come in, then," he said, moving aside.

She blinked when she stepped over the threshold, a soft smile touching her lips. The scar tissue on the left side of her mouth pulled slightly. Scar tissue that had been given to her by the man she was going to marry. Oh, it had been an accident, and Jonathan knew it. But with all the pain and suffering the accident had caused Rebecca, intent had never much mattered to him.

"This is beautiful, Jonathan," she said, her dark eyes flickering to him. "I haven't been here since it was finished."

He shrugged. "Well, that was your choice."

"You don't like my fiancé. And you haven't made much of an effort to change that. I don't know what you expect from me."

"Appreciation, maybe, for all the years I spent taking care of you?" He wanted to cut his own balls off for saying that. Basically, right about now he wanted to escape his own skin. He was a bastard. Even he thought so.

He was sitting in his misery now, existing fully in the knowledge of the pain he had caused Hayley.

He should never have had that much power over her. He never should have touched her. This misery was the only possible way it could have turned out. His only real defense was that he hadn't imagined a woman like Hayley would ever fall in love with a man like him.

"Right. Because we've never had that discussion."

His sister's tone was dry, and he could tell she was pretty unimpressed with him. Well, fair enough. He was unimpressed with himself.

"I still don't understand why you love him, Rebecca. I really don't."

"What is love to you, Jonathan?"

An image of Hayley's face swam before his mind's eye. "What the hell kind of question is that?"

"A relevant one," she said. "I think. Particularly when we get down to why exactly I'm here. Congratulations.

After spending most of your life avoiding being part of the rumor mill, you're officially hot small-town gossip."

"Am I?" He wasn't very surprised to hear that.

"Something about kissing the pastor's daughter on Main Street in the rain. And having a fight with her."

"That's accurate."

"What's going on?"

"What it looks like. I was sleeping with her. We had a fight. Now we're not sleeping together."

Rebecca tilted her head to the side. "I feel like I'm missing some information."

"Hayley was working for me—I assume you knew that."

"Vaguely," she said, her eyes glittering with curiosity.

"And I'm an asshole. So when I found out my assistant was a virgin, I figured I would help her with that." It was a lie, but one he was comfortable with. He was comfortable painting himself as the villain. Everybody would, anyway. So why not add his own embellishment to the tale.

"Right," Rebecca said, sarcasm dripping from her voice. "Because you're a known seducer of innocent women."

Jonathan turned away, running his hand over his hair. "I'm not the nicest guy, Rebecca. We all know that."

"I know *you* think that," Rebecca said. "And I know we've had our differences. But when I needed you, you were there for me. Always. Even when Gage broke my heart, and you couldn't understand why it mattered, why I wanted to be with him, in the end, you supported me. Always. Every day of my life. I don't even remember my father. I remember you. You taught me how to ride a bike, how to ride a horse. You fought for me, tirelessly. Worked for me. You don't think I don't know how tired you were? How much you put into making our home…a home? Bad men don't do that. Bad men hit their wives, hit their children. Abandon their daughters. Our fathers were bad men, Jonathan. But you never were."

Something about those words struck him square in the chest. Their fathers *were* bad men.

He had always known that.

But he had always believed somewhere deep down that he must be bad, too. Not because he thought being an abusive bastard was hereditary. But because if his father had beaten him, and his mother had left him, there must be something about him that was bad.

Something visible. Something that the whole town could see.

He thought back to all the kindness on Pastor John Thompson's face, kindness Jonathan certainly hadn't deserved from the old man when he was doing his absolute damnedest to start a fight in the middle of The Grind.

He had been so determined to have John confirm that Jonathan was bad. That he was wrong.

Because there was something freeing about the anger that belief created deep inside his soul.

It had been fuel. All his life that belief had been his fuel. Gave him something to fight against. Something to be angry about.

An excuse to never get close to anyone.

Because underneath all the anger was nothing but despair. Despair because his parents had left him, because they couldn't love him enough. Because he wasn't worth…anything.

His need for love had never gone away, but he'd shoved it down deep. Easier to do when you had convinced yourself you could never have it.

He looked at Rebecca and realized he had despaired over her, too. When she had chosen Gage. Jonathan had decided it was just one more person who loved him and didn't want to stay.

Yeah, it was much easier, much less painful to believe that he was bad. Because it let him keep his distance from the pain. Because it meant he didn't have to try.

"What do you think love is?" Rebecca asked again, more persistent this time.

He didn't have an answer. Not one with words. All he had were images, feelings. Watching Rebecca sleep after a particularly hard day. Praying child services wouldn't come by to check on her while he was at work, and find her alone and him negligent.

And Hayley. Her soft hands on his body, her sweet surrender. The trust it represented. The way she made him feel. Like he was on fire, burning up from the inside out. Like he could happily stay for the rest of his life in a one-room cabin, without any of the money or power he had acquired over the past few years, and be perfectly content.

The problem was, he couldn't make her stay with him.

This house, his company, those things were his. In a way that Hayley could never be. In a way that no one ever could be.

People were always able to leave.

He felt like a petulant child even having that thought. But he didn't know how the hell else he could feel secure. And he didn't think he could stand having another person walk away.

"I don't know," he said.

Rebecca shook her head, her expression sad. "That's a damn shame, Jonathan, because you show me love all the time. Whether you know what to call it or not, you've given it to me tirelessly over the years, and without you, without it, I don't know where I would be. You stayed with me when everybody else left."

"But who stayed with me?" he asked, feeling like an ass for even voicing that question. "You had to stay. I had to take care of you. But the minute you could go out on your own you did."

"Because that's what your love did for me, you idiot."

"Not very well. Because you were always worried I thought of you as a burden, weren't you? It almost ruined your relationship with Gage, if I recall correctly."

"Yes," she said, "but that wasn't about you. That was my baggage. And you did everything in your power to help me, even when you knew the result would be me going back to Gage. That's love, Jonathan." She shook her head. "I love you, too. I love you enough to want you to have your own life, one that doesn't revolve around taking care of me. That doesn't revolve around what happened to us in the past."

He looked around the room, at the house that meant so much to him. A symbol of security, of his ability to care for Rebecca, if her relationship went to hell. And he realized that creating this security for her somehow enabled him to deny his own weaknesses. His own fears.

This house had only ever been for him. A fortress to barricade himself in.

Wasn't that what Hayley had accused him of? Building himself a perfect fortress to hide in?

If everybody hated him, he didn't have to try. If there was something wrong with him, he never had to do what was right. If all he loved were things, he never had to risk loss.

They were lies. Lies he told himself because he was a coward.

And it had taken a virginal church secretary to uncover the truth.

She had stood in front of him and said she wanted love more than she wanted to be safe. And he had turned her down.

He was afraid. Had been all his life. But before this very moment, he would have rather cut out his own heart than admit it.

But now, standing with his sister looking at him like he was the saddest damn thing she'd ever seen, a hole opened in his chest. A hole Hayley had filled.

"But doesn't it scare you?" he asked, his voice rough. "What if he leaves?"

She reached out, putting her hand on his. "It would break my heart. But I would be okay. I would have you. And I would…still be more whole than I was before I loved him. That's the thing about love. It doesn't make you weak, Jonathan, it makes you stronger. Opening yourself up, letting people in…that makes your life bigger. It makes your life richer. Maybe it's a cliché, but from where I'm standing you need to hear the cliché. You need to start believing it."

"I don't understand why she would want to be with me," Jonathan said. "She's…sweet. And she's never been hurt. I'm…well, I'm a mess. That's not what she deserves. She deserves to have a man who's in mint condition, like she is."

"But that's not how love works. If love made sense, if it was perfectly fair, then Gage West would not have been the man for me. He was the last man on earth I should have wanted, Jonathan. Nobody knows that more than me, and him. It took a miracle for me to let go of all my anger and love him. At the same time… I couldn't help myself.

"Love is strange that way. You fall into it whether you want to or not. Then the real fight is figuring out how to live it. How to become the person you need to be so you can hold on to that love. But I'm willing to bet you are the man she needs. Not some mint condition, new-in-the-box guy. But a strong man who has proved, time and time again, that no matter how hard life is, no matter how intensely the storm rages, he'll be there for you. And more than that, he'll throw his body over yours to protect you if it comes to that. That's what I see when I look at you, Jonathan. What's it going to take for you to see that in yourself?"

"I don't think I'm ever going to," he said slowly, imagining Hayley again, picturing her as she stared up at him on the street. Fury, hurt, love shining from her eyes. "But…if she sees it…"

"That's a start," Rebecca said. "As long as you don't let her get away. As long as you don't push her away."

"It's too late for that. She's probably not going to

want to see me again. She's probably not going to want me back."

"Well, you won't know unless you ask." Rebecca took a deep breath. "The best thing about love is it has the capacity to forgive on a pretty incredible level. But if there's one thing you and I both know, it's that it's hard to forgive someone leaving. Don't make that the story. Go back. Ask for forgiveness. Change what needs to be changed. Mostly…love her. The rest kind of takes care of itself."

Chapter 14

Hayley had just settled back onto her couch for more quality sitting and weeping when she heard a knock at her door.

She stood up, brushing potato chip crumbs off her pajamas and grimacing. Maybe it was Cassie, bringing up baked goods. The other woman had done that earlier; maybe now she was bringing more. Hayley could only hope.

She had a gaping wound in her chest that could be only temporarily soothed by butter.

Without bothering to fix her hair—which was on top of her head in a messy knot—she jerked the door open.

And there he was. Dark eyes glittering, gorgeous mouth pressed into a thin line. His dark hair tied back low on his neck, the way she was accustomed to seeing him during the day.

Her heart lurched up into her throat, trying to make a break for it.

She hadn't been expecting him, but she imagined expecting him wouldn't have helped. Jonathan Bear wasn't someone you could anticipate.

"What are you doing here?"

He looked around. "I came here to talk to you. Were you…expecting someone else?"

"Yes. A French male prostitute." He lifted his brows. "Well, you told me to find another man to tick my boxes."

"I think you mean a gigolo."

"I don't know what they're called," she said, exasperated.

The corner of his mouth twitched. "Well, I promise to be quick. I won't interrupt your sex date."

She stepped to the side, ignoring the way her whole body hurt as she did. "I don't have a sex date." She cleared her throat. "Just so you know."

"Somehow, I didn't think you did."

"You don't know me," she grumbled, turning away from him, pressing her hand to her chest to see if her heart was beating as hard and fast as she felt like it was.

It was.

"I do, Hayley. I know you pretty damn well. Maybe better than I know myself. And… I think you might know me better than I know myself, too." He sounded different. Sad. Tired.

She turned around to face him, and with his expression more fully illuminated by the light, she saw weariness written there. Exhaustion.

"For all the good it did me," she said, crossing her

arms tightly in a bid to protect herself. Really, though, it was too late. There wasn't anything left to protect. He had shattered her irrevocably.

"Yeah, well. It did me a hell of a lot of good. At least, I hope it's going to. I hope I'm not too late."

"Too late for what? To stick the knife in again or…?"

"To tell you I love you," he said.

Everything froze inside her. Absolutely everything. The air in her lungs, her heart, the blood in her veins.

"You…you just said… Don't tease me, Jonathan. Don't play with me. I know I'm younger than you. I know that I'm innocent. But if you came back here to lie to me, to say what you think I need to hear so you can…keep having me in your bed, or whatever—"

Suddenly, she found herself being hauled forward into his arms, against his chest. "I do want you in my bed," he said, "make no mistake about that. But sex is just sex, Hayley, even when it's good. And what we have is good.

"But here's something you don't know, because you don't have experience with it. Sex isn't love. And it doesn't feel like this. I feel…like everything in me is broken and stronger at the same time, and I don't know how in the hell that can be true. And when you told me you loved me… I knew I could either let go of everything in the past or hold on to it harder to protect myself." He shook his head. "I protected myself."

"Yeah, well. What about protecting me?"

"I thought maybe I was protecting you, too. But it's all tangled up in this big lie that I've been telling myself for years. I told you I didn't love people, that I love things. But I said that only because I've had way too much experience with people I love leaving. A house can't walk away, Hayley. A mountain can't up and abandon you. But you could.

"One day, you could wake up and regret that you tied your future to me. When you could have done better... When you could have had a man who wasn't so damn broken." He cupped her cheek, bent down and kissed her lips. "What did I do to earn the love of someone like you? Someone so beautiful...so soft. You're everything I'm not, Hayley Thompson, and all the reasons I love you make perfect sense to me. But why do you love me? That's what I can't quite figure out."

Hayley looked into his eyes, so full of pain, so deeply wounded. She would have never thought a man like him would need reassurance from anyone, least of all a woman like her.

"I know I don't have a lot of experience, Jonathan. Well, any experience apart from you. I know that I haven't seen the whole world. I haven't even seen the whole state. But I've seen your heart. The kind of man you are. The change that knowing you, loving you, created in me. And I know...perfect love casts out all fear.

"I can't say I haven't been afraid these past couple of days. Afraid I couldn't be with you. That things might not work out with us. But when I stood on Main Street... I knew fear couldn't be allowed to win. It was your love that brought me to that conclusion. Your love was bigger than the fear inside me. I don't need experience to understand that. I don't need to travel the world or date other men for the sake of experience. I need you. Because whether or not you're perfect, you're perfect for me."

"*You're* perfect," he said, his voice rough. "So damned perfect. I want…to take you to Canada."

She blinked. "Well. That's not exactly an offer to run off to Vegas."

"You want to use your passport. Why wait? Let's go now. Your boss will let you off. I'm sure of it."

Something giddy bubbled up in her chest. Something wonderful. "Right now? Really?"

"Right the hell now."

"Yes," she said. "Yes, let's go to Canada."

"It's not the Eiffel Tower," he said, "but I will take you there someday. I promise you that."

"The only thing I need is you," she said. "The rest is negotiable."

His lips crashed down on hers, his kiss desperate and intense, saying the deep, poetic things she doubted her stoic cowboy would ever say out loud. But that was okay. The kiss said plenty all on its own.

Epilogue

Jonathan hated wearing a suit. He'd never done it before, but he had come to a swift and decisive conclusion the moment he'd finished doing up his tie.

Hayley was standing in their bedroom, looking amused. The ring on her left hand glittered as bright as her eyes, and suddenly, it wasn't the tie that was strangling him. It was just her. The love on her beautiful face. The fact she loved him.

He still hadn't quite figured out why. Still wasn't sure he saw all the things in himself that Rebecca had spoken of that day, all the things Hayley talked about when she said she loved him.

But Hayley did love him. And that was a gift he cherished.

"You're not going to make me wear a suit when we do this, are you?" he asked.

"I might," she said. "You look really hot in a suit."

He wrapped his arm around her waist and pulled her to his chest. "You look hottest in nothing at all. Think we could compromise?"

"We've created enough scandal already without me showing up naked to my wedding. Anyway, I'm wearing white. I am a traditional girl, after all."

"Honey, you oughta wear red."

"Are you calling me a scarlet woman?"

He nodded. "Yes, and I think you proved your status earlier this morning."

She blushed. She still blushed, even after being with him for six months. Blushed in bed, when he whispered dirty things into her ear. He loved it.

He loved *her.*

He couldn't wait to be her husband, and that was something he hadn't imagined ever feeling. Looking forward to being a husband.

Of course, he was looking forward to the honeymoon even more. To staying in a little apartment in Paris with a view of the Eiffel Tower.

For him, trading in a view of the mountains for a view of the city didn't hold much appeal. But she wanted it. And the joy he got from giving Hayley what she wanted was the biggest thing in his world.

Waiting to surprise her with the trip was damn near killing him.

"You have to hurry," she said, pushing at his shoulder. "You're giving the bride away, after all."

Jonathan took a deep breath. Yeah, it was time. Time to give his sister to that Gage West, who would never deserve her, but who loved her, so Jonathan was willing to let it go. Willing to give them his blessing.

Actually, over the past few months he'd gotten kind of attached to the bastard who would be his brother-in-law. Something he'd thought would never be possible only a little while ago.

But love changed you. Rebecca had been right about that.

"All right," he said. "Let's go then."

Hayley kissed his cheek and took his hand, leading him out of the bedroom and down the stairs. The wedding guests were out on the back lawn, waiting for the event to start. When he and Hayley exited the house, they all turned to look.

He and Hayley still turned heads, and he had a feeling they always would.

Jonathan Bear had always been seen as a bad boy. In all the ways that phrase applied. The kind of boy no parent wanted their daughter to bring home to Sunday dinner. And yet the pastor's daughter had.

He'd definitely started out that way. But somehow, through some miracle, he'd earned the love of a good woman.

And because of her love, he was determined to be the best man he could possibly be.

* * * * *

*The last man casting director Perla Sambrano wants
to see is Gael Montez. But the handsome A-lister is perfect for
her new show. Now, snowed in during a script reading, will he
become the leading man in her heart just in time for Christmas?*

Read on for a sneak peek at
Just for the Holidays…
by Adriana Herrera.

"Sure, why don't you tell me how to feel, Gael, that's always been
a special skill of yours." She knew that was not the way they would
arrive at civility, but she was tired of his sulking.

She could see his jaw working and a flush of pink working
up his throat. She should leave this alone. This could not lead
anywhere good. She'd already felt what his touch did to her.
Already confirmed that the years and the distance had done nothing
to temper her feelings for him, and here she was provoking him.
Goading an answer out of him that would wreck her no matter
what it was. And he *would* tell her because Gael had never been a
coward. And he'd already called her bluff once today.

He moved fast and soon she was pressed to a wall or a door,
she didn't really care, because all of her concentration was going
toward Gael's hands on her. His massive, rock-hard body pressed
to her, and she wished, really wished, she had the strength to resist
him. But all she did was hold on tighter when he pressed his hot
mouth to her ear.

"I've told myself a thousand times today that I'm not supposed
to want you as much as I do." He sounded furious, and if she hadn't

known him as well as she did, she would've missed the regret lacing his words. He gripped her to him, and desire shot up inside her like Fourth of July fireworks, from her toes and exploding inside her chest.

"Wouldn't it be something if we could make ourselves want the things that we can have," she said bitterly. He scoffed at that, and she didn't know if it was in agreement or denial of what she'd said. It was impossible to focus with his hands roaming over her like they were.

"I don't want to talk about it." *It. I* and *T*. She had no idea what the *it* even was. It could've been so many things. His father's abandonment, their love story that had been laid to waste. The years they had lost, everything they could never get back. Two letters to encompass so much loss and heartbreak. It was on the tip of her tongue to demand answers, to push him to stop hiding, to tell her the truth for once. But she could not make herself speak, the pain in his eyes stealing her ability to do so.

He ran a hand over his head, like he didn't know where to start. Like the moment was too much for him, and for a moment she thought he would actually walk away, leave her standing there. He kissed her instead.

Don't miss what happens next in…
Just for the Holidays… *by Adriana Herrera,*
the next book in her new Sambrano Studios series!

Available November 2021 wherever
Harlequin Desire books and ebooks are sold.

Harlequin.com

*After a decade apart, COO Sloan Outlaw isn't looking to get back
with ex Lesley Cassidy. But with her company facing a hostile
takeover, he offers his assistance…if she joins him at his luxury
cabin. But when they find themselves snowed in, the heat ignites…*

Read on for a sneak peek at
What He Wants for Christmas
by New York Times *bestselling author Brenda Jackson.*

"What do you want to ask me, Sloan?"

He drew in a deep breath. "I need to know what made you come
looking for me last night."

She broke eye contact with him and glanced out the window,
not saying anything for a moment. "You were gone longer than
you said you would be. I got worried. It was either go see what was
taking you so long or pace the floor with worry even more. I chose
the former."

"But the weather had turned into a blizzard, Les." He then
realized he'd called her what he'd normally called her while they'd
been together. She had been Les and not Leslie.

"I know that. I also knew you were out there in it. I tried to
convince myself that you could take care of yourself, but I also
knew with the amount of wind blowing and snow coming down
that anything could have happened."

She paused again before saying, "Chances are, you would have
made it back to the cabin, but I couldn't risk the chance you would
not have."

He tried not to concentrate on the sadness he heard in her voice
and saw in her eyes. Instead, he concentrated on her mouth and in
doing so was reminded of just how it tasted. "Not sure if I would
have made it back, Les. My head was hurting, and it was getting

harder and harder to make my body move because I was so cold. Hell, I wasn't even sure I was going in the right direction. I regret you put your own life at risk, but I'm damn glad you were there when I needed you."

"Just like you were there for me and my company when I needed you, Sloan," she said softly.

Her words made him realize that they'd been there for each other when it had mattered the most. He didn't want to think what would have been the outcome if he'd been at the cabin alone as originally planned and the snowstorm hit. Nor did he want to think what would have happened to her and her company if Redford hadn't told him what was going on. The potential outcome of either made him shiver.

"You're still cold. I'd better go and get that hot chocolate going," she said, shifting to get up and reach for her clothes.

"Don't go yet," he said, not ready for any distance to be put between them or their bodies.

She glanced over at him. Their gazes held and then, as if she'd just noticed his erection pressing against her thigh, she said, "You do know the only reason why we're naked in this sleeping bag together, right?"

He nodded. "Yes. Because I needed your body's heat last night." He inched his mouth closer to hers and then said, "Only problem is, I still need your body's heat, Les. But now I need it for a totally different reason."

And then he leaned in and kissed her.

Don't miss what happens next in…
What He Wants for Christmas *by Brenda Jackson,*
the next book in her Westmoreland Legacy: The Outlaws series!

Available December 2021 wherever
Harlequin Desire books and ebooks are sold.

Harlequin.com

Love Harlequin romance?

DISCOVER.

Be the first to find out about promotions,
news and exclusive content!

Facebook.com/HarlequinBooks

Twitter.com/HarlequinBooks

Instagram.com/HarlequinBooks

Pinterest.com/HarlequinBooks

ReaderService.com

EXPLORE.

Sign up for the Harlequin e-newsletter and
download a free book from any series at
TryHarlequin.com

CONNECT.

Join our Harlequin community to share your
thoughts and connect with other romance readers!
Facebook.com/groups/HarlequinConnection